CRE

BOOK ONE

ANGEL LAWSON

Book Layout ©2013 BookDesignTemplates.com
Book Cover ©2015 T.M. Franklin

Creature of Habit/ Angel Lawson. -- 1st ed.
ISBN-13 978-1-5369786-5-0

Prologue

He killed again.

Vicious and grotesque, he left the remains where I would find them, like breadcrumbs trailing through the forest. One here, another there. Random enough to confuse the police, but not me. We thought alike, our skills comparable, but at the end of the game our objectives are infinitely different. I was the Hunter and he, the Predator.

Working my way through the dark forest I paused to inhale, pinpointing his exact trail. I caught a hint of blood and sweat mixed with decay from the forest floor. Moving closer, the scent grew stronger, fresher. The kill was recent, but the killer was long gone.

To be safe, I scaled the nearest tree and surveyed the scene below. Blood soaked the damp ground, seeping into the dirt and leaves. A woman's body laid on top, her flesh torn to shreds. She wore athletic clothing and the type of shoes for running. I jumped to the ground for a

1

closer look, the earth tremoring under my feet upon my landing.

Mud covered her exposed knees; she'd kneeled at one point, most likely begging for her life. I bent over her body, sniffing at her hands, at the marks on her neck, the cuts on her wrists. Two others had helped the Predator, and while his scent lingered in the area, it was not on the victim. For some reason, he never touched them himself. That was one of the many questions I had about these deaths. Why murder these women if he didn't join in the kill? Surely he needed to feed?

I scanned the area, searching for a message or a clue—anything from the Predator. As usual, he'd left nothing but destruction and death. The kill itself was his message. He wanted to taunt me on my own territory. Murder people under my watch.

It was something he would soon regret.

1

Amelia

The boxy, four-story building sat on the edge of town, jutting from the asphalt-lined streets. I double-checked the address on the unimpressive building, comparing it to the slip of paper in my hand. The numbers matched, confirming that this was indeed the location for my appointment. My job interview, actually.

Frowning, I looked down the street, empty other than the cars parked along it. The address was right. The appointment was today. I had little choice but to put my game face on. I needed this job—immediately. Why did it matter if I couldn't figure out how a multi-million dollar foundation operated out of the building in front of me? Sure, the building looked to be in good condition, although it was probably close to a century old. Truthfully, I expected something a little more modern. But who was I to judge the quirks of the rich? What did I know? Clearly not much, since I had two weeks before I had little choice but to pack my bags and move back home if I didn't secure some sort of job.

I climbed the steps to the second floor entrance. Nothing identified it as an office building, but there was an intercom on the wall outside the door. I pressed the black, plastic buzzer with my thumb. A woman answered.

"Palmer Residence."

"Hi," I said, searching for a camera. None were visible. "Hello, this is Amelia Chase. I have an appointment at nine?"

"One moment, please," replied the voice on the other side of the intercom.

The door swung open and I was met by an attractive woman who looked to be in her late thirties. Eyeing her drastic, raven-black hair with blunt bangs and blood-red lipstick, I secretly wished I could pull off either and not look like a hooker.

"Amelia," she said. "Nice to meet you. I'm Genevieve, Mr. Palmer's current assistant."

That was the job I was applying for. The one that, hopefully, would keep me in Asheville with my best friend Drew.

"Please come in," she suggested, ushering me past the sparsely decorated foyer. I followed her to a sitting area, our feet crossing from hardwood to a finely woven rug. She gestured for me to sit. "Thank you for coming in on such short notice."

I smiled. Short notice wasn't a problem for someone close to being jobless.

"Mr. Hudson had many wonderful things to say about you," she said.

"Mr. Hudson has been a wonderful supervisor at the library," I said, looking around the room, still a little confused. "So this is the Foundation's office?"

"Oh, no. This is Mr. Palmer's home office."

"Home?"

"He lives on the upper floors. The corporate offices for The Palmer Foundation are in Raleigh."

"That's a three hour drive."

"Yes, which means Mr. Palmer works here sometimes but often spends time out of town. As his assistant, you'll manage household affairs and the home office."

Manage the house? That wasn't how Mr. Hudson had described the job. I assumed I would work at the actual foundation offices. Two phrases came quickly to mind: 'beggars can't be choosers', and the always lovely, 'to assume makes an ass out of u and me'.

"So, if I got the job, I would work here?" I said, taking everything in. Paintings and artwork lined the walls. The room had an elegant feel, and I definitely suspected that the couch I sat on was an antique. Although, it could have been fake or a reproduction. I had never been in a home with such expensive and tasteful décor. But then again, I had never known anyone who had a personal assistant or was the CEO of a multi-million dollar foundation, either.

"Primarily." Genevieve sat down in the seat across from mine and smiled. "Mr. Hudson and I met when we worked together on the fundraising campaign for the art history collection at the University several years ago. When Mr. Palmer was seeking a new assistant, he came to mind for a referral."

I smiled back, feeling relieved that she seemed so nice and casual. "I'm thankful he suggested me for the job. The post-college job search has been a little intimidating."

"Let me start by saying that this is not really an interview. Mr. Palmer has reviewed your resume and Mr. Hudson's recommendation. He thinks you will be a wonderful assistant and would like for you to start immediately after graduation."

"Wait, so I already have the job?"

"If you'd like it. We realize it's below your educational achievements and doesn't require much other than a strong sense of organization and good work ethic, both of which were applauded in your recommendation, but it pays well and is perfect for an entry level job."

"Believe me," I said, "I'm not really in the position to be picky."

"Great."

"Do you mind me asking why you're leaving? I know it seems forward but—"

"No, it's understandable. I've decided to take some time off and go back home to my family," she said. "Because of the short notice, Mr. Palmer would like you to spend some time training with me before I go. Again, it's not a difficult job, but Mr. Palmer is very particular about how he likes things managed. "

"Sounds like Mr. Hudson," I said fondly about my soon-to-be-former boss.

She smiled. "That's why it should be a perfect transition."

Relief washed over me the second I heard I'd already gotten the job. I wouldn't have to move back home and Drew and I could make next month's rent. I fought back a squeal of excitement and plastered on my game face.

"Amelia," Genevieve said, "before you agree, it is important for you to understand exactly what is expected of you for this job. Although Mr. Palmer would like you to take the position, it needs to be a good fit for you as well. If you think you are in over your head at any point, tell me so we can make other arrangements."

"I'm sure it will be fine, but tell me whatever it is I need to know. I definitely prefer being prepared." I dug a small, leather-bound journal out of my bag along with a pen, ready to take notes.

"No smartphone?"

"Oh, I have one of those, too, but I prefer to take notes on paper and then transcribe them onto my phone.

I've had more than one lost document in the electronic world."

She nodded approvingly. "First, let me explain that he is really a wonderful man. I'm sure you're aware of the outstanding work the Foundation does in the community. They support so many programs in the tri-state area."

"I've seen their name on the art building at school."

"Yes, the whole family is a huge patron of the arts. Grant Palmer, in particular, has a strong connection and desire to work closely with mental health services. It's his pet project. Each year the Foundation holds an important fundraiser for the psychiatric hospital."

"He sounds generous."

"He does, and he's very passionate, sometimes to the extreme. He can be singularly focused, which means that, as his assistant, you will need to be prepared for this type of hyper-focused personality."

"Extreme how?"

"Mr. Palmer is very quiet and keeps to himself. Some weeks I don't see him at all." I had no problem with this since I preferred to work in a quiet environment. I gave her an encouraging smile and asked her to continue.

"He will leave you a list of duties on your desk each morning or send you an email if he is not in town. They're not difficult jobs," she assured me, "but he is rather particular about how he wants things done. No matter how abstract, it is important for you to follow his directions carefully. Order is incredibly important to him. I can show you some examples."

Genevieve had such a worried expression on her face that I felt the need to interrupt her. "Genevieve, I promise you that you cannot scare me off. I am pretty meticulous about my work as well, so this sounds like it will be a good fit. Mr. Hudson wouldn't have suggested this job to me if he didn't think I could handle it."

"I agree and am glad you feel that way." She exhaled—the tension on her face lifting. I had the impression that she may be more nervous than I was. "He's an extremely private person. If you want to keep this job you must use discretion about him at all times. He holds a position of prominence in the community and his reputation is very important. Do not go out on a Friday night and talk about him in the middle of a bar. Do not send a gossipy email about how nice his home is. And never speak to the press or any other publication without permission."

I scribbled all this down even though I knew none of those were intentions of mine.

Genevieve continued, "If you break any of these basic agreements he will find out and you will lose your job. You'll be asked to sign a confidentiality agreement before you start. I hope that's not a problem."

"I can't see why it would be."

"Good," she said. "Would you like to see the house?"

I nodded and stuffed my notebook in my bag, following Genevieve out of the sitting room. To be honest, I tried not to gawk and show my inexperience, but it was hard. Despite the plain exterior, the building was gorgeous and absolutely immaculate. Like a museum.

The downstairs held the parlor, a kitchen, a small office for me to use, and a library. I peeked in the library, assessing the sheer number of books in his personal collection. For a booklover like myself, it was a dream. The shelves were lined floor to ceiling, and on the other end of the room I saw rows of record albums and a table with a record player. Nothing fancy, but similar to the kind my parents had growing up.

Genevieve noted my interest. "As Mr. Palmer's assistant you are welcome to read his books or listen to his music. Just make sure you put it back where it belongs. One time I put a copy of Dickens back on the wrong shelf and he spotted it immediately. He has eyes like a hawk."

We made our way to the kitchen and Genevieve opened some cabinets and the refrigerator, which all held minimal amounts of food. She laughed when she saw the questioning look on my face and said, "Mr. Palmer primarily eats out of the home and adheres to a specific diet. You don't have to worry about groceries or food shopping. You're welcome to keep coffee or tea here for yourself and to keep your lunch in the refrigerator, if you'd like."

We moved on to the laundry room and storage areas, and then she gave me a quick tour of the basement garage. It housed several expensive cars. I was completely clueless about cars, other than to fill mine up with gas when the light turned on.

"Will the cars be part of my responsibilities?"

"Mr. Palmer tends to take care of his own automotive needs. In general, it is not something with which you need to concern yourself."

We went back inside and she explained that the house had a front and back staircase. We took the back staircase to the second floor and she quickly pointed out the areas I was prohibited from entering. Genevieve waved her hand down the hall to two closed doors. "Those are Mr. Palmer's private rooms. Do not enter them at all. Ever."

"Got it."

"There is a guest room and bath down the hall if he has a visitor, which does happen from time to time, and, well...follow me." Before she opened the door she caught my eye and said, "If you can handle this room, you can handle this job." She pushed open the door and I felt my jaw drop.

We entered a full-sized room that had been converted into a closet and dressing room. All four walls were filled with shelves, drawers, or rows of hanging racks. Full-length mirrors adorned a portion of one wall. Genevieve opened a panel and revealed a long row of suits. I ran my fingers down the fabric, noting it had been arranged by color or possibly season.

I glanced at Genevieve. "This is unbelievable."

There were lines of shoes and shirts and coats, each with its own special drawer or shelf. A ladder was mounted against one wall leading to a series of upper cabinets. It would take several lifetimes to accumulate this much clothing and accessories. I couldn't imagine the amount of time or money it would take to shop for a wardrobe like this. "How can he even wear all of these?"

"Your guess is as good as mine," she replied.

I inspected the items closely and noticed a trend. Several looked vintage. All were in good condition but clearly from another time or era. I pointed to a row of hats on an upper shelf and wondered aloud if he was a collector.

"Collector is a nice way to put it. You'll find that he is something of a hoarder. I don't think he has ever thrown anything away that he has intentionally purchased." She looked around the dressing room. "At least once per month a large package of new, seasonal clothing will arrive. It will be your responsibility to sort and arrange them."

"Wow."

"You think you can handle this?"

I took it all in, the clothes and shoes and neat lines of matching hangers. I thought about the books and music, the way Mr. Palmer seemed to truly love what he owned.

He *was* passionate, I thought. There was nothing wrong with that. "Yeah, I think I can manage this. It's like a library but with clothes."

"Exactly." She showed me a couple more areas of interest and then we walked back downstairs. We worked out a part-time schedule for the next week, allowing time for me to complete my final exams.

"When do you think I'll get a chance to meet Mr. Palmer?" I asked, stashing my notebook back in my purse.

"I'm not sure. Please understand I am not exaggerating when I say he is fairly reclusive. But it's not a bad thing, it's just his nature," she said. "Work is his element. He is very good at his job and he's developed an extensive system to ensure communication with his employees that, at times, may come across as a little brash and impulsive."

"I'm sure it will be fine."

She escorted me to the door and I walked out to my car, feeling a little overwhelmed from all the information. I wasn't completely sure what I had gotten myself into. From what I could gather, I had apparently agreed to work for the next year for a reclusive, obsessive-compulsive, vintage-clothes-wearing and special-diet-eating boss.

2

Grant

D aylight faded as I turned my car down the alley that led to the garage. After parking I entered the house and listened carefully. Nothing but sweet, glorious quiet. Genevieve must have already left for the day. That relieved a bit of the tension that had built in my shoulders and neck. After a long day of working in the Raleigh office, I coveted time alone.

I crossed through the kitchen and inhaled, pausing for a moment. What was that? An odd scent lingered in the air. Something lemony. Maybe Genevieve wore a different perfume? I inhaled, trying to narrow down the origin, but couldn't put a finger on it.

"Stop obsessing," I said aloud, mimicking Genevieve's authoritative voice. The fake voice was right, because really, I had things to do, and analyzing perfume scents wasn't one of them.

Walking past her desk, I picked up the report sheet she left me each day, updating me on messages and paperwork or any assignments not completed. The day was perfect, every task checked off and that was why I would miss her working here. She never let me down. Not once—other than the occasional book mix-up. Nothing related to work, for sure.

I did see the notation that Amelia Chase, the new PA, had come in. She'd passed her initial interview and was set to return next week under Genevieve's instruction. Good. The less disruption, the better. Between the Foundation and my personal work, I had little time for any interruption in how my offices were managed. I made a mental note of her start date and headed upstairs.

In my dressing room I was struck by the same scent from before. Faint, but enough to taste on my tongue. I caught my reflection in the mirror. The pulsing dilation of my eyes told the true story. I was famished. Unfortunately, I had work to do first.

After changing and dropping my soiled clothes into the hamper, I entered my office. I inhaled. No lemons here. Just perfect, quiet, nothingness. I set the iPod, and spread the day's newspapers across my desk, flipping through the pages, looking for the details on the murder I'd heard about in the news today. The police didn't have much—only a body and some lame theories. Their favorite being the ridiculously misinformed 'animal attack'.

The kill made the third murder in six weeks. It was more than what we normally had around here in a year, and the kind of crime that brought unwanted attention to this part of the country. I frowned down at the papers, unhappy with the news. This type of situation was bad for business. That was something I couldn't risk.

I marked the pages I needed and arranged the paper with the others. I considered calling Elijah, asking for his opinion, but a fierce twinge of hunger forced me from my seat.

So much for getting anything accomplished tonight. I stood and walked back into the dressing room and again caught that same delectable smell. No wonder I was hungry; Genevieve's perfume triggered an intense physical reaction. Like chocolate for someone with a sweet tooth.

My research would have to wait, because my sudden, ravenous hunger could not.

3

Amelia

Graduation came and went with the usual caps and gowns, tassels and photos. My mom and dad came up for the weekend from Atlanta. In an instant, my college career was over and my new job as a personal assistant would start. The library job had been completed and I'd spent the last two weeks training with Genevieve. I felt pretty confident I could manage Mr. Palmer's affairs, despite Genevieve's constant reminders of his quirky, hard to predict behavior.

"How is he hard to predict?" I asked one day as she introduced me to his computer system. "If he's so OCD then it seems like it would make it easier."

She shrugged her petite shoulders and simply said, "You'll see."

I never encountered Mr. Palmer during my training period. Genevieve said he spent much of his time at meetings in Raleigh or even flying to other cities, raising or allotting funds for the Foundation. We'd have to meet at some point. It did seem weird to take on a job and never have a formal introduction to your boss, but again, beggars can't be choosers.

Rain fell in sheets on my first day of working solo. I tried to pretend it was good luck, but it only proved to be a huge pain in the ass. I drove up to the building and parked on the street, wishing I'd been given a spot in the spacious underground garage. After a brief fight with my umbrella I managed to make it to the house fairly dry and let myself in with the key that I'd been given by Genevieve. The foyer carried the silence of an empty building, and after hanging up my coat and umbrella, I went straight to my desk.

My desk.

I took a second to sit in the chair and relish the moment. My first real job and my very own desk. Pushing aside the daunting realization I was now a real grown up, I took out my phone and snapped a picture, thinking I'd post it on Instagram later. Genevieve had removed all of her personal items and the desk was clean and free of any clutter. I'd brought a few trinkets from home but reconsidered when I saw the flat, spotless surface. I liked the sense of opportunity.

Just as I'd been told, I found the list written by Mr. Palmer. For weeks now I'd been fascinated with his handwriting. He had the most elaborate, distinct script I'd ever seen. It had a very old-fashioned style. A preciseness, like it had been printed off a computer and not by hand. I was jealous of the smooth lines and curves of his letters and immediately hoped I never had to write something for him in my own loopy, girlish handwriting. Next to the list was a brand-new smartphone with a yellow post-it note stuck to the screen.

Keep with you at all times. For work purposes only.- GP

I slid the bar on the front and it came to life. I noted several apps had already been loaded, most organizational. The address book was loaded as well as the contact pages, including employees at the main Foundation office.

My instructions for the day included gathering his laundry for the cleaners and running some basic errands to the home improvement and drug stores. He also needed a certain type of pen from a specialty shop north of town. I was instructed to go to his PO Box (boxes— there were four) where he had his mail and newspapers delivered. Apparently, Mr. Palmer subscribed to over 15 newspapers a day, local, national, and from surrounding states. He reviewed these each night. I had no idea how he consumed all that information after a full day of work but I guess it was not my business.

Not my business—the first rule of being a personal assistant.

I reviewed the list and the instructions, taking time to call for directions to one of the shops. A shiny, silver credit card was attached to the note pad with a black clip. 'The Palmer Foundation' was embossed in raised letters on the front. A separate note explained I was to use this only for approved purchases.

Six hours, eight stores, one stop for gas, another for lunch, one stumble into a puddle and an argument with the Duds and Suds Laundromat manager later, I was back at the office. I was exhausted and drenched from being out in the rain all day. All I wanted was to go home and get in bed. But I had two hours to go, and needed to put away my purchases and finish the small list of things described to do here at the house.

I spent some time changing the light bulbs out in the library and parlor. Apparently Mr. Palmer decided to switch over to environmentally conserving bulbs. I felt wasteful throwing out the old, perfectly fine ones but that was not for me to judge.

Nope. Not my business.

In the library, I was distracted by the books that lined the shelves wrapping around the room. As with many other things in the house it was a mixture of old and new, and there were even a large amount of books in foreign languages including German, French and Italian. I paused to pick up a series of leather-bound editions of Shakespeare. They were worn and soft. There were copies of Homer and Steinbeck. I also noticed a tidy row of thick medical journals, with cracked leather spines. I knew he was supposed to be a prodigy, having taken over the Foundation in his early twenties, but I found it hard to believe he could read all of these books. If he didn't read them, then that meant...well, increasingly, I had the feeling Grant Palmer was quite possibly a pretentious ass.

But that was the thing I couldn't figure out. Who exactly was Grant Palmer?

Drew and I had looked him up after my initial interview. Google notified us that he was young, smart, and good looking (of course he was handsome). The society pages said he did a bunch of amazing things for charity. The business community loved him and found his methods groundbreaking. Oh, and the gossip blogs? They couldn't figure out who he dated because he came to and left every event alone. He answered every personal question with a simple, "No comment," leaving everyone to their own speculations. Drew and I both felt like this seemed a bit of a stretch. Did I mention he was handsome? And rich? And super generous? He probably rescued drowning kittens, too.

Maybe he required everyone to sign a non-disclosure agreement—including the kittens.

After I finished saving the world one light bulb at a time, I made my way upstairs carrying the laundry and other personal items to his dressing room. My list described a set of casual clothing to fold over the back of a chair. Then I needed to place the newspapers on the dressing counter, lining them up so a small gap at the top revealed the title of each copy. I arranged his mail in the slotted organizer, large envelopes in the back with

Angel Lawson

the smaller in front. Genevieve implied he had an office in the area she'd designated off limits. I found it strange that I couldn't leave the newspapers and mail in there but whatever...

Not my business.

Moving to the dry-cleaning I picked up, I tore the plastic wrappers off and removed the hangers provided by the cleaners. I snorted at the extravagance of using special hangers, thick wooden ones, but god forbid we use anything but environmentally-safe light bulbs. There were enough hangers in this room to make a whole tree. They lined up neatly, sterile and uniform. I swapped the appropriate hangers and placed the clothing in the appropriate location. Style, color, season... I knew it was the right spot because I had a chart, a cheat sheet (or rather, a cheat binder), given to me by Genevieve. Each item was photographed and documented in its proper location.

Pretentious.

I walked around the room, adjusting and making sure everything was in its place. Even though this room was sort of insane, I liked being up here. So far it had been a little lonely being in the house without company all day and being in this dressing room made me feel like I was working for a person, not a phantom. The rest of the house felt kind of impersonal but up here I was able to learn a little more about the elusive Mr. Palmer.

Underneath the perfectionism I found signs of his real nature. Below his dress shirts I discovered a collection of vintage tees hanging on one of the racks. I flipped through each one, reading the names and scanning the logos; The Beatles, The Rolling Stones, The Who, The Grateful Dead, The Doors, Janis Joplin, Pink Floyd, Led Zeppelin, David Bowie, Queen, and KISS. I stopped at the KISS one and ran my fingers over the slick surface of Gene Simmons painted face and ridiculously long tongue. There were too many to go through but they seemed in chronological order and at the end of the row I saw one for Cher, Elton John, Nirvana, and the last one for Madonna's latest tour.

It was an impressive collection, very eclectic. He must have found a specialty shop that worked off original designs. I wondered whether or not Genevieve was in charge of finding and purchasing these.

Ah, the life of the rich.

I left the room, switched off the light and closed the door behind me. I wandered down the stairs to my desk and filled out my daily report. I typed it up, not wanting to reveal my hideous handwriting, and left it on the edge of the desk as instructed.

As I gathered my things I considered that it had been a good day, but I was happy to head home to order a pizza and go over the day's events with Drew. I wondered if I would see Mr. Palmer anytime soon, since my interest was getting more and more piqued as the days went by.

Surely I had to come face to face with him at some point.

4

Grant

Lemons.

The scent assaulted my nostrils the instant I walked into the house. Stronger than before, which meant it wasn't Genevieve and I could only assume it was the new PA. I preferred not to have our first encounter be a reprimand—not that it was a reprimand. It was more a necessity. It's not that the scent was unpleasant, it was simply one of those fragrances that at first it smells appealing but then becomes overwhelming and obnoxious. Distracting. I didn't have time for distractions.

See? I'd already spent too much time thinking about perfume, again.

I would leave her a note tomorrow asking her to stop wearing the scent, claiming it was giving me migraines. That may be a stretch, but the odor messed with my head one way or the other, and migraine sounded as plausible as anything else I could come up with.

In my dressing room, I removed a shirt from my collection off the hanger. I was going out tonight. I needed to. I had the tendency to shut myself off in the house after a day at the office, decompressing from the long days at work. Normally, I didn't go into the office so much, but as it was the end of the fiscal year, there were many meetings with accountants and committee chairs reviewing the budgets and organizations we funded. The hospital fundraiser was only a couple of months away. I had no choice but to show up and fulfill my role as CEO. Either way, it was time for a public appearance. Recluses made people nervous. I went to great lengths to keep people at ease.

I pulled the light blue shirt over my head and tugged my jeans up, buttoning them at the top. I selected my favorite pair of brown boots and a seasonally appropriate, light-weight jacket before walking over to the desk to peruse the mail from today. I held an envelope under my nose and winced as it elicited a sharp pain in my temple.

Damn lemons.

Sniffing the envelope one more time before leaving the room, I tucked several of the papers under my arm and left through the front door instead of the back. It was still misting as I set off on foot in the direction of the more populated and trendy section of town. It wasn't a long walk, a couple of miles, and the fresh air made my head feel better. Yes, the perfume had to go, it was entirely too disturbing.

I crossed the street and continued toward my destination, taking time to observe passing groups and listen to their chatter. It was a Monday so the crowds were thin and thoughts seemed to be on work or other regular life stressors.

Trivial.

I entered the corner café, the one with a patio out front, and greeted the counter worker with a smile. She knew my face and my order, as I was a regular here. Businesses came and went in this area and this particular shop had been here for about six months, which was perfect for my needs. Long enough to be seen but not long enough to make an impression.

"Nice shirt," said the girl working the counter. She looked up at my face and smiled warmly. I noted the tiny birthmark on her cheek.

"Thank you."

She blinked twice with crystal blue eyes that contrasted off her dark skin. "Looks vintage."

"Oh, does it?" I asked, ignoring the encouraging tone of her voice. "I've had it for a while."

"I'll bet," she said with a coy smile.

Out on the covered patio, I placed my papers and drink on the table, and settled into the hard plastic chair. I noticed a phone number scribbled on the side of my drink and the name, "Laurel."

I scanned the first paper, tagging the items of interest with a black pen. The third murder victim had been identified—a young woman from Lake Junaluska. I could only imagine the family's distress. The police would try to convince them that it was an animal attack or some sort of random accident. That there was no way this was connected to the other recent deaths. Unfortunately, they were incorrect. There was a murderer—a serial killer—attacking women, and he was coming our way.

As I read, I was aware of the nagging pain that would not leave me. I wondered if someone else was wearing the cursed fragrance as well. This could be a problem for me if it suddenly became popular. I sniffed the air and realized, with astonishment, that I was the source of the foul odor.

I pulled up the front of my shirt to my nose and inhaled.

A burst of fragrance came from Gene Simmons' upside down, makeup-covered face and my head began to spin. I dropped the shirt for a moment and took a gulp of fresh air.

Okay, better. If anything, I was a master of discipline, and I used everything I had to calm myself. I was better than allowing this to rattle me. In fact, I saw this as nothing more than a challenge.

Grant Palmer loved a challenge.

So I sat and read, marking stories and jotting notes,
ignoring the throbbing pain. Occasionally, I found myself pulling my shirt up quickly and breathing in, under
the guise of checking to see if it was any less offensive.

It wasn't.

But I didn't stop, either.

Like a junkie craving a hit of cocaine, each time I
sucked in the odor I felt a rush, followed by pain, and
then disgust.

After an hour of repeating this ridiculous pattern, I
threw away my untouched coffee and collected my papers. I should go home and toss the offending shirt in
the hamper. I should go home, but the pain increased
and the desire continued to build. I stood on the corner
long enough for two buses to pass. I had two choices. Go
home as intended or go out and satiate my cravings.

The cravings won.

5

Amelia

The computer churned out the crisp sheet of paper documenting my accomplishments for the day. The list was long, a little tedious, but satisfyingly complete. I held back a self-congratulatory cheer. I mean, it wasn't like there was anyone around to hear it anyway.

I had survived my first week of work without screwing up, or even meeting my boss. When the clock struck five I had plans to meet Drew for dinner and drinks—lots of drinks—to celebrate.

Halfway out the door, my phone rang. "Crap," I muttered, scrambling to find it in my purse. In the process I dropped the keys, and then my bag, barely catching the caller before it went to voice mail.

"Hello," I answered, distracted, looking around for the keys.

"Ms. Chase?"

"Yeah, this is Amelia," I grunted. Ah! My fingers connected with the keys.

"This is Grant Palmer." I froze.

Crappity-crap.

I fought to gain some professionalism. "Yes sir, how are you?"

"I'm fine, thank you. I know it is late but I need you to do one more thing before you leave." His voice was very direct, but carried a soothing lilt.

"Oh, of course." I groaned internally, wanting to tell him 'hell no'. He would pick tonight, Friday night, the only night my plans included something other than pajamas and ice cream, to keep me late. "Let me get my notepad to jot this down."

Pushing the key into the lock, I let myself back into the house.

"I'm having the Raleigh office send you some paperwork via email. Once it all comes in, please copy it in triplicate, and have them spiral bound." His words come out in a rush and I ran down the hallway to get a piece of paper to write on. "The cover should be clear, but the backing needs to be opaque. You may choose the color. Black usually works. Each set of documents needs to be numbered, notarized and logged in the file. When you're finished leave them on your desk by the daily report."

I was still scribbling down the information when I realized it was my turn to talk, so I blurted out, "Tonight. No problem," when I was really thinking, " *You have lost your freaking mind! Tonight! It's Friday I have plans! With a margarita!*" Instead I repeated, "No problem. I would be happy to do that."

"Thank you, Amelia." Click. The line went dead.

I dropped my head to the desk and moaned. This was the first direct task he had asked me to do. Well, other than the bizarre note he left requesting that I change perfume. I didn't wear perfume so I had no idea how to fulfill that demand.

I picked up the phone again and texted Drew.

Um so...working late.

How late?

Late.

9:30?

I'll try.

Save you a drink?

Save me five.

I refused to let this ruin my whole night so I sucked it up and prepared to finish my task quickly. I did the best thing you can do when in a hurry, I waited.

Five minutes passed and nothing had come through even though I clicked refresh eighty-eleven times. Maybe I'd lost internet connection? Wifi? Nope, five bars stared at me from the corner. After twenty minutes, I checked the connection to the wall and restarted the computer. Thirty minutes and I went to get a snack out of the refrigerator. Forty-five minutes later my email chimed. *Finally!* I clicked the print button. Impatiently, I snatched the papers as they rolled out, making sure they stayed in order. Once they were all printed I quickly ran out the door to drive to the copy store. There was a 24-hour shop a couple of miles away. I glanced at the clock on the dash as I darted out of the car. It was 6:30. Plenty of time to finish, go home and change and get to the bar.

Since it was Friday night the store was not very crowded and my hopes soared. The university being on summer break made it even better. I took a place in line behind an older man with a small stack of papers. My hope was short lived as I watched the 16-year-old behind the counter approach the customer in front of me. He had ear buds hanging over his shoulders, a dirty T-shirt peeking out from behind his crumpled blue vest. It became immediately clear he did not have a date later that night so he would not understand my rush. I crossed my arms and waited. Again.

According to my watch, their exchange lasted a full 38 minutes. I listened over and over again as the customer explained repeatedly that he needed the paperwork enlarged, but not too large and not too small. They had to make countless copies before the perfect size was agreed upon. I almost clapped when he finally walked out of the store.

I rushed the counter, smiling brightly at the surly teenager in front of me. "Hi." I said, hoping he would put some pep in his step if I was nice.

He barely glanced at me as he said, "Hey. What do you need?" *Hmmm, I may need to up the charm.*

"Oh, I need some copies made and then bound. Here." I shoved the paperwork in front of him with the directions I had written down. "Sorry, I know, but my *boss* really needs it. Ugh, working on Friday night sucks, right?"

He picked up the directions and grunted, turning to the copiers behind him.

I sighed and stole a glance at my watch. It was 7:15. There was no way I could make it home to change but I looked okay, well I thought I did, even if Copy Boy didn't think so.

He could do this and I would get it notarized and then leave it on the desk and race to meet Drew. No problem.

I spent the next 25 minutes pacing the store. I made a bracelet out of paper clips, and wrote my name in White-Out on scrap paper I found in the trash. Just when I thought I was going to completely lose my shit, Copy Boy walked back over. I considered punching him when I noticed hands which were empty.

"Finished?" I asked, hopefully.

He shrugged. "The binding machine is kind of messing up so I had to make new copies for the one that got jammed."

"Does that mean you're not finished?"

He shrugged again and walked away. Okay then.

Twenty minutes later I had my binders and had paid with my shiny silver credit card. I sat in the car and realized I had no idea where to get something notarized at this time of night. I ran back in and asked Copy Boy if someone there could do it.

He thought for a minute and said, "Yeah, Sarah my boss can do it."

I almost leaped over the counter and gave him a kiss. Probably his first one, but I was willing to make the sacrifice.

"Great! Can you give them to her for me?" I asked.

"Uh, no. She's on the over-night shift. She won't be here until ten. Sorry." Stupid Copy Boy. He would die a virgin, I was sure.

Pissed, I walked back to my car. I had no idea what to do. I was banging my head on the steering wheel when my phone rang.

I answered with little enthusiasm. "Hello."

"Amelia, are you finished?"

It was Drew. I could hear the thumping music behind him signaling that he was already at the bar.

"No, I have everything but the paperwork has to be notarized. I have no idea what to do. It's Friday night. Not only am I not going to be able to meet you I will probably get fired since I failed at my first assignment given to me directly by my boss," I whined, on the verge of genuine, freak-out tears.

"Okay, calm down. We can totally figure this out," Drew assured me. I took a deep breath, trying to make myself focus.

Clutching the phone I said, "The notary at the copy place won't be back until 10 pm. The bank is closed and any other official place would be too by now."

There was a long pause on the phone and finally Drew said, "Well, what would his old PA have done?"

"Drew! Yes! Let me call Genevieve and find out what she suggests to do."

I scrolled though my phone, thankful Genevieve had suggested I save her number in case of an emergency. I sighed in relief when she picked up in the third ring. "Genevieve . It's Amelia. I need your help."

6

Grant

To my surprise, it was almost ten o'clock when I arrived home. I had spent the better part of the day in Black Mountain taking care of some family business.

Well, they called it family business. I called it an intervention. For the twentieth time in as many years. Seriously, I had a feeling they looked forward to it, like a normal family would look forward to a reunion.

Due to all this, I was behind on my work and my nerves were shot from all the talking and guilt and the non-stop chatter. I'd spent all these years avoiding them for this exact reason, except they still felt like it was their business to get into my business. Or rather, my personal life. Or my lack of one. Regardless, they were nosy and pushy and it only confirmed the reason I left all those years ago.

I approached the door, but stopped, fingers paused on the door knob.

Thump

A deep, muscle-rattling vibration shook me to the core.

Thump, thump

I looked around and even leaned out the door of the garage facing the alley. Nothing. Silence. Not even a car in sight.

I walked back to the door and pressed the button to the garage door before walking in the kitchen. As I closed the door I was assaulted by a wave of that blasted perfume.

Damn. I swelled with irritation. Earlier in the week I left her a note about the perfume and unbelievably, it actually seemed worse. Was she bathing in it?

Thump, thump

The smell rattled my head, causing it to pound, which was the least of my problems as I felt my hunger growing even though I was well-fed.

thump, thump, thump, thump

I held my breath as I walked through the kitchen to her desk with the intent to simply grab the binders. Then I could retire to my room, away from the obnoxious smell and rest my throbbing head. That was my plan. I always had a plan. Three moves ahead of the other person. How? Because I could always anticipate the next move.

Always.

Except, in the absolute silence of the room I realized, three moves too late, there was a person standing five feet away. Unaware. She was unaware that I'd seen her.

Thump, thump

Five feet.

How did I miss it? Her?

I heard nothing. Not a whisper. Well, that wasn't entirely true.

I'd been so distracted by the smell and intense pounding of my head that I'd failed to see her standing right in front of me until it was terribly, unfortunately too late.

Thump, thump

My reaction was a defensive, low growl rumbling through my chest. I'd broken a fundamental principal. Never let down your guard.

thump, thump, thump, thump

Louder and faster the thumps came. I took a deep breath.

Lemons.

thump, thump, thump, thump, thump

She still hadn't seen me, at least I had that advantage, and I assessed her quickly. She had pale hair and an even fairer complexion. Her hair was braided in a long plait down her back, and I zeroed in on the grayish vein near the curve of her exposed neck. I sucked in a gasp of air. She turned, her very green eyes wide with surprise.

"Oh!" she exclaimed, nearly jumping out of her shoes. "You scared me! You must be Mr. Palmer. I'm Amelia."

thump, thump, thump, thump, thump, thump, thump

Her heart beat faster and her ears burned red, adding another pulse point to the rattling noise in my head. I stared at her face and then down at her hand.

She held it there for a moment, floundering in the air, until she finally withdrew it, surely remembering the rules Genevieve had told her about touching me. Or, rather, never touching me.

I had mere seconds to pull it together, to maintain composure for the woman in front of me.

I squinted, focusing on her face—not her heartbeat, not her scent, but her face—and looked her in the eye. As calmly and softly as possible, I made direct eye contact and said, "Ms. Chase, I think you need to leave."

"Excuse me?"

"I don't mean to be rude." I kept my voice even, pleasant, even though my head was about to split. Had I blinked? Did she? I made sure to maintain eye contact this time, and added, "It's very late and I've had a tiring day. It would be best if you left. Now."

Her eyes were filled with confusion and a slight edge of fear. She gaped for a moment, her eyebrows knitting together. "Um, sure, I can leave. Sorry to inconvenience you."

Again she frowned, fluid glistening in her eyes. She didn't seem compelled but simply affronted. Scared?

44

Whatever her reaction, it wasn't normal. I clung to the edge of the desk, the wood splintering under the pressure. Clarity struck and she took a quick step back before dashing for the front door where I heard her pull something off the hook on the wall and slam the door.

Her motion caused a waft of familiar lemony-scent, laced with the delicious hint of fear, to hit my senses. Within seconds of the door closing, I raced down the hallway intent on stopping her. No, not stop her. To catch her.

A brief moment of discipline overruled my instinct, and I pressed a black button next to the security box. Bolts engaged, locking all of the doors tight. Nothing I couldn't get out of if I tried, but I wouldn't. I couldn't.

Or could I?

Even under the most stringent resolve, I crashed hard into the wood and glass door with my body. The glass splintered into a spider web of cracks, threatening to shatter beneath my strength. I spread my palms flat, pressing against the wooden surface, bracing myself. I couldn't open it. I wouldn't. I fought the instinct, the hunger and desire.

I leaned my back against the door and slid to my knees, clutching my hair in my hands and groaned loudly. *What. The. Fuck. Was. That?*

7

Amelia

"Blow," Drew commanded as he handed me a tissue.

I took it from him and wiped my nose. After I'd been told to leave by Mr. Palmer, I ran to my car and inexplicably cried all the way home. I wasn't a big crier, like, ever, but something about our exchange unnerved me. I felt sick to my stomach and my head hurt. My reaction made no sense. Drew found me a short while later curled up, in my pajamas, eating peanut butter out of the jar. Now we sat on the couch together with my feet tucked under his body. He had brought over his own spoon along with a pack of crackers. When the jar was half empty he said, "Tell me exactly what happened after we hung up."

I sniffed. "I called Genevieve and she hooked me up with a friend who works in an attorney's office who is happy to help out when needed. Needless to say, I have him on speed dial now."

I dipped my spoon into the jar and came up with a hulking scoop of peanut butter. Before putting it in my mouth, I continued. "After that I booked it back to the office trying to salvage part of the night. I was standing at the desk when I heard something, I mean, someone, behind me."

I ate a chunk of peanut butter off the spoon and Drew smeared his on the crackers. I took a huge gulp of milk to wash it down.

"Drew, you know when you get that feeling, like the hairs on the back of your neck stand up?" I asked.

He nodded. "Intuition, your sense of self-preservation."

"Exactly. That's what I felt except it was weird. One minute I was alone and then the next I instinctively knew I wasn't. I mean, it was only Mr. Palmer, so I was relieved, but at the same time he was not happy to see me. The look on his face was totally bizarre."

"Define bizarre."

"Like weird. Creepy as hell. How did he sneak up on me like that? Why did he look at me like I was a freak? I mean, he's the freak."

"Right? It's not like he didn't tell you to work late."

"That's what makes this even more infuriating, he is the one who made me do all that crap after hours! Why was he acting so strange?"

My tears were gone and now I was beyond upset and had moved onto pissed. Not only was my boss obsessive-compulsive and pretentious, he was a jerk, too. I shouldn't be surprised. That closet pretty much explained everything about him.

Drew glanced at me and suggested, "Maybe he was having a bad day? Even hot jerks have a bad day every once in a while, right?"

I rolled my eyes at him and he stuck his tongue out in return. "I don't care, Drew. It is not okay to treat people like that. Even if you are a rich, hot boss."

Drew narrowed his eyes and made a face.

"What?"

"Was he really as hot in person as he was in those photos?"

Leaning back into the side of the couch I groaned before answering, "I only saw him for a second, and I thought I may pee myself, but I have to say hotter. Definitely hotter."

Drew snorted, amused by my plight. I found myself laughing back, enough to break out of my wallowing. I grabbed the peanut butter jar and scraped out the last glob. Just my luck. I'd finally gotten a job with a really hot, young boss, and he was a total ass.

8

##

V*ermeer.*

Monet.
Renoir.
Van Gogh.
Mondrian.
Dali.
Picasso.

I listed the names and conjured an image of each one—taking a breath to calm my nerves. It worked, barely. At the very best, time slowed and my mind wandered, while I pressed my back against the crumbling wall.

It was strange how time moved differently at different phases of life. When I was a school boy the day would go on endlessly. Each minute felt like an eternity. Yet, summer vacation would pass in the blink of an eye. Later, hours passed by like seconds, days like hours, and weeks, like days. In the blink of an eye I would realize a month had passed and while I could recall every instance, the actual time had slipped away with little notice. That was not the case this weekend. From the moment Amelia Chase ran out the front door on Friday evening, my life came to a screeching halt.

Well, this wasn't entirely true. I had one slip where I actually attempted to get out the door. I stopped myself, but not before ripping the security system out of the wall in utter frustration and disappointment. My anger was as much at myself as it was letting Ms. Chase go. I regretted both.

I was better than this. Infinitely better. Stronger. More disciplined. I had control of my...well, I had control of everything. My life, my house, my work—everything was perfectly managed. At least until the unfortunate encounter between me and Ms. Chase.

I forced myself back inside and lay on the floor until I calmed down. Physically I was fine, at least for the most part. The scent still bothered me but that was the least of my concerns at the moment. The girl had changed things for me. I realized I'd been living recklessly and therefore had exposed myself to a great vulnerability. Professionals would call this a 'relapse'.

Matisse

Degas

Cezanne

In my life there was no room for error. Any breach to my personal property would be catastrophic. An intruder in my home was unacceptable. And although Ms. Chase was not actually an intruder, the fact she surprised me to the point that I was unaware of her existence in my own home was more than concerning. It was alarming and quite frankly suicidal.

Around dawn, I managed to contain myself, finally convinced I wouldn't do anything rash. I left the foyer, leaving the mess of the broken door and security system to deal with later. Right now, I needed to figure out how to deal with the problem of Ms. Chase. I hadn't had an impulse like that in decades. Why her? Why was she different? And how had she rebuffed my directions so easily?

Before anything else I retrieved a container of blood from my quarters and ripped off the seal, consuming the contents in a single gulp. Then I opened another. And another.

I hadn't had the need to feed like this in many years—hunting was my preferred method. I deprived myself of many things—the thrill of the hunt was one of the few basic desires I still pursued. But I was always prepared for a potential emergency.

Steadier, I went to her desk. I placed the container next to her keyboard and lowered myself in her chair, looking for something. Anything.

Unlike Genevieve or the PA before her, there were no personal photos or trinkets on the desk. She'd only been here for a week. Was that too early for desk decorating? Possibly. I opened the center drawer and pushed aside the pens and pencils. I found a receipt in the corner of the drawer. I picked it up and began reading.

Ted's Tofu Hut

1-Falafel Wrap....5.99

No Onions

1-Large Herbal Tea (decaffeinated)...$1.99

1-Slice Carrot Cake....3.99

I felt my eyes narrow in concentration. Tofu? She must be a vegetarian. One who didn't eat onions or drink caffeine. But she wasn't totally healthy. Even I knew carrot cake was still cake.

I shut the drawer and reached for the tablet near the phone with curled girlish writing on it. I felt a wave of humor looking at her handwriting. It reminded me of the pathetic love notes sent to me by various girls when I was a student at school.

Apples

TV Guide

Apple Sauce

Socks

Vitamin-Water

Q-Tips

Water with Vitamins? That sounded revolutionary. What kind of store sold apple sauce *and* socks?

I shoved the list away, feeling even more confused about my assistant. I thought about what I did know. I had read her recommendation from Mr. Hudson and her resume. She'd been commended for her work ethic and organizational skills. She wasn't at the top of her class but had plans for furthering her education in the future. Genevieve was impressed and thought she would do well here.

On a personal level I knew she was from Atlanta. Parents still married. No siblings. What else was there to know? Oh, she smelled fantastic.

I spent the rest of the day retracing her footsteps. In the kitchen she had used a glass and a mug from the cabinet. There was a tea bag in the trashcan. In the refrigerator I found soy milk and Greek yogurt. In the storage closet the light bulbs were stacked perfectly and slightly angled to fit on the shelf in even numbers.

She'd been everywhere. Some clearly to perform her work duties. Others seemed to be random wanderings. In the parlor I found imprints of her shoes in the carpet near my Cezanne. She'd been in the library, leaving oily fingerprints on the covers of my Shakespeare. In the bathroom I could smell lemons on the hand towels.

She had marked every inch of my home.

None of this told me much, I knew, but it was all I could do for the moment. I knew what I *wanted* to do. I wanted to go find her and figure out how exactly she'd been able to resist my command. That would be my first question. Okay, realistically that would be my only question. I sincerely doubted she'd live much longer to answer any more.

Unable to do what I wanted, I retreated to my private quarters, cancelling my plans for the weekend. I sent the binders she made by courier to the office and made my presentation by Skype. I delved into my papers and attempted to follow my typical routine. That was how an addict fought a full-fledged relapse. Go back to habits. Ingrain them.

That was how I pushed through the weekend.

I lied to myself, pretending I didn't care to know more about the mysterious Amelia Chase by studiously researching or cataloging information about the murders in the area. Perhaps, I considered, after reading about a particularly bloody kill, I considered she was some sort of test. Something to prepare me for a future battle. Maybe she was delivered by the Divine. Those were the lies I told myself when I left my papers and computer searches to escape into my closet to press my nose to any article of clothing she may have touched.

A test. She was simply a test. One I could successfully pass—like all other challenges over the course of my lifetime.

I ignored my phone and its incessant ringing. I pushed away the outside world. She was outside and I wasn't ready to face anything beyond these walls.

By the end of Sunday I was thoroughly exhausted but had made some decisions. I stretched out on the floor of my dressing room and inhaled the lingering hint of lemon. Amelia Chase was an enigma. That much I was willing to admit. But she wouldn't defeat me or my mission. I would use this as a challenge to further my discipline and focus.

And if it didn't work I would let her go and find a new assistant.

For now I would immerse myself in her smell and struggle to become stronger.

9

Amelia

On Monday I paced the sidewalk outside Mr. Palmer's building and gave myself a pep talk. Like a complete, "*You've got this, Mel!*" speech, which really just made me feel worse and not better.

To a passerby I was sure I looked unbalanced, and I probably qualified. I didn't know many other people who would be willing to go back to a job environment as hostile as this one. Okay, hostile may be an exaggeration. All he did was ask me to leave in the calmest, smoothest, creepiest voice I had ever heard. Call it intuition, but it felt like more than a simple request. I wasn't someone who would quit a job for trivial reasons. Mr. Palmer being creepy, as far as I was concerned, counted as trivial.

It was a beautiful day, the first truly warm weather we'd had this summer. Even in the warmer months it remained cool in the mountains. People had a tendency to take advantage and stay outside as much as possible when the opportunity arose. I secretly hoped Mr. Palmer would be out of the house all day and would stay away from me in general.

So, with one last, "Grant Palmer can fuck himself," mumbled under my breath, I stepped off the sidewalk and up the steps leading to the front door. That was until I saw the front door. Or actually, some of the front door. Okay there was a door, but the glass looked like someone had detonated a bomb, leaving splinters of wood peeling from the edges of the frame.

"What the hell?" I asked. The door looked like someone smashed something into the it like a battering ram. I tiptoed over the mess, crushing glass and pieces of wood under my shoes and breathed a sigh of relief that the key worked. Yes, even through all that the door was locked and beyond that, I really didn't want to ring the bell.

Just inside the foyer an ugly tangle of wires and metal hung from the former security box. Side-stepping the mess, I looked to hang my coat and bag on the hook in the hall. It too had been torn off the wall. Whatever happened here came from the inside, not out.

I listened carefully.

"Hello?" I called. Okay, 'called' may be a little much. Whispered? I didn't really want to alert Mr. Palmer or a robber or the S.W.A.T. team that tore through that door about my presence. I was met with silence. I wasn't sure if that was a good or bad thing. I had previously decided to treat this day like any other, like Friday evening hadn't occurred. Obviously there were bigger problems to deal with.

A list waited for me at my desk and thankfully, none of the notations were for me to pack up my belongings and leave. An additional message was at the bottom of the page.

Ms. Chase,

Please contact Asheville Handymen to come repair the door as well as Smokey Mountain Security. Both of these jobs need to be completed by the end of the day-
GP

I flipped the heavy cardstock note over, but that was it. No explanation other than instructions to stay in the home with the workers at all times. The normal list had plenty of items on it to keep me busy while the repairs were being completed.

Okay, maybe Mr. Palmer wasn't just creepy but downright crazy.

I turned on the computer and found the address book with all the contact information for Mr. Palmer's needs. I called the handyman service.

"Asheville Handymen, this is Jack."

"Jack, I'm calling from Mr. Palmer's office and we are in desperate need of your service."

"Oh! Mr. Palmer! Of course, what do you need?" He sounded like he may have wet himself.

"Yeah, we've got a bit of a problem over here. You're going to have to see it yourself."

"I'll have my best team there in an hour. Probably less."

"What? No, standard 6 hour time frame like the cable company?" I wasn't surprised though. Even in my short time working for Mr. Palmer it was obvious how the rich received special treatment. To be fair, if Mr. Palmer trusted him in his home he probably paid him very well.

While I waited for them to arrive, I busied myself with my latest project; the ridiculously tedious task of updating names and addresses into a new program recently installed on the computer. Mr. Palmer wanted this to be linked to his phone and laptop. I stared at the intimidating list. Sometimes I felt like this house was caught between two worlds. One modern and one a little old-fashioned. Like the current project. I had to take the handwritten names and add them to the database. Why were they handwritten in the first place? Whatever, I thought.

Not my business.

I bit the bullet and began working. I had made it through one and a half pages of Mr. Palmer's perfectly perfect handwriting when the front door rang. Expecting the workmen, I rushed over to open the door, and was surprised to see it was a postal delivery man carrying a massive box in both hands.

"I've got a package for Mr. Palmer," the man said.

"I'll sign for it," I said.

"What the heck happened to this door? You guys get robbed?"

"It was like this when I got here. I haven't quite figured it out myself."

He shook his head and asked where I wanted the box. I pointed to my office to get it out of the way of the mess.

As he was leaving a van pulled up with the logo for the handymen on the side. I waited for them at the front door. Two men close to my age walked up the front steps in jeans and matching work shirts. They stopped before the porch, jaws dropped, taking in the broken door.

"So, I guess I don't have to tell you what's wrong," I said, gesturing to the mess behind me.

The one with the name Thomas embroidered on his pocket spoke up and said, "No, I think we can figure it out. But how the heck did this happen?"

"I have no idea. Mr. Palmer only left me instructions to call you and have it repaired."

The other man, whose name was Mark, swung the door open and shut while scratching his head. "Doesn't matter how it happened, I guess, but I hate to tell you this is going to be a pretty big job."

I frowned. "How big?"

"Obviously you'll need a new door, but we'll have to repair the door jamb first. Once the security system is

back up and running we'll have to come inside and re-
place the interior wall. That's original plaster so we'll
have to touch it up also, oh and the glass."

"Can you at least get it fixed today? Mr. Palmer requested it be finished before the end of the day."

Thomas looked over the damage again. "It's gonna
take us at least until late afternoon to get the first coat
of plaster on. You may want to tell the security guys to
come later today."

"I guess you better get started," I said, turning to
walk back to my desk. "I have a feeling he'd like it done
as soon as possible."

Thomas nodded and then turned back to me. "I'll call
in a couple more guys. Uh, I don't think I got your
name...you know, in case we need you for something."

I turned back toward him and noticed he had nice
brown eyes and a friendly smile, which I returned. I offered my hand. "I'm Amelia. Amelia Chase."

He gripped it in his own. "Nice to meet you, Amelia."

I left them to their work and went back to my desk to
call the security company. They promised to come by 4
PM which would give Thomas and Mark a chance to get
a good head start. Off and on I checked on the guys to
see if they needed water and peek at their progress as
they dismantled what remained of the door off its
hinges. Each time I saw the mess I was left with the same
question, how did this happen in the first place?

10

Grant

Monday rolled around and even though I felt steadier on my feet, I decided to spend the day in my study, leaving Ms. Chase to handle the repair men. At my desk, I switched on the computer and sat back in my leather chair. My study was part work space, part Grant Palmer museum. Collectibles lined the walls, although not expensive ones like I had downstairs. No, these were items I had collected over my lifetime—things I held dear that no one outside of my family had been privy to. In contrast to my personal items, an extremely sophisticated computer system sat on my desk. The system held everything about my life and job. Not just the Foundation but my other, more personal work. Privacy and security were a must and the information most damning to the carefully crafted career and persona of Grant Palmer were all held in this room.

To use a term from popular culture, I was sitting in my very own Bat Cave. Or, probably more accurately, my Fortress of Solitude.

It was a large room, converted out of the former industrial space that the building had originally been used for. I had it customized years ago when I purchased the property. The walls were sound and fire proof, although I was able to hear faint noises through the walls if I focused. Manual and electronic locks secured both the doors and windows, which included sensors and alarms that if triggered were sent directly to me regardless of my location via phone or watch.

As befuddled as Ms. Chase made me, with her unreadable expression and lack of accessible personal information, I did have other methods of observing her. I flicked the switch on the monitors and they sprung to life, filling the screens with images. One was a normal monitor that opened directly to a password prompting page, to which I was the only one who had access. I watched the other larger monitor come in focus and I was able to see multiple locations throughout the building. The entire structure was constantly being filmed by high-tech, hidden security cameras, excluding this room and my bedroom. Normally I didn't allow outside help to come in and do much of the work around the house as part of my public image, but not this. Elijah and I rigged this whole set up together and no one but the two of us knew it was here. Well, other than Olivia, of course. I learned long ago it was pointless to try to keep secrets from her.

Cameras filmed the front door and walkway, the foyer, parlor, kitchen, garage, back alley, the front and back stairways to the second floor, the common area upstairs, and my closet. These cameras were state of the art, military grade, although not necessarily from *our* military. I could see with perfect clarity small movements or the writing on a piece of paper. It was excessive, but I had a desire for the best, and this was it. I didn't use this system every day, but after an attempt of retaliation by a business acquaintance I realized I couldn't rely on my senses alone. Friday night, Amelia Chase confirmed this for me once again.

It had taken all weekend to figure out exactly what had thrown me about Ms. Chase. The fact that her scent was so powerful was strange. I'd heard of irresistible prey before—something so delicious you couldn't pass it up, but this seemed even beyond that. I hadn't even realized she was prey. My head pounded and her heart beat tricked me. It was like she flooded my senses to the point of overriding them.

That was unheard of.

Determined to get back to normal, I spent the early morning hours cross referencing dates, locations and victim names from the previous week's papers. Although many were random, I noticed a pattern emerging, and it looked like it was moving closer and closer to the city. I had a large map on my desk, a charting program and Google Earth up on my computer. I entered the data I'd collected and was able to track his movements. If I was right, he'd make another attempt tonight. This time I would be ready.

At approximately nine in the morning, a figure crossed the security monitor. I watched Ms. Chase stop abruptly in front of the house. I studied her body language, curious to glean anything about her. I noticed her shoulders were bunched up, tense. Her forehead creased with lines. She began pacing back and forth, speaking to someone—or no, I quickly realized, she spoke to herself. I focused on her pink lips and made out the words, 'Grant Palmer' and 'Fuck himself'.

Ouch.

I continued to watch her but leaned back in my seat, running a hand through my hair. Why was she angry at me? Granted, I was a bit abrupt on Friday night, but did I really deserve a 'fuck himself'? That seemed extreme. I'd simply asked her to leave the house. For her own safety. Sure, she didn't know that, but really, the other options would have been terribly unpleasant.

Or, did she know? Did she sense something? Did a primal instinct kick in? The tell-tale hairs on the back of her neck or a tingling sensation warning her about a dangerous hunter nearby?

Things kept getting more interesting. Or rather, *she* kept getting more interesting.

Despite my justifications, her reaction piqued my interest. I observed as she came to the top of the steps and warily eyed the damaged door. I grimaced seeing it through her eyes. That was definitely not one of my better moments, but thankfully the mess didn't deter her from entering the house.

thump thump thump

I could hear the faint, pulsing beats behind my insulated fortress. I shook it off. I'd prepared for this—for her. I settled myself and got back to work.

The Predator liked to accost women on familiar territory. Snatching them in the comfort of fading daylight. I said he snatched, but really, he had others do his work. What was probability of each attempt having been successful? Had any of his victims escaped? Doubtful, but it was an angle worth pursuing. A living victim could break this case.

My eyes shifted to the monitors and I found myself wrapped up in Ms. Chase's moves. I watched. I observed. Okay, fine. I spied. I wanted to see Ms. Chase. I assessed that she wasn't very tall, with curvy hips and thin arms and legs. She had a thick head of blonde hair, which again was tied behind her neck. Why did she wear it this way? Was it easier to work? So many questions passed through my mind as I studied her and her movements, the interactions with the workers that came in and out of the house. I searched for a reason to dismiss her—something inappropriate or unprofessional, but it never came. From my current viewpoint she was the perfect assistant. I needed to resolve my problems and let her do her job so that I could continue with mine, because I had work to do. Important work. Possibly life-saving work. Wait—

I leaned forward. What was that man doing? The handyman. I made out the lettering on his shirt—Thomas. While the other worker, Mark, focused on the task at hand, Thomas couldn't keep his eyes off Ms. Chase.

Adjusting the volume, I leaned closer to the monitor, eyes scanning every angle. It wasn't that Thomas was watching her, it was *how* Thomas was watching her. Where Ms. Chase's body language was hard to read, this guy...well, his motives were clear. The way he held himself, he...what was it called? Flirting. He flirted with her. Smiling and puffing up his chest.

I didn't like it.

Not one bit.

They went to do their respective jobs, the men at the door and Ms. Chase at her desk. I got up from my seat and paced the room for a while, processing the information I had gathered this morning.

My assistant was brave, returning to work even though I had been potentially dangerous to her at our last meeting. This, of course, could also be interpreted as stupid, risky behavior. I also noted she was diligent, hardworking, and surprisingly professional. In my opinion, that countered the stupidity.

And apparently, to the men downstairs, she was quite appealing. Which I supposed I could relate to, although in an entirely different way.

Thomas, from the way he looked and moved around her, liked her face and body. Even through the insulated walls I could feel his heart rate increase every time he came near her. He sniffed, nostrils flaring when she passed—also intrigued by her scent. To that, I could definitely relate. I sat in silence, listening to the way his voice cracked when he laughed and the nervous tremble in his voice. He spoke carefully, searching for the right words. He was trying to impress. He had a full body reaction to this woman. Reactions I couldn't even begin to comprehend.

To be blunt, I did react to her physically, but not like Thomas, who had a slight, yet visible, tightening in his trousers. I felt a comparable desire in the back of my throat. It wasn't so much attraction as hunger—a different form of desire. I recalled her pale skin, so fair it was almost translucent. The bluish veins spreading across her wrists and neck. Every second she was in my home I could see, feel, and hear the pulsing beat of her blood as it circulated though her body.

And then there was her scent. That, I didn't understand. I was accustomed to hunger. Especially the deprivation. That I could handle, but Ms. Chase? Something about her was different. I wanted to know what it was about her that caused this reaction.

All of these things were on my mind as I sat behind my desk viewing Ms. Chase, who was now in the kitchen filling two glasses with ice and water. With one hand I swept the work off the desk, pens and papers clattering to the floor, to lean over the monitors obsessively. Through the screen I watched her as she carried the glasses down the hallway to the front door, kindly asking if the two men were thirsty. They smiled happily. They spoke politely about the weather, how warm and beautiful it was today with the sun finally out, how they were lucky to work outside on occasion.

Fascinated by their simple, polite conversation, I watched how they talked and laughed and communicated. Wide genuine smiles. Easy, light banter. I tried my best to fit in during social interactions, but I doubted I was ever quite this smooth.

The girl collected the glasses and I noticed Thomas' finger lingered for a fraction of a second on her hand. His face maintained innocence, but as I leaned into the monitor, watching his every move, I saw everything. He wanted her.

Ms. Chase turned, walking back inside, and her hair flipped just slightly, and Thomas moved closer and again sniffed the air.

Mine.

Like an animal needing to mark his territory, I leapt from my seat and raced down the hallway. I ceased to inhale, shutting out her scent. I learned quickly that it didn't matter. I felt her in my bones.

thump thump thump thump thump
mine mine mine mine mine

The vibration echoed, over and over in my head, unraveling all of my carefully constructed control and discipline. Like a chain being broken in half, my resolve to stay behind closed doors for the day didn't even last a full morning. My efforts to passively observe crumbled into a heap of failure as I rushed down the stairs, too quickly.

She shrieked, startled by the sight of me suddenly by her side. Aware of my mistake, and in an attempt to maintain a semblance of control, I froze. The glasses in her hands tumbled forward, landing on the glossy hardwoods one at a time.

"Oh my God," she said, glass shattering around her toes. "I'm so sorry. I'll clean it up, right away."

The two men dropped their tools and came running in from the porch, stopping cold in their tracks when they saw me. I positioned my body between them and the girl. Thomas' eyes flicked to Ms. Chase. "Are you okay?"

"She's fine," I declared.

They slunk back to work.

Ms. Chase regained composure and I attempted to do the same. She took a deep breath but I held mine, trying to figure out a way to justify my presence. In seconds, I had completely unraveled. I hadn't planned ahead and now I was faced with an enormous dilemma. Here I was, standing in front of her after seeming to appear out of thin air.

What could I say? The truth? That I rushed down here, like a fool, to claim my territory? That I was ready to fight these other men over her like a dog would fight for his dinner?

Even I knew that wasn't acceptable.

"Is everything okay?" she asked unevenly.

The minute I opened my mouth I would be overwhelmed by her scent. Could I resist her? Maybe. But I also thought I could stay in the house while she was here and not approach her. Look how wonderfully that turned out.

I determined I had two options and quickly decided between them. Option one involved speaking to her. Out of the question. Option two was rude and unprofessional, but at least everyone would get out of here in one piece. I said nothing and silently waited as the girl in front of me calmed herself.

In a matter of seconds her breathing regulated, including her chest moving at an appropriate rate. The flush that ran down her neck and up her cheeks soothed, but not completely. Her green eyes narrowed to suspicious slits and she tilted her head, glancing between me and the mess on the floor.

I stared back, blank faced, looking like the world's biggest asshole.

Ms. Chase chewed over some words, biting them back. Probably another 'fuck him' and leaned over to clean up the shards of broken glass scattered across the floor.

A flare of hope flickered. Maybe she would determine I was a gigantic jerk and she would quit. She could walk away and leave me to my business. I'd hire someone else who didn't have an indescribable allure. Except, just as I'd convinced myself of the possibility, a third, horrific option opened before my eyes. Ms. Chase bent down to retrieve the broken glass. Her fingers moved near the razor sharp edges at the same moment as the shrill ring of my phone cut into the thick, oppressive silence. I didn't answer. I didn't need to. She looked up, leaving the glass on the ground and I lunged, grabbing the edge of her jacket, and said in the most charming voice I could muster, "Please. Let me do that."

11

Amelia

"**P**lease. Let me do that."

I froze. His voice was so soft and smooth, almost mesmerizing. No, it *was* mesmerizing. With only the slightest hesitation, I stopped what I was doing and stepped aside. When I finally found my own voice, it sounded high pitched and squeaky next to his. "No, Mr. Palmer, I can—"

"Ms. Chase," he said, grinding his teeth.

An argument formed on the tip of my tongue, but I swallowed it back. "Thank you. Um, let me get the broom."

He nodded curtly, and as I walked in the direction of the storage closet in the kitchen his phone chimed again. This time he answered. I waited in the hallway, giving him privacy, but I heard every word.

"No. It's fine," he said, without a greeting. "It's under control."

He waited, listening to the voice on the other side, feet crunching glass.

"I know," he said, voice strained, followed by the chime, signaling the end of the call.

I waited a moment before entering the hallway with the broom and dust pan. "I really should do this," I said, thinking, somehow, this would come back to haunt me.

"Ms. Chase, please hand me the broom. I really don't want you to cut yourself. And, it was my fault. I'm the one that startled you."

I relinquished the broom and he swept up the mess scattered across the hallway. I tried to keep the gaping at a minimum, but it was hard. As with everything else, Mr. Palmer continued to surprise me. Each movement he made was quick and precise. His long fingers wrapped around the handle of the broom and I couldn't help but notice how smooth they were. His skin was flawless, like he'd never experienced a moment of manual labor in his life, yet he seemed comfortable with this task.

He wore khaki-colored pants and a white linen button-down, dressed up but not in a suit. His hair was dark brown, but lighter streaks glinted from the sunlight streaming in the open front door. It was styled messy, intentionally so, like a model. In fact, everything about him looked intentional. And perfect. From his disheveled bedhead to his expensive, worn leather shoes. I couldn't see his eyes, as he was looking down, looking for glass. I wanted to know what color they were. Blue?

Green? Whatever they were, I assumed they were also amazingly perfect.

He looked so young but his movements and gestures were that of a much older man. He was tall but he wasn't very big. No. It was more like he was long and lanky without the awkwardness of a young man. I glanced away, forcing myself to stop all the analyzing.

He searched the floor for any remaining pieces of stray glass. He spotted one hidden in the corner, invisible to my eye, and quickly swept it into the pile. He turned and asked, "May I have the dustpan please?"

Our eyes locked briefly and I saw them. Violet.

Not blue.

Not green.

Violet.

"Um...huh?" I asked, unable to speak coherently, transfixed by his rich amethyst eyes.

Amusement twitched at the edges of his mouth. "The dustpan, may I have it?

"Yes, sorry. I think I'm just a little flustered still," I explained. He gave me a quick nod of understanding.

He quickly swept up the pile of debris and stood. "Ms. Chase, I apologize for startling you. I have a horrible habit of sneaking up on people. It's unacceptable."

"It's fine," I said. "I wasn't paying attention."

"I would also like to apologize to you for the other night. My behavior was out of line." He lifted his hands in the air, one occupied by the broom and one with the full dustpan and said, "I'd introduce myself properly with a handshake but unfortunately..."

His voice was still soft, yet there was something missing. He sounded so formal and stiff—slightly robotic. His apology rang with sincerity yet came across as somewhat forced, like words from a script. Nothing about this man made any sense.

"Here, let me take those." I reached out for the broom and dustpan. "And please call me Amelia. It's nice to meet you, Mr. Palmer."

He handed them over to me and I put them away. I returned to find him standing in the same place, unmoved, with an intense look of concentration on his face.

"Was there something you needed?" I asked which caused him to look at me with a confused expression. I pressed. "When you came down here? Did you need something from me?"

Recognition flittered across his face, as if he'd only just remembered why he came down in the first place. "Yes, I heard the delivery man come in and I thought I'd take the box upstairs and ask you to unpack it for me."

"I'd be happy to." I followed him to the parlor. He picked up the large box with ease. It must not have been as heavy as I suspected.

Halfway up the stairs, I heard my name being called from behind. I turned to find Thomas in the hallway. Mr. Palmer was already at the top of the stairs so I quickly ran back down to see what he needed.

"Do you need something?" I asked.

Thomas glanced up the stairs. In a low voice he said, "I wanted to ask you if I could have your number? Maybe I could call you sometime?"

This guy had balls. Asking me on a date in the middle of work hours. I hoped Genevieve was wrong and this was the kind of thing Mr. Palmer wouldn't catch on to. I was already walking on eggshells.

"Here." I fished a business card out of my pocket. In a quiet voice I added, "Call me after work, okay?"

From the top of the stairs I heard a loud noise and I waved Thomas off. I ran up the stairs, two at a time, to find Mr. Palmer. He was on the landing waiting for me with a look of irritation on his face.

Great. Back on the shit list.

Flushed and out of breath, I explained, "I stopped to help Thomas with something, sorry."

Abruptly, he turned away and went into his dressing room. I hesitated for a moment but followed him, unsure of my next step. I wasn't sure why he was irritated with me, it had only taken a second to speak with Thomas and it wasn't like he knew we were talking about non-work-related activities.

I entered the dressing room and he pointed to the box on the floor. I could tell from his stiffness that the slight progress we had made downstairs was gone. Evaporated like water on a hot day.

"This package is filled with clothing and accessories. Please place them in the appropriate areas of the closet. Then take the camera, the one in the bottom drawer over there," I followed the direction of his finger as he pointed to of a row of drawers against the wall. "Photograph each outfit. In the box you will find an envelope with an itemized list that will provide information about what article of clothing goes in which section of the closet and binder." When he finished he turned without another word and walked through a side door I'd been instructed not to enter.

Wow. Okay, maybe he wasn't so much a recluse but just a total weirdo.

Admittedly, he hadn't been overly friendly downstairs but he did, at least, appear sincere. Now he treated me like a child who had been caught with their hand in the cookie jar by a mother with eyes in the back of her head. What had I done? I ran through the possible offenses. Other than speaking to Thomas, and leaving him waiting for a moment, I hadn't done anything wrong.

Whatever, I thought. Genevieve hadn't told me about this side of Mr. Palmer. Quirky? Yes. A little strange? Sure. Standoffish? Definitely. But hostile and jerkish? No. Not at all. Actually, I felt like Genevieve really liked Mr. Palmer. She seemed genuinely fond of him. That meant whatever was going on between us was, well, between us.

I found a pair of scissors and opened the package. Inside were tightly packed stacks of dress and causal shirts, four or five pairs of nice pants and two pairs of jeans. There were also shoes, belts, and other accessories. I took a quick peek at the labels and rolled my eyes at the designer names. Ralph Lauren, Dior, Prada. I was sure the shirt I was holding cost more than my entire summer wardrobe. The items in this box alone would be enough to dress a normal man for a year, not just one summer. Honestly, he was going to run out of room soon to store it all.

It took me several hours to coordinate and photograph all the new items. As the minutes ticked by, I found myself glancing toward his door, wondering if he would ever come back. I'd created an intense fantasy about standing up to him, asking him what his problem was and why he thought he could treat me so badly.

I daydreamed of walking up to him and poking his chest with my finger, which of course would be difficult since he was so tall. I'd probably hit him in the belly, which would be way less effective. Either way, then I would force him to look me in the eye and admit he was being a jerk and that his first apology meant nothing. I wanted to tell him that he was a spoiled little boy who needed to treat people with respect.

That was what I wanted to do.

But he never emerged, so it didn't matter.

I sighed, because I'd never do it. I was too much of a chicken. I gathered a handful of leather belts and hooked them one at a time on a rack hanging from the wall. If I'd known I would spend my summer hanging up clothes, I would've gotten a job at the GAP.

I completed my work in the dressing room and went downstairs. I ate my lunch at my desk, finishing the data entry I'd started that morning. Thomas and Mark left while I was upstairs, and when the guy fixing the security system arrived late that afternoon I simply showed him what needed repairing. Mr. Palmer never reappeared from his rooms.

At six o' clock I packed my bags and left my daily report on the desk. At the front door, I paused for a moment at the bottom of the steps, positive that I could hear the faint strains of music from above. It must be nice to hide away while everyone else fixed your problems.

12

Grant

The buck fell easily and I drained his blood with efficiency. As I wiped a drop from the corner of my mouth I heard the snap of a branch and froze. The other forest animals fled the instant I took down the deer. I should be the only one out here. Too late at night for hunters and too far off the beaten path for hikers.

Just me and my prey, or so I thought.

The air stirred, pushing a gust past me. I inhaled. Musky and cool. The smell would appeal to a human, but for another creature of the night it kicked my instincts in gear.

"Who's there?" I asked. It was, after all, my territory. Silence was the only reply but now I saw the edge of a heavy wool jacket and a flash of short red hair. "Show yourself, friend."

He stepped from his spot, hands up. "Just traveling through," he said. His voice carried a Midwestern drawl. "Heard you on the hunt."

I didn't acknowledge the buck I'd just consumed, but I knew what he was thinking. Feeding on animals wasn't popular among my kind. "Ah, so you're new to this area. I'm Grant Palmer."

"Palmer?" The instant the word left his mouth I caught an additional odor. He wasn't alone.

"Traveling companion?" I asked.

"Nah. More like a snack I'm saving for later. These mountains are pretty dense, not a lot of civilization." Again, his eyes flicked to the animal carcass. "But I guess you already knew that."

"Pickings get a little slim out here. You wouldn't mind giving me a taste would you?"

A muffled squeak came from behind the man's back. In the shadows I made out a small shape—a girl from the looks of it. Her hands were tied with a thick rope. Was this man part of the Predator's group?

He hesitated as expected. Sharing wasn't a priority of our kind. Finders keepers was more like it. I took a step closer and made eye contact with the girl. "You okay?"

She froze but I didn't look away and I heard her weak plea, "Help me."

I nodded and said, "I think she'd rather come with me."

The vampire frowned. "Doesn't work that way, friend. This one is mine and I have plans for her. You'll need to get your own—unless you like eating filthy animals, and something tells me you do."

I clutched the handle of the knife in my hand and moved fast, slicing away at the binds. The girl stumbled back while the vampire sprang into action, rushing at me with full, unbridled force. I swiped at his legs, tripping him. He landed with a thud, sliding across the forest floor—leaves and dirt scattering on impact. With the upper hand I pounced landing hard on his chest. We tussled on the ground, rolling down an embankment, until we got to the bottom. Wrapping my hands around his throat I declared, "You made a mistake coming into my territory. The Palmers run these mountains and kidnapping girls is against our standards."

He kicked and sputtered beneath me. I leaned over and pressed the tip of the knife to his throat. His eyes narrowed and he said, "You're a freak."

"And you're dead. For real this time."

With the blade I slit his throat before tearing it off in one quick move. I wiped the dirty knife blade on ground before looking up at the girl. She stood frozen, eyes wide in terror. I gave her a fast nod and said, "Let's get you home."

***

I left the girl, Maggie, with Olivia, after compelling her to forget most of what she'd experienced. With my face and actions wiped from her memory, I set off toward the coordinates I'd entered in my watch before I left the office. Reaching the location documented in the police report didn't take long. Warring odors assaulted my senses and it only took a moment before I found a smudge on the sidewalk. I wiped my finger over the dark stain and sniffed the coppery blood.

The police hadn't found a body, but a girl was reported missing. Searching the surrounding areas thoroughly, I came up empty, too.

Examining the area, I stopped near a wooden fence separating yards. Scratch marks were gouged into the top of the fence. I spread my fingers over the lines, matching them to my own razor-sharp nails and leapt easily over the six-foot high obstacle. My feet landed in the soft grass next to a handful of other footprints. At the very least, this guy was of similar height and size. I sniffed the markings and caught a whiff of his scent. So the Predator had been here. *What did he do with her body?* I wondered. After finding nothing else useful, I decided to head east, following the pattern I had formulated.

As I traveled I opened my mind to the noises of the night. Passing homes, I heard the sounds of families having dinner and children playing outside enjoying the warm weather. I overheard an argument by two lovers, one bitter over the betrayal of the other. Most of it was mundane, people worried about bills or work or relationships. After all this time I'd become numb to the day-to-day worries of humans. I attempted to respect their privacy when possible, but tonight I was listening for something else.

The Predator.

I'd heard him before. Several times in fact, but I was always too late. He seemed to have a sense of when to move on, of when I was coming. I'm not sure if he knew I was on to him yet or if it was a coincidence. I felt like he knew. He was elusive, always one step ahead.

There were others with him, at least that was my theory. Their voices changed and often combined with the victims, making them hard to identify. Everything about this predator and his accomplices was one step ahead of me. I was fast. He was faster and unfortunately, deadlier.

So, tonight as I walked, I listened for his voice, for the clues I needed to find him before another unsuspecting victim stumbled onto his path. If all went according to plan, I would catch up to him. The pattern fit and my research was flawless.

Oh shoot, I burned the bread....mommy, Jane hit me on purpose...I'm sorry, I really am....Oh. My. God. You will not believe what I just heard...

Humans. Nothing they said was ever of much importance. My thoughts turned to Ms. Chase and I wondered where she was at this moment. Had the worker called her for a date? Had she made plans to see him? Again, I was irritated by my fascination with her and determined I had to move past my obsession.

Did you watch Fallon today...I'm going to the store, do you need anything...please, please, whatever you want...

My mind perked up at the last one and I narrowed my focus. The voice sounded distressed. Low growls echoed in the night.

Do you want my money? Or my car? Here, take my keys.....please...

I zeroed in. They weren't far. Less than five miles away, if my calculations were correct. I inhaled, catching his scent, mingled with hers. She smelled salty—like sweat and her heart beat erratically. Not only from fear but exhaustion. Tiny, but important clues. I couldn't be positive but I took off in the direction of the nearest park. It fit his pattern. An educated guess was better than nothing at all.

"Don't do this...please...oh my god." Her voice rang through the night, clear as a bell.

His reply was gravelly, snide. *"Don't be afraid...you're part of a bigger plan. Remember that."*

I came to the entrance of the park and read the wooden sign.

Lullwater Park
Jogging Trails
Hours 6:00 AM-Dark

The sweat and racing heart signaled the woman was probably a jogger. I tore through the darkness in the direction of the trails. This was the closest I had come to him, the closest I had been to stopping him from continuing his terrorization of this community. I heard her begging for her life, no longer speaking to him, simply rambling during her final moments.

I ran, cutting across green space and rocky paths. I leapt over a small stream, feet sinking in thick, dark mud. Her voice bounced off the trees, leading me to her. They couldn't be more than a mile or two away.

"It will all be over soon, once my friends and I are satisfied."

That was when I heard the others. They too spoke in low voices, punctuated with the occasional growl. These weren't civilized beings. Not like myself and my family. Not even like the Predator.

I focused on him, noting that his voice was deep and rough. His accent was indistinct but the tone of his voice spoke with authority. I broke through the tree line as two of the killers pulled the jogger from her kneeling position to her feet. They held her before the Predator, her arms stretched wide, like a sacrifice. She shivered, eyes wide and terrified, visibly shuddering as he touched her face gently. She never felt the snap of her neck or the cuts as the others tore at the flesh on her exposed arms and wrists.

I was fast but incredibly, they were faster—feeding and discarding her body before I could stop them. The woman was dead. The killers gone, slipped away in a half-dozen possible directions, trailing not only in their scent but that of the dead.

"I'll catch you," I said, in a raised voice, while standing over the body. I pulled out my cell and dialed 911 before retreating back to the safety of the woods, but not before I heard the faintest of words deep in the back of my mind.

"Game on."

13

Amelia

H e was in the kitchen when I arrived the following morning. Uncharacteristically disheveled
with mud-caked shoes and weary, pale eyes.
He glanced in my direction as he washed his hands. The
water in the bottom of the sink was brown and filthy.

"Can I help you with something?" I asked.

"No thank you, Ms. Chase. I'll send your list down immediately."

He dried his hands on the towel by the sink, arranged
it carefully back in place and left the room.

An hour later he brought down the list, clean and re-
freshed. His unruly hair was damp from the shower and
he smelled delicious.

"Is that uh," I started to ask something about shampoo or body gel, but nothing logical came out.

"What?" He looked for something amiss on his list.

"You're uh, um, never mind. I'll get right to this." I
snatched the list from his hands and he promptly disappeared upstairs so quickly I didn't see him go, again.

With the day half over, I sat for a quiet moment in my chair. The clock said I had three more hours of work. I wanted nothing more than to go home. I'd spent the morning running the errands for Mr. Palmer and dreaded the tedious, ridiculous job he had for me that afternoon.

I came each day prepared, once again, to move past our bumps and enjoy my job. I watched *E!*. I understood that rich, attractive people were eccentric and spoiled. Was Mr. Palmer basically a Kardashian? At least I didn't have to sanitize the house from a series of female visitors. Genevieve never implied he had a girlfriend and on face value I couldn't imagine why not. Women should be crawling all over this place. But realistically? A girl-friend seemed unlikely. A one night stand? Possible, but with all the OCD stuff going on....no wonder he was such a jerk. Maybe he just needed to get laid.

Lack of orgies aside, Mr. Palmer was frustratingly difficult. With each passing day I learned his obsessive compulsive habits passed eccentric and lingered toward mentally unstable. On Tuesday he left me directions to reorganize his enormous record collection out of alpha-betical order and into subgroups by artist, genre and date of release. He also wanted the covers photographed and entered into a data base. This project alone would probably take me the entire week and my brain was a puddle of mush by the time I'd gotten through the Ds.

On Wednesday he left me with various chores around the house. My instructions were to straighten and dust all the paintings on the walls. There were additional, detailed, guidelines about how I had to wear cloth gloves and to never, *ever* touch the actual painting itself. I also had a special duster to use for the other antiques. After I completed the artwork I had to dust the common rooms, taking time to hand clean each curio or knick-knack he had apparently collected or inherited from around the world.

I didn't have a history of being clumsy, but all the rules and specifications were giving me a complex. I was sure at any moment I would drop and shatter a priceless heirloom. I should check the bathroom cabinet for Xanax or get a prescription. There was no way I could continue working like this and not develop an anxiety disorder or at the very least, an ulcer.

As I carefully cleaned the panes on a gorgeous Tiffany lamp (real, I Googled it), I began to wonder if Mr. Palmer wanted me to quit. Some of the tasks he'd given me were so outrageous that I felt like this was some kind of giant test. They seemed above and beyond what Genevieve described during our training. Was he waiting to see if I was fool enough to follow his instructions or if I would actually refuse to do something he asked? Beyond that, I wondered if I refused, would have enough justification to fire me?

Amelia Chase was not getting fired.

With a defiant attitude in mind, I spent Wednesday afternoon on my hands and knees with a comb, straightening out the fringe on the antique rugs and carpets throughout the house. Which, by the way, was utterly ridiculous and a complete waste of my time. It was fringe. On a rug. No one cared if it was perfect.

Except Mr. Palmer. He cared.

Now, with three hours left in the day, I rubbed my fingers into my temples and plotted my escape from his particular brand of madhouse. I forced myself into the kitchen, to the large supply closet which would normally act as a pantry. Mr. 'Special Diet' Palmer didn't keep food in the house so the pantry was now a supply closet.

I had purchased new bins and containers for the closet earlier in the day. Apparently Mr. Palmer needed his office supplies separated into specific containers. The paperclips from the push pins, the masking tape from the scotch tape, and so forth. I had to admit, going hog wild at the fancy organizer store with an unlimited credit card was pretty awesome. It was sort of like a dream come true. A dream that got even better when I armed myself with a state-of-the-art computerized label maker since he couldn't just look in the clear container and figure out which one was which.

I plugged in my ear buds, turning it to the local news station. I'd never been one to listen to this type of show but ever since I started spending so much time alone it made me feel like I had a little contact during the day.

At least I was up on current events. The big one, locally at least, was the string of deaths around the state. It was all anyone talked about.

The police have little information other than they suspect an animal attack. Our reporter Jason Childs spoke to Montgomery Amerson, a National Park wildlife expert, and he isn't so sure about that theory. "It's uncommon for a bear or bobcat to wander into suburban neighborhoods and attack a human," he said.

"But it's not impossible?" Jason asked.

"No, but I'd definitely want to see a medical report on the wounds to be sure."

The police had no comment about Mr. Amerson's opinion and warn people to stay away from the local trails and not to approach any wildlife.

"Next hour on Asheville Talk we'll discuss broader theories, like the one sociologist James Norton has about this not being an animal at all but possibly the work of a ritualistic killer..."

The box of staples slipped from my hand and fell to the floor, scattering the small metal pieces. "Seriously, my parents paid eighty-six thousand dollars for me to get a degree and I'm spending it sorting office supplies." I dropped to the floor to pick them up but the hairs on the back of my neck stood on end and I said a silent prayer that it was my imagination. I glanced over my shoulder.

"Jesus!" I cried, when I saw a tall, thin girl with a thick head of red hair standing in the middle of the kitchen. I yanked the headphones out of my ears.

"Hi!" she replied, with a bright curious smile.

I managed to stand even as my heart lunged to my throat, pounding like a freight train. "Who are you?"

"I'm Olivia. Grant's cousin. I let myself in."

"Mr. Palmer's cousin?" I took a settling breath, heart still beating in my ears. She seemed harmless. Less than harmless, I thought, eyeing her flowery dress and strappy sandals that made her tower over me like a giant. "Was he expecting you? Because he didn't tell me you were coming," I said. "Not that you can't stop by, you're family. I'm just a little caught a little off guard—"

"No, he's not expecting me. I thought I would surprise him," she answered with a smirk. "He hates surprises."

"He does?" I didn't like where this was headed. I was already on his shit list.

"Yes, but he loves me, so it will be alright."

"If you say so." I placed the boxes on the shelves and reached for the box of Post-it-Notes. "He's not here right now, but I'm sure it's okay if you wait. Oh," I said, offering my hand, "I'm Amelia, the new assistant."

"Of course. Amelia." My name rolled pleasantly off her lips. She grasped my hand in a firm handshake.

I turned back to my work but felt her vivid, candy-apple green, eyes watching my movements as I continued with the mindless task of sorting the notes by color and size. I resisted the urge to take a stack of squares and write 'I Quit' in color coordinated markers and stick them all over the house in a fit of rage.

I turned to face her again, and asked, "Can I get you something? Tea or coffee? Mr. Palmer doesn't have any food in the house, but I could go get you something if you want. I have some yogurt and a cereal bar in my purse," I rambled. Olivia made me nervous with her watchful eyes. What if he'd sent her here as another part of his crazy controlling mind games?

Olivia shook her head and said, "No thank you. I'll wait in the other room."

"Sounds good," I said. "Do you know the way?"

"I do, but would you mind sitting with me? I had a long drive and could really use the company." For a moment I lost my train of thought. Her eyes and voice were incredibly appealing, very much like her cousin's.

I wasn't sure what to do. I had a feeling Mr. Palmer was going to be super pissed about Olivia showing up like this. Like she said, he didn't seem the type to like surprises or anything fun. Also, I wasn't sure how much I was supposed to entertain his guests. I mean, I had a stack of Post-it notes to deal with and seriously, I was not getting fired over a stupid sticky note. But then again, I would hate to offend his family by being rude. This whole situation was entering uncharted territory.

Olivia must have noticed my unease and said, "Please. Don't worry about Grant. He can blame me if he wants to get pissy about it." She laughed and added, "Which he will. Foul is his favorite mood."

Oh, I liked this girl. I followed Olivia as she led the way into the parlor, taking a seat in one of the large, overstuffed chairs. I couldn't help but check out her long legs and covet the graceful way she sat across from me.

"Really, Amelia," she said. "Don't take Grant too seriously. I know he can be a bit of a grump but he has a good heart. He forgets how to act around people sometimes."

I smiled back but said nothing, not wanting to fall into the trap of speaking about him. There was a moment of awkward silence but thankfully she changed the subject, asking me about my schooling and future plans.

"Well my plan is to save some money and go to grad school to be a librarian," I said, after giving her a brief rundown of my life so far. "Working here seemed like a good way to stay in Asheville and do that." Maybe it was the fact I'd gone days without speaking to anyone like this, but I found Olivia easy to talk to. I had to wonder if she was really this good or was I this desperate. Other than Drew and the occasional store clerk, I spent most of my days alone.

"You said you had a long drive? Do you live out of town?"

"Oh, I live in Black Mountain."

"I've driven through there. It's a pretty town."

"We really love it. My whole extended family has lived there for some time."

"That sounds nice. I'm an only child so it's always just me and my parents. But I guess you and Mr. Palmer are close then?" I was snooping. I couldn't even deny it.

"Very close. The whole family is tight. I'm sure you'll get to meet them someday."

The back door opened and closed. Quiet footsteps walked across the kitchen and I stood up quickly while Olivia remained seated. "He'll probably go directly up-stairs," I said. "I'll go catch him."

Proving me wrong, again, Mr. Palmer joined us in the parlor. He gave Olivia an unsurprised, pointed look, like he knew she was there before he walked in the room. Olivia smiled at him and he rolled his eyes before turning to me.

"I see you've met my cousin, Olivia. She has a way of making herself at home."

"I have and she's been lovely to talk with. Now that you're home I'm going to go back to work." *Those Post-It notes aren't going to sort themselves,* I wanted to add, but held back. "Nice to meet you, Ms. Palmer," I said, backing out of the room, trying to make a fast escape.

"It's Olivia. And it was great meeting you too, Amelia. I hope to see you again soon." She walked over and gave me a tight hug. Oh boy. She was a hugger.

I went back to my work in the closet, but listened to them quietly go up the front stairs, presumably to Mr. Palmer's private quarters. Those two couldn't be more different. Olivia's open and warm nature compared to Mr. Palmer with his stiff, jerkish behavior. It made me wonder how two people who grew up in the same family could turn out so unalike. Although my confusion could be due to the fact I was an only child and didn't have the experience of a close family.

Left alone with my news radio, I finished the notes and checked the time before moving on to another bin. An hour had passed. Just two more to go. If anything, Olivia provided a bit of entertainment in my otherwise dull and boring day. For that, I should thank her. Her visit also gave me a chance to see Mr. Palmer in a different light. Although, I thought, while arranging push pins by size, it would take more than nice words from his cousin to change my mind about him.

14

Grant

"Grant, you didn't tell me Amelia was so fantastic," Olivia said on the way upstairs.

I didn't acknowledge her comment and walked into my dressing room to put my coat up and change out of my work clothes. Although I had to admit, at least to myself, that Amelia did smell pretty fantastic.

"What are you doing here, Olivia?" I asked, pulling a clean shirt over my head. Standing in front of the mirror I ran my hands through my hair, trying to get it how I liked it.

"No 'how are you' or 'I'm so glad you came to visit'?"

I brushed past her and walked into my study and sat behind the desk looking for something to do other than talk to my cousin. My incredibly nosy, persistent cousin. Not by birth. No, all of those cousins were long gone. Olivia was part of my 'new' family. One formed out of both necessity and a general fondness for one another. Olivia was the one person in this day-and-age that I appreciated the most. Dare I say, cared for the most. She definitely cared for me, which was why she was giving me that look. The one I didn't want to deal with right now.

"You can't ignore this, Grant."

I ignored her.

"Stop it, Grant. We need to talk about this." She flopped on a chair across from my desk, arms crossed in determination.

I sighed and looked at her. "What do you want me to say? Do I find her appealing? Yes. Am I going to do anything about it? No. There is nothing more to discuss."

She frowned. "Are you sure you can handle it?"

I glared at her. "Yes. You know I can. I have."

Olivia glared back at me. "You almost slipped with the glass. And the other night, she barely made it out of here alive."

"But she did. I told you on the phone it was fine. You know I'm disciplined. I have this very much under control." I told her hoping my tone would end this conversation.

"I'm not sure it matters anyway. She's going to quit."

"Did she tell you that?"

Olivia tapped the side of her temple. "You know how this works. It's like a freaking crystal ball."

I sighed and slumped into my seat. If Olivia had a premonition then surely Amelia Chase was close to a decision. "I know."

To be quite honest, I wanted her to quit. After my reaction to her and the worker on Monday, combined with the fact I'd failed in my attempt to save the woman in the park, I'd resolved to push Amelia Chase out of my life for good. I spent the rest of the week ignoring her and leaving her with hours of monotonous tasks. I figured after several days she would grow tired and frustrated with the absurdity of my menial projects and resign.

"It's what you really want? Because right now that's the path she's on, but it doesn't have to be. You have a lot of control over this situation. In fact, you're the reason she wants to quit in the first place. Do you really have to be such an ass? I mean, combing the fringe on your rug? That's a bit much even for you."

I glared at her and she glared back with narrow eyes. She knew I didn't like it when she used her powers to interfere with my life. That was the first rule between us. Breaking it now, when I was already so vulnerable, was unacceptable. "Don't do that."

"I can't turn it off, Grant. I can see what's going to happen to pretty much anyone that crosses your path. That girl has been pinging my radar for a week."

I ran a hand over my face. I knew she couldn't stop the visions any more than I could stop the way I manipulated people.

"Believe it or not," Olivia said, "I'm more worried about her than you. I feel an obligation to make sure she's safe and with you acting so unbalanced, I'm keeping an eye on her."

"Understandable," I admitted.

"You never answered my question. Do you want her to leave?"

"It's for the best, you know that. I am under control but it is a distraction I really don't need. Especially not right now. I need to focus on these murders," I said. "I'd rather her to leave on her own terms. I don't want to fire her."

Olivia broke out into laughter, red hair quivering over her shoulders. I quirked an eyebrow at her, waiting to understand what was so funny. She finally controlled herself and said, "She wavers back and forth. At the moment she's quite determined to stay. To prove that you can't break her. But a couple more of these horrific dirty jobs will seal her fate."

"I haven't asked her to do anything I didn't ask other PAs."

"You're such an idiot. Like Genevieve was going to say no to anything you asked. She was happy you let her spend time with you."

"Genevieve asked for the job and I gave it to her. We barely spoke other than through assignments and emails."

She stuck out her tongue and it was all I could do not to grab it. She'd always been like this, ever since I found her decades ago and brought her into the coven. Half clairvoyant genius—half brat. "It doesn't matter. I have no doubt that I can break Ms. Chase. All the qualities I desired for her as an assistant will end up making this so much harder on her in the end."

We fell into a moment of silence now that the main reason for her visit had been discussed. From her expression I could tell she had something else to say—didn't she always? I never lived up to the expectations of my family. It was the reason we lived apart.

"What?" I asked.

"The boys were sad you wouldn't go hunting with them."

"It's not possible right now. You know that."

"It's not the same without you at home. It's never the same."

"Olivia," I warned.

She sighed unhappily.

I hated disappointing her but the decision had been made. She knew that. She could even see it in her crystal-ball-like mind. I changed the subject and asked, "When is Eli coming home?"

She pursed her lips together, clearly not convinced we were finished with the prior topic, but she let it go for now. "Tonight. They're in Montana now."

"I really need for him to come see me when he returns. Will you tell him?"

"Of course. I'm sure he'll be happy to come down."

I got up and walked to her and pulled her out of the seat. She quickly rose and wrapped her arms around me, embracing me tightly. I reciprocated, leaning down and inhaling the smell of her hair and clothes. As much as I resisted, there were moments when I'd regretted the choices that led me to my current lifestyle. This was one of those times. I hated the strain this put on the two of us.

"Speaking of hunting, and well...Amelia, how's your alternate food source?" she asked, stepping back to walk around my desk bending over at the small refrigerator disguised as a file cabinet. She punched in the code and opened the door revealing six containers of dark red liquid. Four down from my standard ten.

"Under control."

She lifted an eyebrow but I knew I'd passed her test. I may have had to tap into my safety reserve but it was better than slaughtering an innocent girl.

Later, after Olivia returned home, I considered our relationship and how much it meant to me. How living in isolation was taking its toll. I knew it was for the greater good, but for the first time in many years, when Olivia left, I felt a deeper loss than usual. Something my family couldn't give me.

15

Amelia

"Drew, I'm home," I called.

I dropped my keys in the dish by the door and went directly to my room to change out of my work clothes and into something more comfortable. I'd just pulled my hair back into a pony tail when Drew came around the corner with a glass of brownish alcohol and thrust it into my hand.

"You have no idea how much I needed this," I said, taking an enormous gulp. Wincing at the burn, I sat on the couch in the living room and pulled the fuzzy blanket my mom gave me for my birthday over my legs.

"I had an inkling when you called on the way home and left me a message chanting the words, 'do not let me quit my job' over and over."

I put my half-empty glass down on the end table and groaned. "I know. That place is such a nightmare. Do you want to know what I had to do today?"

"Does a fat kid want cake?" he asked, with a wicked grin.

Angel Lawson

"After I arranged all the office supplies in the pantry," I rolled my eyes, "I had to go into his garage and sort through all the nails and screws on his work table and separate them into matching sizes. Then, obviously, I had to place them into labeled containers."

"What is his deal with labeled containers?"

"Everything in that house is labeled."

"You've never seen his bedroom, what do you bet he labels the outside of his bedside table, with things like, Porn, or Condoms, or Weed." He snorted, which made us both burst into giggles.

"No way. That guy is way too uptight to read or watch porn and no girls are coming to his place. He would have to sanitize them before and after they left his room. I figure this is why he's so cranky all the time," I said. "And I wish he'd smoke a little weed. It'd chill him out."

"Please take a video of that if it happens. I swear I won't post it online."

Suddenly I remembered something else, "Oh and guess what?" Drew cocked an eyebrow. "What?"

"I met Mr. Palmer's cousin today. Olivia Palmer, from Black Mountain."

"The plot thickens," he said, rubbing his hands together. "So he has a family. Did you get any dirt?"

"Not really. She really was very nice, and totally beautiful. She seemed to know her cousin was a bit of an ass, which made me feel a little better. She had a little of that 'I'm A Perfect Palmer' vibe going on herself."

110

My cell rang, my personal phone, not the one for work. I jumped up to answer. The voice on the other line made me smile.

"Oh, hi Thomas, how are you?"

"I'm great. Just calling to see how your week was going?"

"It's been okay—no more house disasters."

"Too bad, if there had been I could have dropped by."

I laughed. God this was terrible. I willed him to just ask me out. "So what's going on?"

"I was calling to see if you'd like to meet up tomorrow night?"

I looked up at Drew and he shrugged. "Tomorrow night? My roommate Drew and I are supposed to go to The Lion Head tomorrow night."

"The dive bar off Front Street? Sounds fun. How about I meet you there?"

"Perfect."

"Awesome, I'll meet you there around nine."

I said goodbye and ended the call. Drew gave me an inquisitive look. "Well, the good news is that I have a date tomorrow night. The better news is you get to be my wing-man!" I smiled a huge, fake, grin hoping he would play along. "Just in case it goes terribly wrong. If it goes amazingly right, you can bail."

"Sounds like my idea of a perfect Friday night."

I put on my best pouting face and whimpered. "Drew, please? I really want to go but I'm not comfortable going alone. Especially not right now, with his whole serial killer bear thing going on."

"Okay, but only because of that and I want you to be safe. Plus, what else am I going to do while you are out?"

I leaned over and gave him a squeeze around his shoulders. "Speaking of, did you hear any more news about that poor girl's murder? I tried to catch up on the radio today but Olivia showed up." Drew worked in one of the city offices with a dozen chatty co-workers. I thought maybe he'd heard something.

"Well, the big rumor is that the police are totally confused. They can't decide if it was a murder or an attack by a wild animal."

"Yeah, the park guy wasn't convinced on the animal angle," I said skeptically. "Sounds like a cover-up to me."

"April, the girl one cubicle over, heard on the news that the wounds aren't normal or something. I'm with you; animals don't attack in patterns or leave six bodies in the same exact way."

"Exactly."

"Jesus," I said. "This whole thing sounds insane."

Even though it was silly, I wrapped my arms around my knees, suddenly feeling vulnerable. I couldn't help but think about how Olivia had sneaked up on me today; I didn't even notice she'd come into the kitchen. If she was able to walk in without my notice, I was sure anyone could. I needed to make sure the doors were bolted from now on and to let Mr. Palmer know I was taking extra precautions.

My phone rang, the work one, not my personal one and I mouthed "Kill me now," before answering in a fake-nice voice, "Amelia Chase."

"Ms. Chase, I've realized the guest list for the Palmer Foundation charity event next month needs to go to the printers."

"Mr. Palmer, I would be happy to do that for you," I said, rolling my eyes at Drew. "I'll take care of it first thing in the morning."

"Unfortunately, it must be done tonight. The good news is you should be able to access the list from your computer at home."

Yayyyyy. "That *is* good news. I'll get right on it."

"Please have it done before midnight."

I looked at my watch. It was eleven. "Of course."

"Good night, Ms. Chase."

"You're welco—"

He hung up.

He hung up on me.

He freaking hung up on me.

I sat, jaw dropped with the phone in my hand until Drew asked, "What? What happened?"

"What happened? I'm going to happen," I said, rambling like an idiot. "I'm sick of him treating me like a work horse. I didn't sign up for that. What a fu---"

"What are you going to do?"

"I don't know yet, but it's going to be good."

***

It was Friday and all thoughts I'd had about staying at this job disappeared the minute I walked in the front door of Mr. Palmer's home. I was still furious from the night before. Furious but undecided.

Then I saw the list for the day and my indecision became focused rage. The rage turned to a plan, and my plan turned into reality. That was why I now flipped through the row of T-shirts, trying to decide which one to pick. Bruce Springsteen?

Nah. No need to desecrate an American flag.

Coldplay?

Too whiney. I needed somebody with balls. Gwyneth Paltrow probably claimed those in the 'Uncoupling'.

Jimi Hendrix?

I couldn't bear to do it to Jimi.

I flipped through the shirts one by one, before I made my decision and removed it from the rack.

It was soft and worn. But still pristine. Loved and truly unique. Clearly one of his favorites. I held it up to my face and inhaled the soothing smell of his laundry detergent. Mr. Palmer's laundromat used the best-smelling soap.

Entering the bathroom downstairs, I changed out of my blouse and into the T-shirt. I assessed myself in the mirror and noted how his shirt was too big, which wasn't a surprise since he was so tall. It was actually better that the shirt was so big since I needed as much coverage as possible. I didn't want to ruin my clothes.

I pulled my hair on top of my head, pissed I had spent 20 minutes blowing it out this morning since it would immediately get frizzy in the humidity outside. I left my blouse and shoes in the bathroom and walked to the kitchen for my supplies.

Bucket, bleach, and a scrub brush.

The asshole left me orders to clean his patio furniture.

After working all night on his guest list I came into work and found that instruction on his infamous list. He could have told me on the phone last night, giving me the opportunity to dress appropriately. But no. That would have been too considerate. The way I saw it, I had no other choice but to wear something from his closet.

Fuming, I carried the supplies to the enclosed patio off the back of the first floor. It was beyond degrading and defeating. I didn't mind the manual labor or tedious shit he asked me to do, but this crossed a line.

It was the way he asked me, or rather didn't ask me. It was all through his stupid, passive-aggressive handwritten lists left on the desk for me each day. Like he couldn't bear to be near me or lower himself to speaking to me directly. I was educated and smart and he looked at me like I was a repulsive and lowly slave. I wasn't Miss North Carolina or anything but Jesus, give me a break.

Then there was the fact he was so rude. Of course he acted nice to me when Olivia was here or the workers, but other times he either ignored me or treated me like shit. Every day I completed his ridiculous, exhausting demands and never once have I heard a please or a thank you. How fucking hard was it to leave the words 'Thank You' at the end of a note? How hard was it to come down from his private rooms and actually greet me, in a civil tone, once in a while?

I was at my wits-end and refused to be his lackey any longer, so I resolved to finish the day, scrub his damn furniture and quit. But first, I was going to make him pay.

Armed with my supplies, and dressed in Grant Palmer's vintage T-shirt, I opened the back door and walked out to his overly manicured patio. Potted plants, ferns, and ornamental trees surrounded the brick floor. It was sunny today and the bricks felt warm under my bare feet. A huge stone fireplace sat in the corner while white painted wrought iron furniture was placed around the patio strategically, designed for socializing.

I tried to imagine Mr. Palmer out here socializing with friends or his family on a cool fall night, fireplace lit and candles all around. Maybe they had s'mores. Ha! As if. I honestly couldn't see it. I could see Olivia out here holding court, glass in hand, while he lurked inside, hiding from people.

I sat the bucket down and poured in the bleach and pulled out the hose from beside the house. I mixed the up the two and began working. With every minute, every scrub of the brush and rinse of water, I grew more and more furious at my boss. I was more convinced than ever that he was actually trying to make me quit and I had reached the point where I was happy to grant him his wish.

16

Grant

I heard Elijah the moment he pulled into the garage. Ms. Chase was outside, scrubbing the never-used patio furniture, unaware of his arrival. I hoped Olivia was right and this dirty task would be the final straw, resulting in her leaving today and never return. I even had a reference letter prepared to send her next week if she needed it, although her time here was so short I was sure it would be better never to mention it again.

I'd spent the morning going over my maps and the recent news about the murder from Monday night. None of it was very useful, which was why I'd asked Elijah to come see me.

Through the monitors I saw him approach my office door.

"How was your trip?" I asked, opening the door to my office.

He walked in the room and sat in the same seat Olivia had occupied the day before. "Good, although I'll be happy to get home to the family."

They all craved the closeness. The support. They wanted everything I didn't—no, *couldn't* have. Even so, they'd take me back in a heartbeat. The eternal prodigal son.

Elijah stretched his legs out, crossing them at the ankle, and pushed a thick piece of blonde hair behind his ear. His eyes lit up and he began to recall the hunting trip he and the others just returned from. "It was amazing, Grant. You should have been there. Ryan obsessed over one particular antelope and chased him halfway to Wyoming. Just when he thought he'd caught it he miscalculated and fell fifty feet off a cliff, landing in the river. He ruined his new phone in the water. It's the third one this month. I doubt either Sebastian or I have ever laughed so hard."

I found myself laughing with him. Ryan could be such a fool sometimes, but at heart he was an absolute competitor. No way would he have stopped a kill for a replaceable object.

"You should have come. You know making fun of Ryan is better when you're there."

The smile slowly slid from my face. "I know. I wish I could have, but Elijah, something is going on around here and I need your help. Have you been following the news?"

He nodded and said, "Yes. Miles and I were watching it this morning. The national press has picked up on it. What are you thinking?"

I waved him over to look at the map spread across my desk. I pointed out the pattern, which he was able to spot easily. I showed him the descriptions of the bodies found and I told him what I'd heard and seen the other night. Eli stopped my explanation and clarified, "So you think there were three of them, one leader and two others?"

I nodded. "Yes, that was all I could hear, but the scents were not the same as they were from the other sites. The Predator has left his distinctive mark at each location, but the others seem to change."

Elijah sat back in his seat and was quiet for a moment. I saw the faint lines appear around his eyes, the ones he got when he was stressed. Only one thing stressed him, other than Olivia, and that was his past.

"What are you thinking?" I asked.

"I'm not sure, but it feels familiar yet still kind of...off. When I ran with the gangs, sometimes there were one or two guys that would get off on patterned kills. You know, like, Jack The Ripper style or something," he explained. "But this sounds even more intense than that. Those guys were loners—they never should have been with the gang in the first place."

"The group dynamic is making me uncomfortable too," I agreed.

"The Council has made it clear that this area is protected by a coven. I can't imagine someone with this much organizational ability not having an awareness of that."

"From the little I've gleaned from the Predator, I don't think he cares about the Council or anything else, especially our coven." I picked up a newspaper and pointed to a couple of grainy photographs. "What do you think about the missing people? Abductions? Kidnappings? Do you think they're connected?"

"Possibly. If he really has organized his own gang he may need new recruits."

I walked over to the window and looked out, thinking about the information we had and how to piece it all together. "Stupid ones, too. If Miles calls in the Council there will be trouble for everyone—including myself."

Elijah sighed. None of us wanted to move. Not yet. "You're positive the bite marks on the arms were from vampires?"

"I'm sure, but what I don't understand is why does he let the others eat while he simply breaks their necks?"

He shook his head, still caught up in thoughts of his past. "I have no idea, Grant. But it begs the question; if he isn't feeding on them then who *is* he feeding on?"

We spent some time discussing strategy, how I should step up my patrols, and ways to get to my target faster. "If he can beat you then he must have some enhanced sense."

"I had a similar suspicion." All vampires had enhanced senses; hearing, strength, smell...that sort of thing. Others were quite gifted. While I had the ability to convince people to just about anything and an almost debilitating level of obsessiveness that touched every part of my life, Olivia's mind operated like she was a member of the psychic friends. Eli's gifts were what could be best described as an enhanced enhancement. Smell, taste, hearing. His photographic memory was astonishing allowing him the skill we needed to keep up with technology as well as history. He was similar to a walking Encyclopedia. "There's no doubt he can communicate telepathically. Anytime I get near he taps into my head. It's incredibly unnerving."

"Unnerving but not enough to give him that much of a jump on you," he said. "You're one of the best fighters I know. No way he beats you without some sort of additional juice."

"I hate this bastard." I clenched my fists.

"We'll catch him."

He stood to leave but I stopped him. "Can you look at this for me? I want to be able to access my assistant's computer downstairs from this one, but I don't want her to have access to mine. Can you help me set this up?"

"Sure, let me mess around a little." He walked around the desk and sat in my chair. "You don't trust her?"

"It's not that. I'm simply not sure how much longer she'll be here and I need to secure the information for my next employee."

Elijah continued working on the computer, his fingers moving swiftly across the keys, never looking up. "So you want her to quit?"

I grunted low in my throat and muttered, "Olivia is a blabbermouth."

"She worries."

I rolled my eyes but nodded. "What do you think?"

"I think you've experienced challenges like this before. You'll do the right thing." He reached over and flipped on the monitors, enlarging the one for the back patio. "Frankly, if you were going to kill her it would have happened already. You've got this."

We watched as Ms. Chase crouched in front of a chaise lounge and scrubbed the arms and legs of the chair with a thick brush. Her hair was plastered around her face and I could see sweat dripping down the sides of her neck. Her skin was flushed. Pink and inviting. I watched as she stood up and rubbed her brow with the back of her hand.

I swallowed back the first hint of desire.

I heard Elijah choke and stifle a laugh and I shot him a questioning look.

"Oh, man. Your shirt."

I looked closer and saw Amelia was wearing my classic 1969 Let It Bleed Rolling Stones T-shirt. It was wet and I saw spots of bleach splattered across the fabric.

"What the fuck?" I growled.

Eli leaned back in my chair and began laughing uncontrollably and said, "Stop. It's too funny and you're making me angry and I want to laugh at you instead," he said, gasping for words. "Please don't make her quit. I like her already."

I turned back to the monitor and watched her as she lifted the hem of my shirt and wiped her chin with it. The tiniest sliver of pale white skin popped out from underneath and I ran a hand through my hair while shifting uncomfortably in my seat.

Mine.

Elijah's laughter faded in the background and I heard him, faintly in the background. "Grant?"

Transfixed, I eyed the hem of the shirt grazing against the soft curve of her thighs.

"Grant."

The hollow pit of my stomach clenched.

"Grant!"

Something hard hit my shoulder followed by the clatter of metal against the hardwood floors. I flicked my eyes toward Eli, "What?"

"What are you doing?" he asked barely above a whisper.

I immediately was flooded with guilt and began apologizing, "I'm sorry. It must be overwhelming for you to be around. I've never experienced hunger like this before."

His eyes were filled with confusion still and I searched his mind. I shot back from the desk, pacing furiously around the room as I settled in on his thoughts.

I locked eyes with him for a moment trying to understand. His eyebrow arched, curious. "Dude..."

"What?" I snapped again.

"That's not hunger. Well, a little bit of hunger, but that is not the main emotion bouncing off you..." he trailed off, skirting around the word. His fingers drummed the arms of the chair and he struggled to keep his eyes on mine.

"What the hell are you talking about, Elijah?"

I paused in the middle of the room and ran my hands though my hair. I looked directly at him to make sure he wasn't playing a joke on me or trying to piss me off. His dark eyes were filled with sincerity and a touch of shock. The shock was probably a reflection of my own.

"That feeling? The one rolling off you in waves so hard I could ride one on a surfboard? That's not hunger. That's lust."

"Lust?"

"Lust."

The word hung thick in the air.

Lust.

17

Grant

The word, no, *idea* brought about a range of emotions that coursed between Elijah and me like a rubber ball. I had no idea what to do with *feelings* like that.

He continued working, glancing down occasionally at the monitors, updating the system like I'd asked him to. I was across the room, as far away as possible, as though that made it less likely for him to read me.

The minutes ticked by and he finally spoke. "Grant, it's not a big deal. Well, it is a big deal, but not the way you're thinking. I mean you like her. She's cute and for some strange reason not afraid of you," he said, breaking out into a huge grin. "This makes her either the coolest girl you've ever met or the dumbest. I'm not sure which." He glanced down again at the monitors and I could see her reflected in his eyes, spraying down the furniture and cleaning up the mess she had made on the patio.

My shirt hung over her shoulders and her jaw was set. There was a look of something, determination, possibly, in her eyes. I wasn't sure. Again, the fact I couldn't read her well was disturbing. I mean, really disturbing. This situation opened up a whole other equation I'd never considered. Lust? I rubbed my hands back and forth across the top of my legs, trying to squelch the feelings bubbling from inside my chest.

Although I was confused, I was utterly intrigued. In all my years I truly had never experienced pure lust. Not like this.

Desire was something all creatures experienced. We experienced even more than others, it usually manifested into blood-lust rather than sexual craving. Love wasn't out of the question—Olivia and Eli proved that, but even so, after more than a hundred years that particular feeling had eluded me.

Sex? That was a different matter. I had experience, although always with my own kind. Relationships with humans were strictly forbidden by the Council—as they should be. Humans were too pliable. Too easily manipulated. We were genetically superior. We were also, as a species, in hiding. Revealing ourselves and leaving survivors was considered a crime in our society. Beyond that, having actual feelings for a human was incomprehensible.

To be fair, on one level as far as I was concerned, Amelia was different. She was obstinate. Frustratingly independent. I had not been able to manipulate or compel her to do anything. She rebelled against me—only drawing the line at appearing unprofessional. I seemed to have no upper hand with her at all.

Through the reflection in Elijah's eyes, I watched her complete her work outside and return to the house. She meticulously placed the cleaning supplies in the cabinet before she fell out of camera range in the bathroom.

Staring down at my knees, I finally broke. "She doesn't react to my demands," I said, barely above a whisper. He heard me of course.

There was a tinge of a smirk on his face. "So she's immune to your compulsion?"

"It appears so."

"It happens occasionally. I've had humans I couldn't read clearly. Olivia encounters people she can't see more than a hazy fog. Although from what I understand Amelia isn't a problem for her. Or me. I can sense her feelings vibrating through the floor." He lifted his brow, and stretched back in his seat, placing his hands behind his head. He was clearly enjoying my discomfort. "But for you this has to be very different, right? Not being able to control everyone around you."

"I don't try to control everyone."

He snorted. "You've got the hots for this girl, yet you can't penetrate her free-will. The others will find this very interesting."

I glared at him. "Yes. It's fascinating. Tell me then, what is she feeling right now?"

He ignored my sarcasm, strong willed and powerful. "Not the same things you are, my friend."

"Elijah, so help me, I will tear you limb from limb. Tell me what's going on behind...all that."

His lips tugged at the corners, even though he was about to break. He could only hold off on my demand for so long.

"So what's really going on here...is you like a girl," he taunted. "Grant likes a girl..."

In an instant I was up and over the desk, throwing my weight against him. I pinned him and the chair against the wall. "Tell me, you idiot. What. Is. She. Feeling?" I was going to kill him.

He pushed me off, his foot firmly placed against my chest, and I flew backwards across the room. I arched over the desk and landed on my own chair, shattering the wood under my weight. I leapt to my feet, tangled in splinters of wood and leather ready to rain down on him, but Eli was in front of me already, hands on his hips and a huge grin on his face.

"Man, I'm impressed. You cleared the desk. I was sure you were going to take out the computer," he laughed, picking up the leg of the chair and flipping it in his hands.

I stared hard at him for a moment—two beats—before I shook my head and laughed. "I know. I wasn't sure if I could make it, either. At the last second I twisted a little."

I walked across the room to get a trash can. We bent down to clean up the pieces of pulverized leather and wood scattered across the floor. Together we cleaned up the mess and put all of the debris in the bin. Elijah, apparently done tormenting me for the day, finally gave me what I'd asked for.

"She's pissed, Grant. Like really, really, pissed. Her feelings range from bitterness to rage. Oh, and I'm picking up on a little bit of smugness since she ruined your shirt and she knew it would make you mad. But she's definitely going to quit. She's 100% done with you."

I nodded. Her anger was for the best, even though I wasn't sure it was what I wanted anymore. Since when did I get what I wanted, anyway? And this? Whatever this was fell into a realm of impossibility. My life had been about sacrifice and discipline, especially the last couple of decades. Amelia Chase was simply another sacrifice I had to make.

18

Amelia

I looked in the bathroom mirror and saw a sweaty, red-faced mess. I took a finger and rubbed at a swipe of dirt smudged across my face. All that did was make a darker red mark on my already red skin. Wisps of hair stuck to my cheeks and neck. I tried to tidy up but that only made it worse. Shifting my gaze downward, I saw the full destruction of Mr. Palmer's shirt. The fabric was splotchy with bleach and smeared with grime.

Good.

I didn't feel bad.

The controlling bastard deserved it.

I had two hours left before the end of the day, but I was done. My plan was to leave Mr. Palmer my pre-written letter of resignation on my desk where he could find it when he came by for my daily report.

Daily report: I QUIT.

The thought of leaving that note and the look of confusion on his perfectly featured face made me smile for the first time all day. Sure, I could walk away without leaving the note, but I had a tiny scrap of professional dignity remaining. Barefoot and dirty, I left the bathroom like a hillbilly and walked to my desk, placing the letter on the corner where he would definitely see it.

I had my bag and my shoes and I needed to stop in the kitchen to remove my food and other items. I wanted to leave Mr. Palmer's home the way I found it and remove every trace of my presence. So that I would be nothing more than a blip in his life. Two weeks of disturbance in his routine and stagnant existence. Maybe next time he'd hire a robot instead.

I had my head in the refrigerator when, to my absolute horror, I heard feet on the back stairs. Crap. There went my scrap of dignity.

Mr. Palmer stood at the bottom of the steps and I noticed his hands were full of trash. I saw a tall, lanky man standing behind him carrying an arm load of what appeared to be parts of a chair. Mr. Palmer wore the normal, pained grimace on his face that I'd come to expect.

We stood for a moment in silence while his eyes traveled down my body, taking in his T-shirt and my disheveled appearance. I held my breath for a moment waiting for his reaction. The absurdity of my behavior crashed down on me. I felt like a child. A child who desecrated something very important to the bastard in front of me.

Okay, my guilt didn't last long.

Oh, also? The fact he was overwhelmingly gorgeous when he was mad only made the situation worse. Or better? I had no idea. I lost all sense of rationality when I saw the tense lines of his jaw and the spark of fire in his violet eyes.

I felt the heat rush to my face as I realized he could call the police and have me escorted off the property or arrested. Maybe I hadn't thought this all the way through.

I heard a stifled cough from behind Mr. Palmer. The other man leaned around Mr. Palmer and I saw that he, too, was incredibly handsome. The hint of amusement in his eyes was not lost on me.

Perfect timing to grow a backbone, Amelia.

Cutting our awkward standoff short, Mr. Palmer walked past me out the garage door without a word. The other man followed but gave me a wide smile and nod of encouragement, leaving me alone in the kitchen.

I let out a deep, rattling breath, realizing at that moment, I'd been holding it for some time.

"Nice knowing you, jackass," I said, to the empty room, before escaping out the front door.

***

Figuring I had nothing else to lose, I decided to cap off my epically fail day by going on my date with Thomas. It wasn't the worst idea, except for the fact I couldn't shake the bad feelings from earlier today plus, for some crazy reason I decided to wear heels. Why did I wear heels? God, they're uncomfortable.

I swallowed the last of my drink and peered into the bottom of the glass hoping a refill would magically appear.

Where was that waitress?

"Superman or Captain America?" Thomas asked the table. They'd been playing 'Superhero vs. Superhero' for an hour.

I glanced around the room for the waitress. She'd vanished. Like the contents of my drink.

I slumped back in my seat, dreaming of my couch and comfy clothes. Although my fingers still smelled like bleach, I'd had to scrub to rid myself of the filth that covered my entire body. I was hoping it would remove some of the horror and humiliation I'd experienced as well, but sadly, soap didn't fix shame.

My bad mood lingered as I sat between Drew and Thomas and pretended to be interested in their conversation. I'd never quit a job before and left on bad terms. I felt terrible ruining Mr. Palmer's shirt. Sure, he was an ass, but it was immature and I was embarrassed by my behavior.

Fucking hindsight.

I fingered the paper coasters on the table and pretended to listen to Thomas and his friend, Jess, argue the pros and cons of superheroes.

"Superman can fly. It always comes down to that," Thomas said.

"Captain America is a Captain. Like, he's the boss of all the Avengers. Even Nick Fury defers to him."

They rambled on and I groaned internally and searched the table for a sharp object to gouge my eyes out with, but came up empty.

What I did see was Drew making sex eyes at Jess and pretending this was the most fascinating conversation ever, which I knew for a fact, it wasn't. He raised an eyebrow in my direction, motioning with his mouth for me to smile. I rolled my eyes at Drew but plastered a grin on my face and returned my attention to Thomas.

I knew I wasn't being fair. It wasn't his fault my boss was a douche. I appraised Thomas, noticing how he looked nice in a blue shirt that matched his tan complexion. He really was cute and nice. The problem was, he was a bit boring. At the moment he was animatedly informing Jess of the virtues of Superman. "Superman has super strength and heat vision. He's an alien—the perfect representation of immigration to this country."

I watched with mild interest as Jess took a deep breath and said, "That's the whole point. Superman is an alien—he was born with super powers. Steve Rogers was a normal man—a weak man, who dreamed of being so much more. Look what happened when Red Skull underwent the same Gamma Ray transformation. He became evil. Steve became a hero. He had that moral compass inside him all along. Plus, he jumps out of planes without a parachute, which is like flying but even more badass."

Jess leaned back in his seat and took a long, smug, pull from his beer. He and Thomas eyed one another trying to determine where to take this next. I had to admit, I was impressed. Not so much from this conversation, but from the fact people actually knew this much random information about something I cared so little about.

"What do you think, Amelia?" Thomas asked.

"Me? Um..." I glanced at Drew who was fighting off laughter. This wasn't really my game, but no one likes a party-pooper so I gave it a shot. "Which is the one with all the muscles?"

Jess frowned. "All of them?"

"Has a hammer?"

"Thor," Thomas said, looking a little disappointed I didn't know the difference. "He's a demi-god. That's a whole other competition."

"Ah, okay," I said but offered a weak smile. "Sorry I'm being a drag. I quit my job today and didn't leave on good terms."

"You quit?" Thomas asked. "Wow, not sure I can blame you. Palmer is a pretty terrifying boss. I'm not sure I would have lasted as long as you did."

"Palmer?" Jess asked.

"Yeah, Amelia works—well worked—for Grant Palmer, that totally rich guy I told you about. That's how we met. He gives me the creeps but holy cow, he pays well. So well I need to shut my mouth."

"Gives you the creeps how?" Jess said, not ready to change the topic.

Thomas wasn't saying anything else and I didn't blame him. Mr. Palmer was a good customer. Me? I was in the clear. Zero loyalty to that jerk. "Like he creeps around and has all these freaky OCD habits. Like super extreme. He's rich and hot and I think he's just gotten his way his entire life. Spoiled rich guy, that's all."

Jess' eyes narrowed in concentration before asking, "Is he more like Tyler Durden or Patrick Bateman?"

Oh God, they tricked me into one of their games. One I did not want to play but tossed out, "He looks like Tyler Durden, but possibly may be Patrick Bateman." Who knew what he kept upstairs in those locked rooms. Or what his abs looked like under that crisp shirt.

The waitress came over and took our order for another round of beer, and then Thomas introduced the next topic of who would win a death match, Hawkeye vs. Green Arrow. I excused myself to the restroom.

At the sink I pulled out my hair brush and was attempting to stick strands of hair back in the ponytail when a woman next to me washing her hands said, "Wow, your perfume is amazing, what kind is it?"

I laughed and said, "Oh, I don't wear perfume. It gives me a headache. It must be someone else."

Angel Lawson

In the mirror I watched as she smiled and ran her fingers through her short, dark hair. Her skin was pale. Flawless. Completely smooth. She had on large, 70s style, rose tinted glasses. I admired her tight dress and ridiculously high heels. How does someone even walk around like that and not break their neck?

Unscrewing the cap to my lip gloss I said, "I love your glasses, I could never pull off something so dramatic."

She flashed me an ultra-white smile. "Thanks. I have sensitive eyes so I wear them all the time."

"Well, they work for you."

The girl ran a hand through her hair, tugging at several spiky pieces on top. "So I saw you out there with that guy. Are you here on a date?"

I sat back against the sink. "Ugh, yes. I mean, he's cute and all, but boring. You would not believe the argument he and his friend have been having all night. And what is worse, my friend has hit it off with his friend so I have a feeling it's going to be a long night."

She threw her head back and laughed the most charming, fantastic laugh. She was really beautiful; interesting-looking, like a model. "Yeah, sounds pretty tragic. Well, you come find me if you need an escape. My boyfriend is supposed to meet me later but he tends to be a little unreliable."

I put my brush and make up away and followed her to the door. Stopping just before pushing the door open to the thumping beat of the outside music she turned and said, "By the way, my name is Sasha."

19

Grant

With my standard props in place I was able to successfully stake out the corner of the business district on what seemed to be a busy Friday night. I'd been here for about an hour, my coffee now cold and my newspaper thoroughly read, color-coded Post-it-Notes in place. Everything was as it should be.

Everything except her lingering scent on my clothes and the memory of the sight of her skin, creamy and white. Oh, and the fact I apparently wasn't only hungry but behaving like a typical, horny twenty-year-old. Other than that it was a regular day in the life of a 115 year-old vampire.

I couldn't believe it when I came down the stairs to find Amelia in the kitchen. I'd held my breath when I left my rooms and attempted to ignore her heartbeat. With Elijah there as a distraction I was doing fine until I stepped into the room and saw her standing there, flushed and red. She was so small, draped in my decimated shirt, so incredibly human—*so female*. I stood still and fought the urge to reach out and rub my finger over smudge of dirt on her face or touch the throbbing vein in her neck.

Thank God Eli nudged me in the back, snapping me back to reality.

Hours later I focused on my job, walking through downtown Asheville, past the lively bars and crowds of people. The small city had a jubilant night life—mostly college students and tourists. The tracking pace I'd determined on my maps indicated the Predator would enter the city limits soon. Probably in the next three days. I cleared my head and listened to the crowds. It was a typical Friday night and most people were determined to have a good time. Humans acted foolish, though, in their quest for fun. The excessive drinking, suggestive behavior, or questionable decision-making always caused more pain than they expected. It all began as light-hearted fun in the minds of young people, but often spiraled quickly out of control.

Wow, I wonder if Amanda saw Robert, he looks really hot tonight...Finally, Friday night! TGIF! Why did I wear these shoes they're killing me...Now, where did I put my car keys...or my car...

Their voices carried through the night, bouncing off the brick buildings and concrete streets. The last one piqued my interest and I found him after a brief search. He stumbled over a bump in the parking lot across the

street. I approached him. He reeked of gin and ciga-
rettes.

"Hey, man, let me call you a cab." He struggled to find
his keys in his pocket. I stood by and watched as he
fished them out and promptly dropped them on the
ground. It was easy to help intoxicated people since they
were not clear enough to notice the differences between
me and them.

I quickly picked them up and held onto them. "Who
the fuck are you? Gimmie my keys," he slurred, swiping
a meaty hand toward me. I stepped back.

"Just making sure you get home safe."

"I'm fine," he replied, swaying to the side. I left him
for a moment, struggling to maintain his balance and
walked to the curb, waving down one of the many cabs
trolling the area. "Come here. Get in the cab," I directed,
making eye contact this time. His obstinate attitude sub-
sided and he allowed me to assist him into the vehicle. I
reached in and gave the driver more than enough cash
to cover the fare.

The driver nodded and pulled away from the sidewalk. I watched the tail lights as they trailed down the
dark road and continued my patrol of the bar district.

*I can't believe he was looking at the waitress that
way...asshole....spilling his drink on my new dress...I
wonder if she'll give me her number...those murders are
freaking me out...stupid manager making us park in the
back of the lot...*

I honed in on the last one and within moments found the girl dressed in a uniform signaling employment at a local restaurant. She darted to her car located in the shadowy corner of the parking lot. She was safe from the Predator tonight, but I kept an eye on her to make sure there were no drunken frat boys around.

She got in her car and locked the doors. I wondered why she chose to go alone. Why didn't she bring a co-worker into the dark night? The danger people put themselves in was usually their own fault. Completely avoidable.

My mind flashed to Ms. Chase and I wondered if she took risks like this. All humans do, but some were worse than others. My stomach recoiled at the thought of her unprotected.

The waitress drove away and I turned behind the businesses, to the edge of the dark alley clustered between the old buildings. It smelled like garbage and the constant wetness gave the whole area a funky, bad odor. I held my breath to keep the disgusting scents at bay.

The night was fairly quiet, as I'd expected, and I realized for the millionth time the absurdity of my policing this area. Why was I, a monster and a murderer, wandering the dark streets helping people to their cars and shoving them into cabs? Why did I leave the comforts of my home and my family to comb the beer-soaked alleys of the inner city? At times it seemed trivial—a waste of immortal life, but tracking the Predator steeled my resolve.

Having purpose was important. For countless years I'd lived in my own world, focused on myself and my needs. After mastering our alternative lifestyle and adhering to the societal rules established by the Council, I assimilated into the lifestyle Miles demanded for members of his coven.

I passed a group of young men and women, coupled off. One of the women looked in my direction, and did a double-take—lured in by my appearance. Her partner noticed me as well but shifted positions with his girl, stepping between us. I nodded in greeting and he gave me a tight one in return. "Hey man," he said.

"Good evening."

The girl glanced over her shoulder at me long after they passed. How easy it would have been for me to follow them home, climb into their windows and destroy their innocent world.

Miles and I noticed the trend of rogue vampires hovering around the edge of cities. Although he didn't like me living on my own, or fronting the Palmer Foundation, both of which he found too risky, we did agree to expand the territory that we monitored. I was determined to go on my own and focus on how to use my supernatural abilities for a greater purpose. There had to be something more than the nothingness from before. I began roaming the city at night, alone, for the first time in many years. It wasn't long before I found a person in need. I helped them. Finally, I had a sense of purpose.

The majority of humans needed saving from other humans or from themselves. But vampires still roamed the country—many inclined to feed from the innocent. Their kills were less noticeable to the authorities but fairly easy for me to identify. The deaths appeared random, products of an accident or the fate of living close to an urban area.

As the years passed, I honed my gift and vampire abilities. I finally listened to people instead of tuning out their voices. I learned how to pick up on the subtle differences in their tone, determining what signaled fear and what did not. At first, I was terrible at tracking and was unable to follow the scent or clues left by those I hunted. Eventually, though, I developed a system of physical skills and research that was unparalleled to others of my kind. I used the money I'd earned over the years to fund my mission, and with the help of my family I was able to help more people and save more lives. I was faster and better prepared than those I sought out.

That was how I got to the position I was in currently. Trolling the streets of Asheville on a warm Friday night, blocking out the foul stench wafting from the dank alleys. I waited patiently to help the next poor soul that crossed my path when in need. That was my mission. My life.

20

Amelia

"Amelia, would you like to dance?" Thomas asked, and held his hand out expectantly.

My eyes went to his hand and stared at it for a moment while I tried to come up with an excuse to say no. Too tired? Drunk? Would prefer not to encourage my boring date from hell any further? As I considered my options I realized a fair amount of time had passed and his hand was still out there, waiting for me to take it.

"Amelia's a great dancer," Drew chimed in.

I shot Drew a look of "WTF" and he gave me a double thumbs up in return. I narrowed my eyes at him trying to decide if I should thank him or tell everyone he once left a party with women's underpants on his head. He saved me by coming with me tonight, but not before throwing me under the bus. In reality I *was* a great dancer, but there was no need to encourage Thomas at that point.

"Aw, Drew is being too kind. I am an okay dancer, but these babies," I lifted a spiked heel off the ground, "are lethal. To me as much as you. Please, dance without me. I'm happy to sit on the sidelines and watch."

Drew took my permission and ran with it, grabbing Jess' hand and dragging him into the crowd of sweaty, pulsing bodies. Thomas cocked his head to the side and said, "Are you sure? I don't mind sitting with you. We could talk some more."

And listen to him talk about his costume for Comic-Con next year? Too quickly I responded, "No really, go! I'm totally fine." I gave him a reassuring smile and waved him off. He gave me one final smile and disappeared into the sea of people. I let out a deep sigh of relief.

Ten minutes later I felt a tap on my shoulder and braced myself for Thomas. I prepped myself for an exaggerated yawn and arm stretch to signal my need to go home, but to my surprise it wasn't Thomas but the girl from the restroom.

"Hey! I saw you sitting here all alone and came over to keep you company." She slid into the bar stool next to me, her bracelets clanking down her arm.

"Sasha, right?" I pushed the empty glasses out of her way and smiled. "I'm Amelia."

Sasha flashed me another blazing smile. "How's the date?"

I pointed through the dancers to Thomas who was attempting to grind on a small blonde in the middle of the floor.

"My date is occupied, which is honestly more than I could ask for." I laughed. "He really is nice, just not my type."

We watched the dancers for a minute. I could see Drew's huge grin all the way over here at the table. He was really hitting it off with Jess, which I was truly happy about. They had identical looks of infatuation on their faces so I felt the night was a success for both of them. Well, at least one of us had a successful night. I turned to Sasha and said, "I think I'm going to head home. It's been a really long day."

"I'll walk you out. I'm supposed to meet my boyfriend outside."

I darted over to Drew, telling him my plans to leave and asking him to let Thomas know that I had to go. He waved me off, motioning for me to leave, too involved in Jess to really notice. We both knew he owed me for setting him up with an awesome guy and in return he would do a little damage control for me with my less than spark-inducing date.

I met Sasha by the door and we walked out of the air conditioned bar and into the warm night. In the bright lights in front of the bar I could see Sasha clearer than before. Again, I was struck by her features. Strong and...maybe it was the confidence? Standing next to her made me feel awkward and out of place. She was the kind of girl I could see Mr. Palmer with. Long legs, perfect face, super model hair, sleek manicured nails. I wondered for a moment if she liked obsessive compulsive men.

"So you're waiting for your boyfriend?" I asked. "Too bad, I'm pretty sure my boss would be perfect for you."

"Nope. Taken. We've been together forever." She smiled. "Caleb called while you were saying goodbye to your friend and said he couldn't come. But I told him about you and he really wants to meet you."

"Wait, what did you say? He wants to meet me?"

She stopped and looked at me, her perfect ruby red lips twitched. "Yes. He really does. We can meet him now if you want?"

Suddenly I realized how unnerving it was to be unable to see her eyes hidden behind those tinted glasses. Was she kidding? Or serious? I had no clue, but I did know that the internal alarm system we all have inside was beginning to frantically clang with warning.

I took a small step back and said, in the steadiest voice I could muster, "You know, I realized I have Drew's keys and I wouldn't want him to get locked out..." My words trailed off into an uncomfortable silence between us.

Well, I was uncomfortable. Incredibly so. Sasha seemed calm. Controlled.

Bored?

I took another step back while keeping a fake smile plastered across my face. She reached out and touched my arm. I jerked at her touch and my eyes widened. Fear rippled down my back and my stomach dropped.

"Amelia," Sasha said as she took of her glasses and pushed them to the top of her head. "I need you to come with me."

I realized too late that we were alone, near the corner of two buildings that were separated by a small, dark alley. I was looking for my escape when I noticed her eyes in the head lights of a passing car.

Black. Soulless.

I choked back my fear and began to run but she cut me off, stepping in front of me, far too quick for a normal person. She pushed me once, hard in the shoulders, and I stumbled into the shadow of the buildings. Her long red nails dug into my flesh, threatening to break the skin.

"Oh!" I gasped, startled by her strength but not enough to lose my head. I turned and ran again, this time down the alley, since she was blocking the exit. Even in my desperation, the cliché of the moment was not lost on me. I was alone in the dark, cornered by a deranged, sick woman who wore creepy black contacts, who preyed on ridiculous young women.

I stumbled again in my heels, this time scraping my knee and palms on the gritty pavement. Stupid fucking shoes. Picking myself up, I could hear her behind me, slowly following me in the darkness.

"Amelia. Please don't do this. It's no use. Once I told Caleb about you, he insisted on experiencing you himself." Her heels clicked against the pavement. "We both think you'll be a perfect fit."

Faint light spilled from beneath the back doors of the bars that used this alley. I dashed in the direction of the loud thumping music. Behind the closed doors, people were nearby. Safety. I reached the door and turned the knob. Glaring music and light poured into the alley. I took a step toward safety and a pale arm shot out and slammed the door shut.

Out of breath and scared half to death I let out a slight cry as Sasha leaned in front of me.

"What are you doing?" I whispered between quick, short breaths. "You're fucking crazy."

She grabbed my wrist and pulled me forward. She bared her teeth and to my horror she ran her tongue across the front of them before laughing exuberantly. I twisted my arm away, but she held firm, tightening her grip. I buckled under the pressure.

"God, you smell good." She ran her finger from her free hand across my cheek. Her lips were so close to mine for a moment I thought she might kiss me. For a heartbeat I wanted her to. That desire passed when she said, "He is going to love you. All yummy and full of fire. He likes his girls spunky, you know. You will make a wonderful addition."

"Please don't hurt me," I whispered.

"It will only hurt for a minute, but I promise, the result will be worth it."

"You're crazy."

She didn't reply as the back door opened, flinging against the brick wall with a bang. Sasha and I were knocked apart. A sharp hiss left her lips. I scrambled away and pressed my back to the wall, rubbing the swollen skin on my wrist.

A man stepped out and filled the space Sasha and I had occupied a moment before. He stood tall and confident. Familiar.

"Mr. Palmer?"

"Amelia, go." His voice was tight but soft.

Wide-eyed, I looked from him to Sasha. Her eyes were angry, narrowed with rage. His back was to me now and I heard him speak again, with terrifying force, "Now."

I stumbled on the threshold, falling backwards into the open door. I ran down the hall with only a quick glance backwards. Framed in the doorway they faced off. As much as I wanted to know more, now wasn't the time. I ran away from the dark toward the bright lights, loud music and safety inside.

21

Grant

I kicked open the door, forcing the two of them to stumble away. Ms. Chase scampered into the darkness.

thump, thump, thump.

My senses flooded with her excruciating scent, which was amplified by her perspiration and fear. I paused for a millisecond to brace myself but oddly, the desire to consume was trumped by the overwhelming need to protect.

I stood between them, assessing the injuries to Ms. Chase and maintaining a position of offense on Sasha. I clenched my jaw as I smelled the blood from her scraped knee and watched her rub her tender wrist.

"Amelia, go," I directed, turning to the vampire.

She paused behind me, heart about to rip out of her chest. Defiant as always, but this really wasn't the time.

Without looking back I spoke again, "Now."

I felt her pass by me, a wave of her scent assaulting my nostrils as she disappeared into the building.

Sasha and I were alone now.

She was plotting, I could see the wheels turning as she ran through scenarios, quickly rejecting one after the other.

I could kill her. Quite easily, as she underestimated my abilities. It wouldn't take but a moment, unfortunately I needed information from her first.

"Where is he?" I asked.

Confusion flitted across her face. She wasn't expecting that. "Who?"

I sensed her respect and allegiance for him. "Do you think he feels the same for you?"

"You have a lot of questions," she deflected. "None of this concerns you."

"Yes, it does. You're in my territory, drawing attention to yourselves and me by association. Not only by the police but the Council as well."

She laughed, fake and hollow. "I think this is about more than your territory, don't you see that?"

I ignored her psychotic rambling and tried to figure out how to destroy her in this populated area.

Her confidence grew in my silence and she stepped closer. "You'd better get used to us. We're not leaving. In fact, we've got plans for this little town and you. Oh, and that delicious little human, too. She's lovely."

"If you leave now, I will let you both go without retribution."

She frowned. "You don't get it, do you? We don't care about retribution. The risk only makes the reward so much better. And make no mistake, you led Caleb right to that little pet of yours. She reeks of you, and you," she ran her hand down my shirt, nostrils flaring, "are completely consumed by her."

I charged her and pushed her to the wall, my hands clamped around her neck. Her eyes bulged but the smirk on her face remained, daring me to make her a martyr for her cause. Her nails scratched against my sides.

I leaned into her ear, baring my teeth and growled. "You will stay away from her and you will stay away from the city. These murders stop now or I will tear you apart limb by limb." I pulled her off the wall and shoved her in the direction of the street. She stumbled before gaining footing. "Go. Take that message back to him and pray you never cross my path again."

She looked ready to pounce, hissing in anger, but I stood firm, and seconds later the back door opened and two bartenders began carrying out bags of trash and re-cyclables.

Sasha used the opportunity to disappear into the darkness and I let her go to deliver my message.

22

Amelia

I stood outside the kitchen door, next to the bar, waiting for him to come back in. I wasn't sure if he would but I had nowhere else to go. I was too scared to walk to my car alone and I was too freaked out to go back into the bar and look for my friends. So I waited by the kitchen door, pressed against the wall, hoping Mr. Palmer would come back inside and tell me what the hell was going on.

Who the heck was that girl and what the hell was she rambling on about? She said something about me being a good 'addition' and several things about her boyfriend, Caleb. She looked so crazy with her black, soulless eyes and scary teeth. Someone needed to get back on their meds.

The kitchen door bumped open and I jumped to see if it was him, but instead it was a short girl carrying out a large tray of drinks and food. I discreetly snagged one of the drinks as she passed and downed it in one freaked-out gulp. The warm buzz wasn't enough to help me reason out how Mr. Palmer found me in the first place.

He wasn't the type to go out or party as far as I could tell. And why would Grant Palmer, esteemed CEO of the Palmer Foundation, be in the kitchen of a mid-scale bar? He probably had smashed up food in the soles of his fancy shoes and would expect me to clean them out on Monday.

Monday.

I slapped my hand over my face and groaned. I'd forgotten for a moment I'd quit. Well, I was sure he could find someone else to do the job. Surely, there was a temp agency for rich guys, right?

The door swung open again and I watched Mr. Palmer's tall frame walk by. I pushed off the wall to follow him and he swung abruptly around to face me. Mixed with the typical grimace of pain his eyes relaxed in relief.

"Ms. Chase, I'm glad you waited. Are you okay? Injured?"

I nodded slowly, not really sure what to say.

"Right," he said, seeming to understand my lack of words. He glanced down at my bloody knee and back to my swollen wrist. "Why don't you go clean that up? I'll wait right outside the door. Then I'll escort you home."

Again, I said nothing, but I went in the women's room anyway. I'd been threatened by a woman outside the bar and my former boss, who was rude to me all week, actually saved my life. Now, on top of all that, he was concerned about my scraped knees. If he offered me a Band-Aid I'd probably snap.

Sure enough, when I walked out he stood stiffly across from the bathroom door. A girl with a low neck-line passed him on her way into the restroom and gave him a flirty smile. I observed with fascination that he completely ignored her.

His eyes were fixed on me.

Okay, I thought they were on me, but I nervously glanced over my shoulder looking to see if something more interesting was behind me.

Nope. Just me.

He gestured for me to walk ahead of him and we made our way through the crowd and out the front door.

On the sidewalk he attempted to act casual, but something was off. His hands were shoved in his pockets and he rocked slowly back on his heels. His actions appeared forced and deliberate. Was he always this awkward? My gut told me yes.

The neon lights from the bar signs cast a hazy glow over us, highlighting the red in his hair and accentuating the sharp line of his jaw. Which was a lot more appealing when he wasn't clenching it in fury. We stared at one another in an uncomfortable silence.

I let out a deep breath and said, "I have some questions."

His eyes tightened but he nodded as though he expected this. I opened my mouth to speak but my feet swayed under me. Mr. Palmer reached out and caught me by the arms and held me upright.

Neither of us moved for a moment. He was frozen, hands clamped around the thin fabric of my shirt. Again, we briefly locked eyes until we both looked away, embarrassed by the situation. I wiggled from under his grasp and he quickly withdrew his hands, stashing them behind his back. My face flushed and I said, "I'm okay. Thanks, feeling a little woozy. Could be the drinks or maybe the attempted kidnapping? It's a toss-up."

My attempt at humor did nothing to ease the tension. Stone-faced he replied, "I think I should drive you home."

What? No. "Can't you just follow me?"

He shook his head. "No, I don't think so."

His tone implied he was not happy about the situation either, but I really didn't have the desire to drive by myself, so I nodded and followed him down the street to his car.

When we reached the parking lot he pressed the remote to unlock it and he opened the door for me.

"Thanks," I said, lowering myself into the car.

I'd barely buckled up when I realized Mr. Palmer was already in the driver's seat with the car started, staring straight ahead. He deftly flicked switches and pushed the levers in his over-the-top expensive car. I inhaled the rich leather scent as I sunk into the soft, buttery cushion. Fine, over-the-top, really comfortable, expensive car.

Through half-lidded eyes I observed that his car was spotless, no trash or coffee cups. Not even a leaf stuck to the floor mat. Even here there was nothing to provide a glimpse of the real Grant Palmer. Whoever he might be.

I nervously ran my fingers across the dashboard and fingered the lever on the glove compartment door. I twisted my neck and saw him watching me and I pulled my hand back quickly and placed both my hands on my lap.

"I live on Third and Main," I directed, breaking the quiet of the car. He nodded again, still not speaking. "In that apartment complex that backs up to the river."

The quiet hum of the vehicle lulled me but I had questions and very little time to get them answered. "Will you answer my questions now?"

This time he looked over at me and replied, "Yes, if I can."

"Who was that woman?"

"I don't know."

"Where did she go? Did you call the police?"

"No, she ran away once I approached her." He must have seen the panic in my eyes because he quickly added, "I have a friend in the police department. I'll call them first thing and see if we can save you the trouble of spending the night at the police station."

I let that sink in for a minute and watched his hands manipulate the steering wheel. His fingers were long and slender, arched over the curve of the leather. We rounded a curve and he gracefully moved his hand to the gear shift.

I decided to go with another line of questioning. "How did you find me?"

"I heard a commotion in the alley and went to investigate."

"So you normally hang out in the back kitchen of bars?"

"No, I wasn't 'hanging out'."

"Then why were you there?"

Silence.

I shifted my body so I was looking at him even though he continued to keep his eyes straight ahead.

"Are you going to answer me?" *Answer me!*

He pulled the car into the parking lot of my apartment and stopped. He angled his body toward mine slightly, hands still gripping the wheel, his knuckles tense and straining. The leather creaked.

"No." He sighed.

"What do you mean 'no'?"

"There's nothing else I can tell you about tonight. But I do have a question for you." He looked me in the eye. "Why did you quit?"

Nice deflection.

"I, umm..." I stuttered, trying to come up with a response. He held up one perfect hand and motioned for me to stop.

He took a deep breath and said in his thick, soothing voice, "I apologize for being rude to you. I treated you unfairly and I was completely unprofessional. Sometimes I don't realize what is and is not appropriate to ask my employees to do while at work. And my tone has been unbearable. I've allowed some...personal problems to interfere my relationship with you. It's unacceptable."

"No kidding."

He laughed lightly and said, "I tend to get a little self-absorbed at times."

"A little?" I asked, stunned at his revelation. I looked at my hands and sighed. "Thank you for the apology. And well, I owe you one, also. I have no idea what came over me. I totally ruined your shirt. Like, really ruined it."

Even in the shadows, I could see the flash of anger pass across his face at the mention of his shirt. It was brief, only a there for a moment. Okay, maybe we hadn't worked through that yet.

"Well, yes, you did massacre my shirt. But I guess that makes us even?" he said this as a question and his jaw arranged in a slight grin.

The grin softened his features and I noticed his eyes pulsed, dilating a shade darker. The weariness I'd seen earlier was back, obvious in the dark rings under his eyes. I wondered if he was as tired as I felt. I leaned my head back and rubbed my inflamed wrist, suddenly overwhelmed by exhaustion.

"Does it hurt badly?" he asked and gestured to my arm, his voice soft with concern. I closed my eyes for a moment and soaked up the richness of his voice. My mind wandered for a moment and I wondered if he could sing. "Amelia..." his voice pulled me out of my thoughts.

"No, it's okay," I said, and held it up for him to see. "I bruise easily, I'm sure it appears worse than it actually is."

He stared for a moment at the splotchy skin. Suddenly he blurted, "Will you come back to work? I'm afraid in the two weeks you've worked for me I've become quite dependent." I checked his expression to see if he was serious and to my astonishment, he appeared sincere. "I promise to back off some and act like an appropriate boss. And no more scrubbing the furniture." His lips curved into the most dangerous smile I'd ever seen.

"I'll think about it," I said, not sure, but afraid if he kept smiling at me like that I would agree to just about anything he asked.

He frowned but wrapped his fingers around the door handle, pushing it open. I followed his lead and got out of my side of the car.

"I'm fine from here. Thanks for the ride."

"Don't be ridiculous. I'm walking you in," he said. His demeanor back to annoyed.

"Fine," I replied, once again trying to determine if I wanted a seat on the emotional roller coaster of Grant Palmer.

We walked together up the stairs to my second floor apartment. I fished for my keys in my purse and pulled them out. He offered a courteous, "Let me," and he quickly took the keys from my grasp and unlocked the door. I had a terrifying moment of wondering if I should ask him in but sighed with relief when he dangled the keys in front of me to take.

"Goodnight, Ms. Chase," he said. "Please consider returning to work. If you decline my offer, I will draft a referral letter and send it to you next week."

"Goodnight," I replied, unable to commit. "And thank you."

I watched as he stepped around the corner. Exhausted and spent, I closed the door and stumbled into bed.

23

Grant

Later, I stood in the shadows listening to the sounds of the night as a slight breeze whispered across my face. I touched the key in my pocket, rubbing the grooves over and over, memorizing the pattern.

It was late. The apartment was quiet except for the sounds of sleep. Drew had come home an hour earlier and fallen into bed without checking on Amelia. His breathing and heart rate were steady and even. Clearly, he was unaware of the horrors his roommate had suffered that night.

I'd returned out of some instinctive need to see her. If I had to explain why I wouldn't have the words to do so. Her home was locked and safe. I'd delivered her there myself, yet I felt the compulsion to see her. I slipped the stolen key into the lock and silently twisted the knob until I felt the click of the chambers as they released.

I moved inside, shut the door, and quietly replaced the key on Amelia's key ring by the door. I entered the living room and inhaled deeply. The result was a burning desire, harsh and painful, but it signaled the one thing I wanted.

Amelia.

I wanted her alive much more than I wanted her dead. That wasn't to say her scent didn't ignite my hunger. It did. The difference was that I could resist it. I wouldn't harm Amelia. Now I wanted to immerse myself in her. Protect her.

I crossed the living room until I stood outside her door. Entering quietly, a thin sliver of light traveled across her face. She slept in her bed, curled on her side, wrapped in a mass of sheets. Her blonde hair was tangled and snarled, splayed across the pillow. My eyes traveled the lines of her body, assessing how her hands were clenched under her chin, balled into tiny fists. Her bruised wrist pulsed with heat in the dark.

I picked up the blouse she had worn that evening and pushed it to my nose, burying myself in her exquisite aroma. Dizzy with lust, I found another shirt on her dresser and inhaled. Intoxicating.

Amelia shifted in the bed, rolling to the opposite side, moaning. I dropped the shirt and froze.

I watched her lips and waited, the pink tint visible to my sensitive eyes in the dark. I held my breath, unnecessarily straining to hear that sound escape her lips again. It only took a moment before another low whimper left her mouth.

I was instantly flooded with desire. Unexpected desire, strong and all-encompassing. The reaction traveled down my body signaling, with no room for doubt, the true nature of my cravings. Horrified and shamed, I forced myself to retreat though the apartment. It was one thing to prey on sustenance, it was another to spy on a woman and yearn for her body. Aware of the difference, I left Amelia, the object of my ultimate desire, to her unsettling dreams and prayed we would cross paths again.

***

The last time I called a family meeting, I moved out of the house.

Now I required the coven's help.

In both situations they came willingly, each person taking their particular seat, until the large table was full. Together we formed a formidable group. Five men, two women and centuries of experience.

"Thank you for coming together on such late notice," I said, greeting each member of my family. Miles sat at the end of the table, flanked by Ryan and Sebastian. Brothers, twins actually, that came to live with us in the mid-1930s at the age of sixteen. Italian by decent, the boys had matching dark curly hair. Ryan was strong, built like a giant and immensely powerful. Sebastian was smaller in physique, but had an identical face—other than the massive scarred gash that ran from the space between his eyes, down the left side of his cheek, all the way to his jaw. Similar, grotesque scars marked his chest and lower body as well.

Elijah sat at the opposite end of the table from Miles, laptop open, and Olivia sat by his side, making no effort to hide the concerned frown on her face. Genevieve sat directly across the table from me, placing her glass on the table. To the casual observer the liquid looked like red wine. Of course, it was blood. Human blood. She'd agreed to stop killing humans when she joined our coven but animal blood was out of the question.

"Genevieve," I said, in greeting. "How are things with the Council?"

Genevieve and Miles met at the Council two hundred years ago. They both maintained positions of authority although she took a brief sabbatical to work as my assistant over the last two years. I hadn't been happy about her taking the position as we'd had friction in the past, but Miles insisted. After hearing her forewarnings to Ms. Chase about my behavior, I suspected she was more than happy to return to her original job.

"Just catching up on what I've missed over the last couple of years."

I nodded. "I'm sure that won't take long."

Although Miles was the "oldest" in the coven and brought us all together, in our home we collaborated as equals. His long-standing position with the Council made it easier for us to operate as an approved coven. He sat at the end of the table, bald head reflecting the dimmed overhead lights.

"Grant would like to talk to us about the murders taking place near Asheville," he said. "Things have escalated."

"As Olivia may have informed you, last night the Predator, who I learned is named Caleb, sent one of his companions to kidnap my assistant while she was out socializing with friends."

Sebastian and Ryan glanced at one another—obviously they had not been informed.

"In a public location?" Sebastian asked.

"Yes."

A small crease appeared on Ryan's forehead. "Did you intervene?"

"With Olivia's help, I managed to get there in time. Other than a few superficial injuries Ms. Chase seems fine," I said. "The assailant, Sasha, made a variety of threats but it was clear killing Ms. Chase was not the intention."

"Then why kidnap her?" Genevieve asked. "Did he want to use her as a hostage?"

"No, not exactly," I replied.

"He wanted to change her," Olivia interjected.

"As a companion?" Sebastian asked.

"Unlikely," Miles said. "From this, and other information Grant has gathered, it seems like he's building his own coven."

Elijah shook his head. "It's not a coven as much a gang. Loosely formed based on one strong leader and a couple of lieutenants. I've also developed another theory; that the majority of the gang is made up of fledglings."

"Fledglings?" Sebastian asked. His eyebrows furrowed together. With the scar he looked downright terrifying. "Why would you want to wrangle a bunch of feral vampires?"

"They're expendable," Elijah said. "And scary as hell. They're hard to fight off even for an experienced fighter like one of us. Difficult to manage, but if trained appropriately they can ultimately be an effective weapon."

"You think Caleb wanted Ms. Chase as one of his fledglings?" Miles asked.

"I have no idea what his true intentions are, but Sasha made it perfectly clear they would not be leaving the area any time soon and were looking forward to an altercation of some kind. She also made it clear that Ms. Chase is under continued threat."

"Why didn't you end her right then, Grant?" Ryan asked, fist clenched.

"I wanted a warning to go back to Caleb. I've given him one opportunity to leave this territory, if he doesn't take it then I have to go forward with a full assault. I felt like this would go over better with the Council if they became involved." Miles nodded in approval.

"And that's what you wanted to meet with us about?" Genevieve asked, always the bureaucrat. I can see why some would consider us a good match. Neither of us had much time for lengthy discussion.

"I need to know if everyone is willing and prepared to help me with this battle." The group nodded and murmured their support. I sighed and added, "I also need to know you will help me protect Ms. Chase at all costs."

"The girl," Sebastian asked, as though he'd missed something.

"Yes," I said, refusing to make eye contact with Elijah. "Although she no longer works for me, I feel responsible for her involvement. Sasha made it undeniably clear their interest in her is because of me."

"You fired her?" Genevieve asked, leaning forward. "Grant, she was perfect!"

"Not exactly."

"She quit," Olivia chimed in.

"Olivia," I warned.

"What did you do?" Ryan asked. Miles simply looked intrigued. Sebastian shook his head like he knew it was inevitable. Was it not? Were my behaviors truly that predictable?

Angel Lawson

"It wasn't a good match," I lied. "And that's not the point. Are you willing to help me protect her? I have requested she come back to the Foundation—just to be safe, but it's doubtful she will accept my offer."

Sebastian narrowed his eyes and asked, again, "Seriously, what did you do?"

"Grant, we will assist you in any way you need. Protecting humans has always been a priority. That isn't going to change now," Miles declared. "I have to ask, did she recognize Sasha as a vampire?"

"No. She was too scared and confused."

"Did you compel her memory? Wipe it, per protocol?" he pressed.

I looked down at my hands. "She is difficult to influence."

"No way," Sebastian said, glancing at his brother.

"Wouldn't be so sure about that," Olivia whispered so low only I heard.

"I had no idea," Genevieve said, holding back a snort of laughter. "No wonder she wasn't a good fit, you can't pull her strings like a puppet."

"Genevieve," Miles said, before returning to me. "Please notify me if she becomes aware of our nature. If she's truly immune to your gifts then we'll need to be prepared to take alternate measures. Be careful, Grant. Keep your distance from the girl. The situation with Caleb is already too public. We do not need any other issues."

178

"Not a problem."

Elijah coughed at the end of the table. This wouldn't be an issue except, typically, vampires do not cough. It was time to wrap it up before more of my inadequacies were revealed. "Thank you for your support. I know together we can stop this bastard." I looked around the room at the family I knew so well. "Anyone want to go for a hunt? I've got a little pent-up energy I'd like to release."

"Hell yes!" Sebastian cried, glancing at Ryan. The boys leapt up and ran to grab their gear.

"I'm in," Elijah said.

"Miles?" I asked. It really had been too long.

He smiled. "I thought you'd never ask."

24

Amelia

"You look terrible," Drew informed me as I felt the bed give under his weight.

I had my head back on the pillow and my eyes closed tight. Groaning, I pulled the blanket over my face and snuggled into the bed further. Maybe, I rationalized, if I stayed in bed it could all be a nightmare. Drew picked up my hand. I could feel his fingertips gently touch the swelling on my wrist. It definitely wasn't a nightmare.

"What happened?" he asked. "Holy shit, Mel, are you okay?"

I pulled the blanket off my face and looking into his worried eyes I felt my own start to burn. I sat up, leaning back into the headboard. I wiped my eyes and nose with the hem of my shirt. "I'm okay. Really I am. I don't really know what happened. It was all so strange."

Drew and I sat on the bed for over an hour as I told him about my encounter the night before. His eyes were big as saucers the entire time and I got to the point where I convinced myself that I must be exaggerating.

"Do you think she was high?" Drew asked. "Maybe she was off her meds."

"That's what I thought, too! But I don't know. I mean, who says that kind of stuff?" I kicked off the blanket to reveal my scraped knee. "I fell when she was chasing me, and then I have these." I pulled the neck of my shirt to show the finger shaped bruises and small scrapes from Sasha's nails.

"Woah. Do you want to go to the doctor? Those look pretty nasty."

"No. I'd rather just forget it ever happened." I went on to explain the part where Grant Palmer showed up and saved the day.

"I saw him last night," he said. "He was looking for you."

"Well, he found me, although I'll never understand how. One minute I was at the mercy of a deranged woman and the next, my boss, well, my ex-boss, was saving me." I snorted at the irony.

We both sat quietly for a moment until Drew cleared his throat. "So he just swooped in like some kind of Superman and saved you. Don't tell Thomas you have your very own superhero, he'd nerdgasm all over the place."

I grunted. "Yeah, if Superman had OCD and was a pain in my ass."

We looked at each other for a moment and burst into laughter, collapsing back on the bed. Drew sat up, shoulders heaving, and said, "I wonder if Superman had separate tiny drawers like how Mr. Palmer separates his socks."

I had described to Drew how Mr. Palmer had a whole dresser full of socks. There were athletic socks, and dress socks. Thick wool socks for hiking or backpacking. Colorful stripes, argyles and plaids. Each style had its own tiny sock-sized drawer in his dressing room.

I rolled my eyes and said between giggles, "Drew, Superman wears tights, not socks. I guess Clark Kent wears socks though to the Daily Planet. I'm not sure, but I suspect Clark Kent is a little OCD. He seems kind of uptight."

Drew nodded, "I don't know if Superman is a good fit, though. I'm thinking he is a little more like The Boy Wonder. You should have seen his face when I yelled at him last night!"

I sat up straight. "Drew, you didn't."

He smiled smugly. "I did and I don't care. He had it coming. Of course I had to force myself to look away from his gorgeous eyes. You're right. He is better looking in person." His eyes glazed over for a moment. I couldn't blame him. He had the exact same effect on me. "He apologized, right? And offered you your job back? Are you going to take it?"

I shoved the pillow under my chin, using it to prop my body up while I sat cross-legged and thought about his barrage of questions. I wasn't sure if I wanted to go back and work for Mr. Palmer. He was such a pig before, but at the same time there were some nice moments where I felt like I saw the kind person who came to my rescue last night. He had promised to behave better and didn't I owe him the opportunity to prove it?

I glanced sideways to the Rolling Stones T-shirt hanging over the edge of my hamper. It probably wouldn't hurt my reputation to go back and prove myself as well. Part of me felt a sense of gratitude for last night. How do you turn away from the man who saved you from a psychopath? I wasn't sure I could. And even though I was putting on a brave face for Drew, I was scared of Sasha and her threats, and Mr. Palmer made me feel safe.

I sighed and said, "I have to think about it, but I may. I feel the need to do this the right way. If I have to leave again it will be on better terms."

He nodded and stood. "Let's go get some lunch. I need a major dose of carbs after all those drinks last night. Plus, I have to tell you all about my night with Jess and then tell you about the silly girl Thomas left with!"

"He left with another girl?" I couldn't decide if I was offended or not.

"To be fair, you left with another guy."

I got off the bed and straightened up the blankets and pillows. I put my dirty laundry away, shoving it on top of the ruined shirt, and began gathering my things for the shower. I heard a tap on my door and Drew cracked it open with a thoughtful expression on his face.

"You know, I couldn't help but think about what The Boy Wonder would look like in a cape?" he asked.

I grinned mischievously. "I already have. And he's hot."

I turned back to my dresser and began rummaging through my clothes, looking for something to wear that would cover all my wounds. The injuries were a horrible reminder that Sasha was still on the loose, and I shuddered at the thought of her finding me. I really was lucky Mr. Palmer had found me in time. The alternative was too disturbing to think about. Superman or Boy Wonder, I wasn't sure, but last night, in the dark alley, he was definitely my guardian angel.

***

I walked up the steps, standing under the protective covering near the office door, nervously deciding if I should do this. 'This' involved me going back to work, sucking up my pride, ignoring my instincts to turn around and walk away forever. I'd left my key with my resignation letter when I walked out on Friday so someone had to let me in. I pressed my finger to the buzzer and shockingly, Grant Palmer opened the door. I figured he would've found that robot already.

He stood in the doorway, hair in disarray, wearing a gray V-neck sweater and his standard crisp black pants. His violet eyes looked brighter than before and his complexion had a healthier hue. He had the appearance of a man who had a refreshing, well-rested weekend.

At least one of us had.

I knew I was staring, mouth agape, partially from the shock of seeing him in the doorway, partly from his overwhelming hotness. Gray was definitely his color. Okay, anything was his color but gray took things to another level. I tried to close my mouth and appear nonchalant, like my appearance today had been expected.

Mr. Palmer widened the door and gestured me inside. "Good morning, Ms. Chase. Please come in."

"Thank you," I responded, relieved that he was welcoming and hadn't changed his mind about asking me back to work.

I shrugged out of my raincoat and hung it on the rack in the foyer. Mr. Palmer disappeared around the corner so I walked back to my desk as though everything was normal, as though I hadn't walked out of here in his dirty, ruined shirt, leaving my resignation letter on the desk in a fit of self-justification.

The desk was clear, the letter gone, yet my key was sitting on top, next to the credit card and phone I'd left on Friday, along with a new list of daily instructions.

I felt rather than heard him standing in the doorway. I peeked at him from the corner of my eye. He awkwardly leaned against the door frame, legs crossed at the ankle, hands shoved in his pockets. He appeared causal, informal, yet his posture was stiff and forced. Mr. Palmer looked like the type of person who dined at the Ritz but at the moment forced himself to stay at the Days Inn, like he was uncomfortable in his own skin. I got the feeling he would rather be anywhere else than right here.

I didn't blame him. The situation over the weekend was probably disturbing to him and possibly made him question my ability to make good judgments. What kind of girl gets herself into that kind of trouble? I prided myself on making good, strong decisions. He probably thought I was an idiot for wandering off with a strange person like Sasha anyway. The more I thought about it the more irritated with myself I became. For Christ's sake, there was a serial-animal-attack-killer out there.

His eyes were still on me, waiting for me to turn and acknowledge him, but I pretended I didn't notice and sat at the desk, reviewing my duties for the day.

"Ms. Chase," he said quietly.

I turned slightly, acting surprised at his presence. "Oh, Mr. Palmer. Can I help you with something? I was about to tackle this list." When I faced him, he was standing in the exact same pose as before. He hadn't moved a muscle.

"Yes. Well, I noticed you parked on the street. And after Friday evening, I wondered if you would prefer to park in my garage." Was that a hint of concern in his eyes? If I had to guess I would say that it was and I had no idea how to handle such a completely unexpected gesture. I thought for a moment of my dingy little car, mingling with the beautiful machines Mr. Palmer possessed. I wasn't comfortable with this idea at all.

I smiled appreciatively, "Thank you for the offer. It's really thoughtful, but that's okay. I don't think anyone will bother my car. It's a total hunk of junk."

His eyes clouded and he opened his mouth slightly. I waited expectantly for him to speak but the words appeared stuck in his throat.

Oh no. I'd offended him. He reached out to me and offered me something of his to make me more comfortable and I shot him down. I felt the heat rush up my face as I, once again, managed to screw things up with my boss.

I managed to keep the polite smile on my face the entire time and finally, he grunted, "It's not your car I'm worried about, Ms. Chase." He turned abruptly on his heel. Astonished, I listened to his feet rapidly ascend the stairs, and the sound of a door clicking sharply.

He was worried about me.

I was definitely surprised and admittedly more than a little flattered. I sat for a moment, considering what to do. He was right. It was safer for me to park in the garage, away from the busy street. Away from unstable, creepy-eyed women and their morbid fantasies.

I decided to take him up on his offer and move my car but I wasn't sure how to go about approaching Mr. Palmer in his home. In the past, he had always just appeared at some point. I had never sought him out.

I wasn't exactly sure of the protocol. *Do I simply go upstairs and knock? Should I call him on his cell phone? Do I leave him a note and run my errands and hope he notices it while I'm gone?* I groaned. Why was I waffling over such a simple matter? Everything about this man was complicated. His work, his antiques, his closet, his socks, and now parking—or rather, communication. With a resigned sigh, I decided to take the bull by the horns and just go up there and knock on his door.

I tentatively climbed the steps and reasoned that he was already annoyed with me so it would make no difference anyway. This would either be the right thing to do or one more notch on my not-so-stellar career with Mr. Grant Palmer.

At the landing, I hesitated, deciding which door to use. The one from the wardrobe? Or the one from the hallway that entered his private rooms?

Again I chided myself for over-thinking such a minor detail. It was utterly ridiculous.

I clenched my fists and walked with determination through the dressing room and went directly to the door on the opposite side of the room. I lifted my hand up and rapped forcefully, hoping he would hear me.

I waited a moment, holding my breath and counting the seconds, pondering what to do if he didn't respond. Should I knock again or should I just turn around and leave? Ridiculous.

Fifteen...twenty...twenty-five...my face was undoubtedly turning red due to lack of oxygen. I was going to have to make a decision.

I raised my arm again, knuckles clenched to knock, but without warning the door swung open and I found myself face to face, or rather, face to chest with Mr. Palmer.

I dropped my hand to my side and peered up to see the expression on his face. He didn't seem too annoyed or angry so using my most convincing voice, I said, "That was very thoughtful to offer me a spot in your garage and you're right, it is safer." I gave him the smile I used on the barista when I want extra whipped cream. "Does the offer still stand?"

After a tense moment of scrutiny under his swirling violet eyes, he nodded and dipped his fingers into his pocket and extracted out a small black square.

"Let me show you how to work this." Again, faster than I could respond, he was gone, back down the stairs, leaving me to follow in his wake. I raced after him to keep up, but only managed to slam my arm against the bannister. A sharp flash of pain traveled up my injured arm.

"Ugh," I muttered, and rubbed my wrist. It was still sore and tender from Friday night. I had worn a long-sleeved shirt hoping to hide it from view. I glanced up and Mr. Palmer stood in front of me. How did he get back up here so fast?

"Did something happen?" He looked at my fingers rubbing the red flesh with distaste, his jaw locked and stiff. In that moment, standing in the hallway, at the bottom of his steps, tired of his judgmental glances, and cold, gruff attitude, I snapped.

"Mr. Palmer," I said, pulling his attention away from my arm and back to my face. "If I'm going to continue working here, there are a few things we need to discuss."

His brow furrowed in concentration as though I was speaking a foreign language but he quietly said, "Proceed."

"The tension between us? It has to stop. I am an educated, smart, hard-working woman. I'm not sure how old you are Mr. Palmer, but I highly doubt it is much older than me. I will be respectful to you but I will not be treated as though I am less than you," I announced with conviction although even I could hear the shake in my voice.

He lifted an eyebrow this time and I watched incredulously as his posture relaxed, and he leaned lightly against the wall. I knew my face was red and my eyes were burning, tears betraying my anger. I sucked them back in and heard him say, "Please continue," in an encouraging tone.

Oh shit. I was starting to panic a little at his change in demeanor. There was no way this was going to end well. Resolved in my self-destruction, I figured I may as well put the final nail in my coffin.

"Well," I heard my voice crack so I cleared my throat and began again, "If you want me to do something, I will. If you want me to clean your gutters or wash your windows, that's fine. If you want me to sort your ties alphabetically, by color, brand, and location of purchase," I rolled my eyes before continuing, "I will do it. But you give me the common courtesy of a day's notice so I can be prepared. And from now on, I expect you to say please and thank you when applicable. If there is one thing I'm not, it's your doormat. And if you can't handle these simple requests then I will gladly pack my things, again, and go."

Finished with my tirade, I now just wanted to disappear. I glanced nervously for an escape. All I had to do was grab my purse and coat on the way out the door.

Or not.

Mr. Palmer was still watching me intently but now a slight smile played on his lips. I was entranced by their deep red tint, curving upward, taunting me with their perfection. "And if I do these things you'll stay?"

I lifted my eyes from his mouth, and stuttered, "Wha...what?"

The amusement lit his eyes. "If I submit to your requests, you'll stay."

"Yes. I will stay."

"Good. Ms. Chase, will you please come with me to the garage so I can so you how to work the garage opener? It is a bit different from a normal system, since it's linked to the security system."

I nodded and was shocked at the change in tone. It was still formal but he did say 'please' and he asked nicely. He gestured for me to walk ahead of him so I took the lead, adjusting my ponytail as I passed him and walked toward the back door.

***

On my way back to Mr. Palmer's from the post office I stopped at the little coffee shop I had begun frequenting on my lunch breaks. I maneuvered my car through the crowded street looking for a place to park near the building. I typically preferred to walk to the business district, since it was so close to Mr. Palmer's home, but I wasn't comfortable since the attack.

Things were better at work but still not perfect. Mr. Palmer had stayed true to his word and adjusted his attitude. His treatment toward me was slowly improving.

I was showered in 'please' and 'thank you', offered compliments on my work and given nothing excessively outrageous to perform.

The problem was not his effort to treat me with more respect, the problem was him.

The man truly puzzled me. He was physically so beautiful and graceful. Yesterday I found myself mesmerized by his elegant hands as he pulled a record out of its sleeve, gently cradling the edges of the black disk, careful to never touch the grooves on the surface. I watched as he held it close to his face and inhaled the distinct odor of vinyl. A small smile of contentment crossed his lips.

Yet, when I asked him what song was playing or more about the musician, his body stiffened for a moment and the natural grin on his face was replaced by a more superficial one. He answered politely, but robotically, before he hastily retreated from the room.

He was just so freaking weird.

I found a parking space on the street and walked to the coffee shop. I paused for a moment at the door, noticing a sign plastered in the window. It was a photo of a girl, maybe fifteen or sixteen, dark hair, happy blue eyes and a huge smile. She was wearing a gold cross pendant on her neck that hung in the middle of her chest. Over her picture were the words MISSING-HAVE YOU SEEN ME? I felt my stomach turn and I saw a flash of

Sasha's wicked face flitter across my eyes. I saw at the bottom it said the missing girl's name was Jenna.

I shook my head, pulled the door open and walked to the counter.

"Hi." I smiled. "I would like some tea...preferably something calming?" A wave of nausea passed over me and I forced the image of the girl on the poster out of my head.

"We have a really nice Chamomile, would you like that?"

"Sounds perfect," I said, and waited while she prepared my order, drumming my fingers on the counter. "What do you know about that sign in the window? The missing girl?"

"Her mother came by and put that in the window. Apparently she went missing one night when she was out with some friends at the movies. She left her seat to go get something from the concession stand and never returned. The police think she ran away but her mother is convinced something happened to her."

"That's really sad. I hope they find her."

The girl nodded and pushed my cup of tea across the counter. "Did you recently move around here or something? I've noticed you coming in fairly often."

"No, I don't live around here, but I took a job in the area a couple of weeks ago."

"Oh really? Where?" she asked as she rang up my purchase on the cash register.

"I'm working for Mr. Palmer as his personal assistant. I don't know if you know him. He doesn't go out much." I explained and took a sip of my drink.

"Grant Palmer? Sex hair? Jaw that could cut glass? Wickedly aloof? Man who makes my uterus ache at the sight of him?" she laughed. "That Grant Palmer?"

She nailed it, although I wasn't sure about the uterus part. "So you do know him."

"He comes in a couple of times a week, orders the same thing, smiles at me, and heads to his favorite table outside. I've dropped hints a couple of times trying to let him know I was available, but," she sighed wistfully, "he doesn't seem interested."

I was shocked. I looked at the girl in front of me. She was pretty, with long black hair, smooth brown skin, and legs you could climb. Her eyes were a gorgeous blue and she had a stunning birth mark on her cheek that looked like a tiny bird. If we were in LA or New York I would think she was an actress or model. "Really? He is a little socially awkward, maybe he didn't notice you were flirting."

"No, I was more than obvious. He is definitely not into me."

"I wouldn't take it personally, he's not the most sociable person."

"Not to sound egotistical, but I've come up with another theory," she said, flipping her hair over her shoulder.

"Oh really?" I said, conspiratorially. "What kind of theory."

She laughed again and leaned forward as if telling me a secret. "It's quite simple. Any man that good-looking, that rich, and that single who can resist this," and she pointed to her chest, snugly wrapped in a tight black t-shirt with the name of the shop across her ample boobs, "is playing for the other team."

"You think he's gay?" I asked, incredulously.

She nodded confidently back, a smirk on her face.

I had a distinct memory of Mr. Palmer, holding a trash can full of broken furniture, with the tall gorgeous blond behind him on the stairs coming down from his private rooms. I could almost envision the two of them behind closed doors, standing close together, reveling in one another's tall, muscular beauty. I swallowed hard at the thought.

It made perfect sense.

All of his odd behaviors and quirks could be explained by this simple fact. He had a huge secret he was keeping and this could make anyone tense and stressed. Add a high profile life to the scenario and it made things even more complicated. No wonder he seemed lonely. And angry. I felt angry for him. No one should have to hide their true nature.

"Fucking establishment," I said. "I can't imagine what would happen if people found out he's gay. I mean, we're in the Bible belt and everything."

"You have no idea," she said. "The town I come from? He'd be tarred and feathered."

"People are jerks."

I paid for my tea and gave her a final wave, heading back to work with a completely different outlook.

25

Grant

es Olivia. She's fine."

Olivia. She had called me twice a day for the last week, harassing me about Amelia, but with no solid details of her own to share.

"Is she there?" she asked. "If she isn't there you can't be sure."

"No, I can't see her at this very moment, but it is sunny and hot outside so I thought it was a safe day to send her to the post office without fear of another attack." I clenched my hand in my hair, trying to remain calm. The phone call was exactly the reason I didn't live at home any longer. I needed my space and people out of my head and my future. I decided to be proactive. "Have you had another vision? Is that what you're trying to tell me?"

"No. I haven't," she admitted.

"Olivia," I said, pondering something that had been bothering me since the meeting with the coven. "What does Miles really think about Ms. Chase?

Angel Lawson

"Have you not discussed it?"

"No," I said.

"That's unlike you. Normally you two have gone over everything a dozen times." From literature to religion to medical practices, Miles and I tended to have extended conversations on everything. Olivia was right, I'd been avoiding the subject of Amelia.

"Well, what do you think he's thinking?" I asked.

"I suspect he's worried about the Council. You've already pushed their stance on involvement in the human community with the Foundation. He's gone to bat for you before."

"You don't think he will again?" I asked.

"I think you may want to talk to him about Amelia, tell him your true feelings and concerns."

I laughed. "You don't think that will make things worse? Miles is open-minded but consorting with humans is a pretty big violation. The biggest, in fact."

"I think Miles is fair and I think your happiness is very important to him, but you and I both know he takes the rules of the Council seriously and you're precariously close to breaking them. You should tell him before it goes any further."

"I haven't made any decisions."

"No," she said, and I heard a small snort. "Honestly, I think you're safe for a bit. You and Amelia never seem to be on the same page anyway."

She *had* seen something. "What are you talking about?"

"You know the rules—your rules, in fact. No peeking into Grant Palmer's life."

"Olivia," I warned, running my hand through my hair.

"Be careful, Grant. This isn't a situation you're used to."

I sighed. I could concede that I was way out of my league. "I will."

I disconnected and continued to look though the files I'd stored up on the third floor. The only entrance to this level was through my private study. I kept huge filing cabinets up here for old newspapers and other information on the 'cases' I worked. Once upon a time this was supposed to be my studio and remnants of that life were currently shoved back against the wall and covered by a huge cloth. Another reminder of the life I gave up for the one I chose to live now.

I went back six months and began looking for any weird incidents I may have overlooked the first time. Anything that sounded like the altercation between Amelia and Sasha. I'd only searched at that time for information concerning the ritualistic murders but nothing else. I'd been so focused on Caleb that it was entirely too possible other crimes had slipped through the cracks. I laid the papers out on the floor and began the tedious process of tagging anything of interest.

With different colored Post-its I marked each event that seemed even remotely suspicious including, but not limited to, vandalism, muggings, or abductions. Halfway through the March papers, I realized I'd run out of stickers and went downstairs to the supply closet in the kitchen.

As I approached the second floor stairs I braced myself for the onslaught of Amelia's fragrant scent and presence. I'd heard the garage door open moments before and I knew she had arrived at the office. I arranged my face into what others considered socially appropriate and walked into the kitchen.

"Good afternoon Ms. Chase," I said, observing her attempt to get a coffee mug off the top shelf.

"Hi," she grunted, straining to reach on the tip of her toes.

I processed the moment, watching her struggle with the height. *Oh, right,* I thought, with a sudden flare of irritation at myself for being so dense. "Let me get that for you." I easily plucked the cup off the shelf and placed it on the counter.

The small gestures stumped me every time. Simple things like holding the door, allowing the person to walk ahead of me, or offering to carry in the boxes and bags from the car. Things I hadn't considered in many years. It made me question how other humans felt about my interactions with them...had I failed?

I walked over to the storage closet and rummaged around, quickly finding the notes I needed due to Amelia's excellent organizational skills. I was prepared to turn around and tell her this when I noticed out of the corner of my eye that she was watching me. Oh the irony.

Her eyes were questioning, tightened at the corners, and I felt them linger. Her interest excited me because no one ever paid me much notice—not for long at least. When they did I could tell what they were thinking by their increased heart rates or listening to their whispered comments. Women were impressed by my appearance and men were in awe of my intimidating nature. Everything about me drew people in for a moment but then, just as quickly, those same qualities made them uncomfortable and they scurried away.

Amelia stood behind me, her heart rate even and breathing normal, inspecting me. Again, I had no clue what she was thinking and the thought of that was thrilling.

I turned finally and faced her, noticing a light pink tint to rush up her neck.

"Thank you for organizing the closet so well. I found just what I needed." I held up the pad of garish pink notes.

"You're welcome," she said, the same quizzical look on her face as before.

"I'm going to be upstairs and would prefer not to be disturbed. If you need me call my cell, okay?" I said under her scrutinizing gaze. I shifted my feet, feeling slightly uncomfortable.

We stood in a sort of tense stand-off until she turned her back to me and hunched her shoulders while she stirred her cup of tea. I took a step backwards, ready to leave the room when she spoke suddenly and stated in a low shaky voice, "I know you have a secret."

My still heart plummeted to my ancient stomach, igniting a feeling of absolute dread and horror. These were the words of my deepest fears. Miles had warned me—this is what Olivia was trying to tell me. I'd gotten too close. My mouth became dry and I had to force myself to breathe in order to appear normal.

I steadied my voice. "A secret?"

The sound of her metal spoon, tracing the edge of her cup, was the only noise in the room until she said, "The signs were all there. I mean, they're stereotypical but stereotypes are for a reason, right?"

"I'm, uh, not following."

"Well, you're freakishly neat and tidy. Your closet alone should have sent up a red flag."

Okay. This was true. I had an extreme case of obsessive compulsive disorder, but that was hardly an identifiable trait of being a vampire. It was more of a personal quirk exaggerated by the vampirism. I braced myself for more.

"Obviously your body is like...killer." Her heart beat like a hummingbird's wings and I could almost feel the heat of nervousness rolling off her body. Only this silly woman would be embarrassed as she destroyed my life. Abruptly she said, "I mean, killer. I know a lot of men who would die for your physique."

She thought I looked amazing. A smug grin crept across my face before I shook it off, wondering for the millionth time what thoughts were running though her head. I was aware women found me attractive, as it was one of the lures that made humans such susceptible prey. To hear Amelia say those words brought about a rush of feelings I wasn't used to, but was it really important to say right now?

"Your skin is flawless, unblemished. And your hair...it's a work of art."

"My hair?"

I hated my hair. Loathed it. It was the one thing that drove me absolutely insane post transition, but that alone was nothing definitive. I mean, look at Miles. He was bald. Forever.

She stepped closer and peered at my neck and chest. "You man-scape, right?"

I shook my head silently, afraid to speak. I had no idea what this 'man-scaping' thing was but I knew I didn't have it.

"Huh," she considered and turned back to the counter, her long hair swaying a bit as she took a sip of her tea. "You probably have more clothes than Kanye West."

The uneasy knot in my stomach quickly morphed into one of confusion. Kanye West? Who?

She continued, rambling now. "Sometimes you speak like you've never been around a woman, and you never have company, and the only time you did it was a man. Who, coincidentally, was also unbelievably gorgeous."

What? I literally was unable to follow her train of thought. What man was she talking about? I searched my memory and came up with the only male visitor we'd had.

Elijah.

She stilled, palms flat on the counter. When she spoke it was low and with conviction. "Like I said, I know what you're hiding, Grant."

Here it comes. Images of what would come flashed in my mind. Would she run screaming? Would I have to kill her? In over a hundred years I'd never had a moment of exposure like this.

"I want you to know that I support you—no matter what."

I waited for a beat. I waited for the earth to stop. For the fear to sink in her eyes.

"Uh, what?"

Amelia spun around and looked me in the eye. The wrong emotion was written across her face. Instead of fear she looked, as she had just proclaimed, supportive? "You're gay."

I was stuck in the moment, hands clenched, prepared for exposure but I heard her words echo in my ears. Gay?

"I, um...what?" I stumbled over my words. I never stumbled over my words. Everything about this woman completely bewildered me. She reduced me to a bumbling idiot.

Apparently a gay, bumbling idiot.

She took a step forward, bringing a fresh wave of her scent toward me, the excruciating aroma of lemons filling my senses. Her normally pale cheeks were flushed with embarrassment. Her eyes were shining and her lips were puffed out with satisfaction, having 'outed' me.

I'd never found her more attractive.

"You're gay," she said again. "It's okay. I totally support you and your decisions. Well, not decisions since I feel we are all born one way or another, but regardless, I think it's great."

She thought it was great that I was gay. I supposed that was a preferred alternative to me being a blood sucking monster.

She was still talking and I picked her up mid-sentence, "...and you know, I hate sounding so stereotypical but you really do just have way too much clothing for a straight guy. Not to mention the fact the girl at the coffee shop, the really cute one? She told me she has never seen you with a woman, either. And that she has slipped you her number more than once only to find it still on the table when she cleaned up. I mean, she's really pretty. Come on, you're young, single, incredibly gorgeous, rich, successful. You," she stepped closer and jabbed a finger in my chest, "are totally gay."

The minute her warm fingertip made contact with my chest, even through the barrier of clothing, sparks of heat spread across every inch of my body.

Focus, Grant. Now was not the time to get the warm and fuzzies for this girl. She thought I was gay and apparently so did everyone else. I'd severely underestimated my presentation to those around me.

She withdrew the tip of her finger and I instantly missed it. I absently rubbed the spot with my thumb trying to feel the sensation again.

She stepped back and picked up her tea and said, "No wonder you're angry all the time. Keeping a secret like that must be exhausting. Then to make matters worse, I'd caught you red-handed with that hottie the other day! Don't worry, I won't tell anyone. It's your decision when you want the world to know." She smiled and winked leaving me alone in the kitchen.

I stood for a moment fighting the urge to tell her otherwise. As ridiculous as it sounded, this was possibly the best mistake she could make. My real secret, that I was an eternally frozen twenty-two year-old vampire that kept up a charade of normalcy by posing as the CEO of a multi-million dollar organization was beyond horrific.

Add on the fact I had a side job of fighting crime and tracking bad guys during my long, endless nights, and things became absurd. The only thing more absurd was that I was currently battling conflicting desires of hunger and lust over the most fragile girl I've ever encountered.

I ran my hands up my face and fisted them in my hair. I wasn't sure when my life had turned into an epically bad horror film, but clearly it had. Oh wait. I did know. It was the day Amelia Chase entered my life. That was the cosmic fate that now added the term 'gay' in front of Vampire CEO Crime Fighter.

As much as it pained me, instead of denying her theory I quickly decided I was going to remain non-committal. If my being gay explained my odd behaviors or physical appearance, then I could live with it. The theory gave me a bit of freedom and it ensured a reason to keep my distance. I needed a good excuse to force me away from the feelings and emotions that had been building since the day she tainted my home. It was all one more lie in my elaborate charade but I needed her to stay close to me while maintaining the image I had crafted. If this meant from now on, in my home, Grant Palmer was gay, then so be it.

I snuck one last look at Amelia at her desk, twirling a strand of her hair around her finger, reading emails on her computer before I climbed the stairs. Watching her

sitting there feeling safe and content for that one moment made me realize I had bigger things to focus on,
and I went upstairs to get started.

26

Amelia

"**Y**ou said what?"

Drew sat across from me at a table at my favorite restaurant, Little Bird Café. It was the best place to get organic, vegan food in town and I could only talk Drew into coming when I had some really interesting gossip to share. He complained the whole time that it tasted like cardboard. I'd been a vegetarian since I was nine and my class took a field trip to the meat processing plant. Once I found out exactly what was in a hot dog, my carnivore days were over.

"Shhhh...or you will get me fired. For real this time," I hissed. I knew I wasn't supposed to tell details of my job to Drew or to anyone else but I couldn't help myself. The whole day had been too much.

He looked around the nearly empty diner and whispered, "You actually accused him of being gay?"

I nodded, stuffing a hunk of falafel in my mouth. It was the same day as my confrontation with Mr. Palmer. I knew I had been somewhat inappropriate with my boss by questioning his sexuality, but I honestly hoped it would make us more comfortable around each other now that his secret was out in the open.

"What did he say?" he asked.

I swallowed and took a sip of my drink. "He didn't say anything. But he definitely didn't say no. And what guy wouldn't deny that he's gay if it wasn't true?" I reasoned.

Drew shrugged. "True, but as much as I'm glad to hear my chances have gone up exponentially, he totally doesn't ping as gay to me."

"You would if you'd seen his boyfriend the other day. He is equally gorgeous and so tall...." I let my mind wander to the shaggy-haired man who visited last week. "The tension between them was thick. They're perfect for each other."

Drew didn't look convinced.

"Whatever, it seemed to do the trick. He was a lot nicer to me after that. What's going on with you and Jess?"

The change in topic was what Drew needed to stop focusing on Mr. Palmer. I listened as he went on about Jess and how they were meeting up later this evening to go see a movie. That piece of information sent an unwanted chill up my spine.

"You guys be careful, okay? Earlier I saw a poster at the coffee shop about a girl who went missing from the theater."

"Wrong profile, honey. I don't think kidnappers are into men," he said.

"Just be careful, okay? After the other night everything is giving me the creeps."

"Yeah, okay. We will definitely watch a movie at his house instead, even if that means I have to sit with Jess and Thomas all night for another round of lame games." He wrinkled his nose and I shook my head glad it was him and not me. "I guess I don't have to tell you to take precautions."

"Nope, I've got that covered."

I'd taken to triple locking the door. The door, deadbolt and chain were locked every time I was home. I compulsively checked my windows and the balcony door. Plus, I practically ran from my car to the apartment every time I came home. I would have actually run if I hadn't been afraid of tripping in the middle of the parking lot. I really did appreciate Mr. Palmer allowing me to park in the garage. I felt much safer and I had the sense he was going out of his way to make me feel more comfortable.

"You know, how about you and Jess come to our place tonight? I was going to read anyway so you can have the TV to yourself. No need to hang out with his roommates and play video games all night."

"Really? That would be great." He pulled out his phone to text Jess the change of plans.

The possibility of Sasha finding me was slim. She'd probably been locked up already for whatever mental-breakdown she'd had. Even so, I couldn't shake this feeling that someone was watching me. I had it at night and sometimes at work. Drew's phone buzzed and he smiled. "He's coming over."

"Good," I said, already relieved we'd all be in the same place.

***

Several days had passed since I'd outed Mr. Palmer and things were, to my pleasant surprise, much better than before.

He seemed a little more relaxed and less tense when he was near me. My attempts at small talk were received better and I actually was able to get him to tell me a little more about his work at The Palmer Foundation. To my disappointment, he clammed up when it came to any personal information.

Understandable, I guessed, since he was my boss. We'd had such a rocky start, but at the same time it was awkward to work so closely with someone in their home and know so little about them. Therefore, it became a personal challenge to get him to reveal any small tidbit of information about himself. I'd decided to use his art, music and antiques as a method to find out more.

It was Friday, the day for dusting and general house cleaning. I'd asked him to work a designated day into my schedule so I could dress accordingly. He happily obliged and we even sat down with our calendars earlier this week and planned together. Little moments like these helped me get a chance to know him better. I realized he had a biting sense of humor when he relaxed enough. I also noticed, as we sat across the table from one another, that he smelled like no other man I'd encountered. It was all I could do to not walk over to him and run my nose up and down his body. For once in my life, I maintained composure and stayed in my seat.

For cleaning day, I wore jeans and a loose tank top with flats. It was casual but not inappropriate, and it made it easier for me to clean when I could get around on the floor and climb the step ladder in comfortable clothing.

There really was little to do so I understood why Mr. Palmer didn't pay for an additional cleaning person. Plus, it was becoming more and more apparent he didn't want company in the house. I'd heard him more than once telling Olivia on the phone not to come visit, that he was fine and very busy. His tone was terse and he always made excuses to get off the phone quickly.

As I dusted the paintings in the parlor I stopped at a particular painting that had caught my eye over the last couple of weeks. It had beautiful blues and reds and I could faintly see the shapes of two figures, although they were very abstract, mingled in with shapes and designs. I peered at it a little closer, looking at the thick paint, intrigued.

"It's called "Male and Female"."

Startled, I spun around, glad I had nothing breakable in my hands. "Dude, you scared me."

"Sorry."

"The painting's beautiful. There is so much going on, every time I come in here I find myself drawn to it. Who painted it?" I asked.

"Jackson Pollock painted it in 1940," he answered. With his long, graceful hands he began pointing out details.

I listened to him describe the painting with fascination. "There is some confusion as to what exactly is in the painting. Some people feel it is a man and a woman. Others think it is one figure but defined two ways. Pollock was very ambiguous in his artwork. He didn't feel the need to explain his paintings to anyone."

"Isn't he the guy with the splatter or drip painting?" I asked searching my brain for filed away art history lessons.

For once my questions seemed to work and his typically smooth face became animated as he spoke. "Yes, but this was an earlier work. He didn't start with the drip paintings that are more recognizable now until later in his career. I prefer this style to the other. When you look at it, it can be almost anything you want it to be. You can find what you're looking for in it each time you see it." He looked down at me through the hair dipping down over his eyes. "I feel this is how most people live their lives, seeing what they want to see, not what is really there."

We stood for a moment, absorbing the painting quietly until he asked, "What do you see?"

"I do see the male. Here is his strong, sharp jaw and thick brow. His hair, it's bushy and golden brown." I tilted my head and studied him for a moment. "He resembles you."

Mr. Palmer studied me back before flicking his eyes back to the painting. "And the female?" he prodded.

"I'm not sure about the woman," I said, pointing to the figure in red. "Her facial features are much less refined, yet her body clearly implies her gender. She's very vague, almost like she is something just out of reach."

I leaned in further trying to make sense out of Pollock's chaos but deciding, ultimately, for this day I was satisfied. I faced Mr. Palmer to find him looking intently at the painting, perhaps dreaming of his own version of what the artist was trying to convey.

I said softly, "Thank you for sharing that with me. I'm going to get back to work now."

Mr. Palmer glanced my way, his eyes never fully leaving the canvas. "You're welcome, Ms. Chase."

I took a last glance as I left the room Mr. Palmer was still standing in front of the piece, hands in his pockets, completely still. I realized this may be the first time since I'd met him he seemed completely at ease and comfortable with me and our surroundings.

Later that afternoon I was surprised to hear the doorbell ring. Mr. Palmer had retreated upstairs to his offices and I had been entering in more names, dates and addresses into the database on the computer. We were not expecting deliveries.

I hopped up and ran to the door, hoping whoever was outside had an umbrella since it was raining quite hard.

I pulled the door open and was happily surprised to see Olivia standing on the stoop under a bright green umbrella. She wore a matching raincoat cinched at the waist with a belt. Next to her was the tall, lanky frame of Mr. Palmer's blonde friend, who was wearing a gray trench coat to stay dry.

"Good afternoon, Amelia. Hope we aren't interrupting."

"Of course not, please come in," I said. "I didn't know you were coming. Hurry and get out of the rain."

"Spur of the moment visit. Don't worry about Grant. We'll handle him."

"Let me take your umbrella and coats," I said, taking them and hanging them up on the hooks by the door. "Please make yourself comfortable and wait in the parlor while I fetch Mr. Palmer."

I bolted out of the room as quickly as my feet would take me and ran up the stairs to Mr. Palmer's door. I knocked gently and he opened the door a moment later, an expectant look on his face. His lean body filled the space between the door and the frame, blocking me from seeing further into his room.

Watching him lean in the door way was one of those moments and a bundle of butterflies exploded in my stomach. God, he was handsome. His hair was pushed back off his forehead, except for several small pieces, and my fingers twitched with the desire to bush those back with the rest. I felt my face warm at the ridiculous thought and said, "Sorry to bother you but Olivia and your friend are here. I asked them to wait downstairs."

"My friend?" He blinked twice. "Oh, you must mean Elijah. I didn't hear them arrive." He shut the door behind him and waved his arm for me to go ahead of him down the stairs.

At the bottom of the steps I turned to him and said, "Elijah is really cute. Good job."

"Amelia." He grimaced, but I waved him off.

"I'll behave," I promised. "But seriously, double thumbs up."

In the parlor Eli and Olivia sat together on the love seat engaged in quiet conversation. Mr. Palmer entered the room behind me and when I glanced back I saw the pained expression on his face. He and Olivia shared some kind of silent communication. She lifted a perfectly sculpted eyebrow. Confused at the energy in the room, I glanced at Eli, who only looked amused.

Wow. Whatever was going on with this group didn't need my involvement. I backed out the door and said, "If you need me I'll be at my desk."

I heard a low rush of words and possibly a hiss from Mr. Palmer as I passed him. I was almost safely out the door when he called, "Amelia, wait. In the chaos the other day I forgot to introduce you to Elijah."

I stepped back in and noticed Mr. Palmer was looking at the ceiling. Olivia had picked up Elijah's hand and smiled at him. I smiled, a little confused at their affection, but said, "Nice to officially meet you, Elijah. I'm Amelia."

He gave me a breathtaking grin and said, "Hi, Amelia."

My eyes shifted from Elijah to Olivia and then to Mr. Palmer. I had the sudden, sinking realization that I was the ugly duckling in a room full of extraordinarily attractive people.

Mr. Palmer coughed and grunted, "Olivia," under his breath.

Olivia smiled warmly at me. "Amelia, Elijah is my husband."

I felt my jaw drop a little and I looked between Olivia and Mr. Palmer trying to figure out what was going on.

Mr. Palmer was still not looking at anyone. In fact, he was strategically looking anywhere but at me, Olivia or Elijah.

"Your husband? No, I had no idea you two were married," I replied through clenched teeth. I hissed in Mr. Palmer's direction, "No idea at all."

The tension in the room was thick. I was pretty sure it was due to my immense embarrassment since I had accused Mr. Palmer of having an affair with his cousin-in-law or whatever they were. I wanted to melt into the carpet and disappear, or at least I thought I did. Except my humiliation dissipated and I was struck with a sudden wave of giddiness. A nervous giggle slipped through my lips and I slapped my hand over my mouth. I realized everyone else was laughing; even Mr. Palmer had a sliver of a smile on his face that he forcibly tried to squelch.

"Nice to meet you," I said again. Then I excused myself from the room and went back to my desk absolutely befuddled. I had no idea what had just happened but I went from feeling horribly humiliated to downright giddy in a matter of moments. It was awkward but preferable to the alternative. I heard the trio go up the steps together and shut the door behind them, leaving me mixed-up and alone downstairs, wondering why Mr. Palmer lied to me about Elijah and what the heck did those people do upstairs all the time anyway?

27

Grant

"**G**rant, if you and Elijah need some time alone I would happily give it to you," Olivia declared in an innocent voice.

I chose to ignore her and walked over to my desk chair while the two of them sat on the couch.

"It could have been worse. Ryan could have been here. Or Sebastian," Elijah said.

"Does everyone know?" I asked, my fingers automatically moving to the bridge of my nose in irritation. Olivia described the scenario in detail: My entire family listening to her as she relayed the conversation Amelia and I had concerning my sexual preferences. Ryan responded typically. Utter amusement and doubled over in laughter. Sebastian actually said, "I knew it" out loud before walking out of the room. Miles kept a straight face, while Genevieve flipped through a magazine as if she couldn't care less. Trust me, she couldn't.

I sighed and slumped a little in my chair.

Olivia came over, sat in my lap and draped her arm over my shoulder. "It's okay, Grant. It's not a big deal and you really had no choice. You had to protect yourself and the family from being exposed."

"You took one for the team. Of course, I'm not sure which team that is anymore. It does explain a lot of things though," Elijah chimed in. He was a dead man. Or a dead vamp. Whichever.

Olivia must have seen it coming because she jumped off my lap and for the second time in so many visits, I lunged at Elijah. He anticipated it this time, dodging me easily, and I landed on the couch with a loud thump. I leapt up in a defensive position. He narrowed his eyes, plotting his next move.

Olivia quickly dashed between us. "Stop it. You know it's funny and we know it's not true." She reached her hand out and pressed it to my lower chest. Her touch was firm—nothing like the warm, searing feeling of Amelia's fingertip.

I nodded and relaxed. I walked back to the couch and sat down and Olivia sat next to me this time, making sure I didn't have plans to go after her husband again. Elijah moved to the computer, ignoring the two of us, probably trying to stay off my radar.

I looked at Olivia and asked in a desperate whisper, "What do you see?"

"With Amelia and Sasha?" she asked.

I gave her a tight nod.

"Right now everything is very murky. I get flashes of the Predator and several others but nothing specific.

224

They haven't decided on a course of action, but they are working on something. I do get the sense it involves Amelia."

I leaned into the couch, slowly rubbing my palms up and down my legs. I hated the fact I hadn't stopped this group of rouge vampires earlier. I should have and I blamed myself for not seeing the larger pattern. It took every ounce of willpower to keep myself from going downstairs to pick her up and lock her away in this safe room until I'd eradicated the danger. I imagined doing exactly that, carrying her in my arms up the stairs. I'd inhale her delightful scent, and touch her soft, creamy skin. She'd be safe up here and in the meantime I would learn all her secrets and she would know all of mine.

I felt Eli watching me and glanced his way. He had an eyebrow raised in concern. "Grant, what is going on? Primal lust was one thing and hunger and desire are another, but this? She's human."

"I know." Every moment I spent with her I wanted her more and more. I wasn't just feeling lust or protectiveness. I wanted more. Companionship?

"Dude, she's human. Off limits. Do not touch. Do not engage. I let it go last time because if anyone was strong enough to fight the temptation it would be you. But if anything, you've gotten worse. You do realize you can't pursue this, right?"

"I know," I repeated, growing agitated. This was exactly why I'd left home. Well, one of the reasons. Between the three of us there wasn't a shred of privacy. Your successes and failures were available for everyone to see and criticize. I couldn't handle it then and I definitely couldn't now.

"Grant, I'm serious. Don't fuck around with her. If something happened to her, the police, her family...they would all come to you first."

Olivia shot Elijah a warning look, cutting him off mid-sentence. In her quiet voice she said, "It's okay, Elijah. Grant isn't going to do anything wrong." It was too late though. Elijah's questions set me on edge. All it took was a tiny stumble and Amelia's fate was clear.

"I'm just saying," he added. "We all know how this will end if you pursue it."

Amelia would be dead. He didn't say it. It wasn't necessary. It was the absolute truth. The only truth.

She turned and looked at me with concern. "I don't agree. I have no idea how this will end, Grant."

I pushed off the couch and left the room, closing the door behind me and entered my bedroom. I knew Elijah was right; the thoughts and emotions I'd been struggling with were outrageous. Dangerous. I had no right to think of Amelia in any way other than as my employee—a human who needed my protection.

I'd been okay with that. I was even dealing with the absurd notion (okay, maybe not that absurd) that she thought I was homosexual. I thought this social barrier between us as man and woman would separate us further, keep us apart, make things more uncomfortable, but I had been wrong. It had the opposite effect. This bit of information made her more comfortable in my presence. She spoke to me about music and art or literature. She forced me to sit down and plan out our schedules, which led to us making jokes and familiarizing ourselves with one another. This caused a bigger problem than I'd ever expected.

I liked her. Very much.

I liked her sense of humor, her desire to learn, her curiosity.

I was intrigued by her lack of fear, her complete and utter disregard for self-preservation. I liked that no matter how much noise I tried to make, I startled her every time I walked in a room because she was so engrossed in her activity she was completely unaware of me. I liked the fact she was unaware of me. That my physical appearance and typical lures didn't seem to work on her the same way it did on other humans. And I liked that place on the side of her neck, right below her earlobe, that tinted red the minute I walked in the room.

I'd been pacing around the room, but at this thought I crumbled on my knees in fury. I could no longer deny I wanted Amelia the way a man wants a woman and it infuriated me. I was furious at Elijah for being right and at myself for being so weak. Enraged at the forces at work that placed this woman in my path when I had no reasonable chance to be with her.

I'd resolved to live alone, without my family or others. To protect those who needed it without reward or acknowledgement. Why did this insightful, strong, beautiful woman have to walk in and knock down my carefully arranged fortress?

I heard a tap on the study door and Olivia swung it open. She sat on the floor next to me and I couldn't bear to look at her. I was precariously close to betraying my family and that was something I couldn't inflict on them.

"Grant, you know I think you can be a real asshole sometimes. Like a total asshole. That shit you pulled on Amelia when she started was ridiculous." She lifted my chin and we looked at one another, family, forged to-gether by damnation and the loneliness of eternal life.

"Is this your idea of a pep talk? Because it's really ter-rible."

She lightly slapped my cheek. "See? Asshole. You be-have this way because you're obsessed with some non-vampire moral code. A code that you created and doesn't have a place in the real world. Amelia walked in that door and knocked you off your feet. That means some-thing, at least to me it does."

"I don't know what to do," I confessed. "She's hu-man."

"And she has incredible free will." Her bright and alert green eyes penetrated mine. "Grant, for once in your life do what you want to do, not what you think you should do. Everything will turn out okay." I buried my face in her lap and felt her fingers weave through the strands of my hair.

I wanted to believe her, but the consequences were too severe. It was one thing for me to live the life of the damned. It was another to inflict it on Amelia.

Olivia and I were quiet for some time, talking in our private language for a while, letting my frustration pass. I allowed myself to be soothed since she really was the only one who could reach me that way.

"Grant, come here," Elijah called from the other room, and I stood up, lifting Olivia with me.

"I'm going to go downstairs while you two play superhero," Olivia said. Before I could argue, she added, "I'll be good, I promise."

I found Elijah sitting behind the desk, focused on the computer screen. He pointed. "What do these latest entries mean?"

I walked around and read the information on the screen. It was the data I had asked Amelia to enter earlier that day. "After Amelia's incident on Friday night, I went back through the old papers I have upstairs looking for any type of suspicious accidents I may have missed."

His brow furrowed in concentration. "And these names and dates correlate to those events."

"Yes. These abbreviations." I pointed to a series of letters next to each name. "They match to the type of crime committed. AR stands for armed robbery, MP, for missing person, A for assault and so on."

Elijah leaned back in the chair, his long legs stretched out under my large desk. He ran his fingers through his hair for a moment and I waited for him to explain. "You definitely think that more than the murders are connected to these vampires?"

"Yes, Sasha's attempt on Amelia made that quite clear," I told him. "The missing person reports have gone up dramatically in the last three months. It fits.

"And you're convinced she was not going to kill Amelia that night but take her to the other vampire, the male?" he continued.

"Yes."

"How many vampires do you think he's added?"

"According to my numbers, at least seven or so. But there could be more experienced vampires like Sasha around, whom he collected from outside the area."

"Do you really think he's forming a gang?"

"Or an army. One of the two."

I heard Olivia on the stairs and in a second she was in the study, alarm etched on her face.

Elijah and I both went to her immediately, and he wrapped his long arms around her torso, supporting her as she slipped into another vision.

"What is it, baby?" he asked. He kissed her temple.

Olivia replied, voice hazy. "The Predator, Caleb, is taunting another victim. This time a male."

"Is Sasha there?" I asked.

She shook her head and said, "No, I keep searching but I can't find her. Caleb is with another vampire, dark skinned, with long black hair and possibly one other, but not Sasha."

I considered this. "The long haired vampire was there last time. When I just missed him. He fed on the woman in the park while Caleb watched."

Olivia nodded and said, "Yes, this is what I see happening again."

I scowled. "Where does it happen? Can we get there in time?"

"I see rushing water and stacks, smoke stacks, some kind of factory or plant." She closed her eyes, trying to visualize it.

"Sounds like the paper mill. By the river." I ran to my closet and changed into boots for the long run ahead of me. We could still save this person. It was dark in her vision but it was still dusk outside. We had time.

"We're coming with you," Elijah said. He opened the long cabinet on the far side of the room, revealing my vast array of weapons. Olivia picked up a canvas bag and together they loaded in what we needed.

"Amelia," I said to Olivia.

"She'll be fine, she's safe. She's meeting friends for dinner and then going straight home. I see no problems at all."

Packed up and ready, we filed down the backstairs. Olivia and Elijah quietly slipped out the backdoor. Amelia sat at her desk, printing out her daily report. I took a moment to inhale her sweet aroma and let my eyes roam. I cleared my throat this time to give her notice. She flinched slightly before turning my way with a small smile playing on her soft, pink lips.

"Good night, Amelia," I said warmly. The fact I was making small talk with Amelia moments before tracking down a vicious monster felt surreal.

"Have a good weekend, Mr. Palmer," she replied, cleaning off her desk. I loved to watch her movements.

"Thank you. Please be careful, and call me if you need anything."

She nodded slowly and I took that moment to go back into the kitchen toward the garage door. I knew that every second in her presence made it harder for me to leave her. The urge to stay with her was getting stronger and stronger each day.

I forced myself to go, for both our sakes. I had no right to her life and she wanted no part in mine.

Minutes later, I sat behind the wheel of my car, barely aware of Elijah programming the GPS or Olivia, eyes closed; searching for any information she may have missed. I promised myself this would be the last time I would let Caleb elude me. I assured myself that the city and Amelia would be safe under my watch.

28

Grant

I accelerated onto the street leading to the paper mill, the one that was edged by the river. Caleb and his companions were in the area, their victim minutes away from a horrific death.

I pulled to the side of the road, away from street lights. No need for any passersby to become suspicious. Olivia's vision had been specific enough for us to easily find the location. Before we got out of the car, I asked, "Can you see anything else?"

Olivia's eyes were wide and her entire demeanor was on edge. Her red hair seemed darker in the shadows of the car. Her eyes had turned a shade darker. She hadn't fed recently. "Yes. Only one of the vampires is a fledgling. He's wild. Almost completely feral. The other is older. He is very much in control and I'm pretty sure he's training the young one. These two will feed on the human while the leader, Caleb, watches."

Elijah and I exchanged looks before moving outside the car. I spoke quickly and quietly, handing out instructions. "I want you and Olivia to take the fledgling and the other one. You have the most experience with them and Olivia can anticipate their moves if necessary." I looked them both in the eye to make sure they were prepared to follow my directions. They both nodded yes without argument and let me continue. "Caleb is mine. I've been tracking him too long to let him slip away now, and hopefully I can get some information from him before I end him."

We moved quickly through the night, hiding in the shadows. It was still wet from the earlier rain. I caught Caleb and another vampire's scent mingled in with the damp, marshy air and the sulfur from the mill. The wind whipped around us, bouncing off the walls of the building, making it hard to locate their exact trail. I closed my eyes for a moment and strained to pinpoint their location.

"What the fuck?" a man, a human, said off in the distance. A heartbeat matched his voice while another less human voice spoke up. "Hayden, you must control yourself. Caleb has not given you the approval to feed...patience..."

"Olivia what do you see?"

"There's a man dressed in a uniform. A security guard perhaps? He's backed into a wall, under a towering pile of lumber." Olivia described his attempt to draw a firearm. His fingers fumbled with the latch, wasting precious moments on a weapon of no use.

"The fledgling is barely hanging on by a thread," Elijah said. "No other thought than kill. We need to get there faster."

The three of us made our way to the back of the mill, toward the loading docks where the lumber was stored. We darted though machinery and stacks of materials, trying to find the exact location.

A strong breeze blew past us and I hissed, "To the right." We wove around to the other side of the platform at top speed. I kept my thoughts on the vampire who patiently taunted the security-guard.

Another scent wafted by, this time familiar.

"Caleb," I announced, breathing in. "The Predator is here." But as I made the announcement I knew we were too late. A loud, guttural scream bounced off the brick warehouse walls and the scent of thick, coppery blood tinged the air. We rounded the corner as the two vampires ripped the flesh from the arms and neck of the human they held captive. Blood poured to the ground and the vampires made no move to stop when we came in view. A ring of red stained the fledgling's mouth and he only moved away when pulled by the older vampire. The victim's panicked screams were cut short by the undeniable sound of his neck snapping. Caleb merely glanced in our direction as he dropped the man's head and proceeded to wipe his stained hands on his pants.

The vampire abandoned the body as we came into view and motioning for Hayden, the fledgling, to do the same.

"Finished with dinner?" Elijah asked in a causal voice. The fledgling growled. "Your handlers should teach you some manners. You've made quite a mess."

Elijah never missed a beat and lunged at him, snatching a piece of his ear as he flew over his shoulder. Hayden took the bait and ran after Elijah in a flash of feral anger, clutching the side of his head. He snarled in pain, but his hunger and rage outweighed any other feeling. They disappeared from view, the sound of their fight muffled by the wind.

The handler, with his ebony skin and black, hollow eyes, dismissed Olivia's size and chased after Hayden, also disappearing from view. Caleb's eyes were on Olivia, I watched as he licked his lips and leered in her direction.

She scowled at Caleb and said, "In your dreams."

I feared for a brief moment that she would ditch our plan, and go after the Predator, but she turned away from Caleb, chasing the vampire through the plant. Caleb watched her go, eyes pinned to her back, only shifting his attention when she darted out of view. He walked forward with a confident swagger. Seemingly unconcerned about his fighters, he casually glanced over his shoulder, his long, greasy hair swaying behind his back and said, "They should keep each other busy for a while."

He angled his body in a relaxed pose and announced, "Grant Palmer. We finally meet." The smarmy grin was still in place and it was taking every ounce of strength I had not to rip it off his face. "I've been following you for some time."

Following me? Impossible. I scoffed at him, unbelieving.

He smirked and said, "I've been keeping track of your side venture much longer than you have been aware of me and my little exploits." My eyes were glued on him as he gestured to the lifeless body on the ground. "At first, I thought you were a rumor or a myth. That the stories told of a vampire who protected this city from others of his kind was nothing more than an urban legend."

He rocked on his heels a bit, shoving his hands into his back pockets. He was filthy, his face and hair covered in dirt and debris. His clothing was worn and tattered and he had the appearance of a homeless person. It was the standard look for those of our kind that lived a more nomadic life as it allowed them to go unnoticed and able to move more freely. His voice and his appearance were contradictory. His tone was refined, the words he uttered calculated and educated, yet his entire presence was abominable.

How had he found me? I thought of all of my systems in place, the security, the 'human' life I lived. The fact someone had penetrated my efforts had me dumb-founded.

When I didn't respond to his musings, he continued. "I admit, I was intrigued. I stumbled upon other vam-pires who assured me it was true, and that not only were you helping humans, you hailed from a nest of non-flesh eaters. A large coven. So I conducted my research and to my astonishment, they were correct."

He paused and I heard a crack, the sound of a hole tearing in my psyche. A vivid image of my family home in Black Mountain flashed through my mind like a bolt of lightning. Just as quickly though, the image disap-peared and my thoughts were once again blank.

"How?" I tried to grasp what transpired between us. I'd heard his voice before but nothing like this.

He smiled. "Like that? It's a little trick I picked up along the way. Are you saying you haven't noticed be-fore?"

I considered the way he'd taunted me—how this seemed so personal between us. A link? I wasn't sure, but I'd seen crazier things.

"I've seen how the seven of you live, mingling with society. Co-existing amongst humans. Even your leader who works for the Council specializes in human-super-natural relations. It's as if all of you feel like you can meddle in the affairs of the rest of us."

This information left me unnerved, rattled at him be-ing in my head. It was one thing for this vampire to know about me. It was another entirely for him to have information about my family and our work. A glimmer of amusement crossed his face.

"Oh yes, I know all about your family. Some of them more than others in fact." He raised an eyebrow tauntingly and sent me a flash of a dark room, rows of iron framed beds, pushed flush against the walls. *A prison? Was this where he kept the abducted?*

"I know you left them some time ago to live this renegade life. That twice in your afterlife you have rebelled against your family. The first time killing less than desirable humans and then later, now, living above the rest of us, attempting to control and manage our nature."

Caleb tilted his head, his stringy ponytail spilling over the shoulder of his cracked leather jacket. "You have lived such a troubled life, struggling between good and evil. I, on the other hand, embrace my inner demon. The irony is where you like to save and sympathize with the humans that surround us, I relish the moment their heart pulses its final beat."

The flood gates opened and a thousand deaths ticked from his mind into mine. I attempted to push away the images of murder after murder, throats torn, limbs shredded, the bodies of lifeless innocents cast aside for one demon's hunger.

"You are not a God, Grant Palmer, and you will not tell me where I can and cannot hunt." His voice was clear and determined. He looked over at the dead security guard and shook his head, "In fact, this man here, you can take the blame for his death."

I took the bait. "How so?"

"All of this, the murders, the kidnappings, it has all been to bring you to me. All of these deaths were to lure you into my game. To teach you a lesson about playing God."

I cocked an eyebrow at him and asked, "If you knew everything about me why didn't you just come find me and take me out when I wasn't prepared?"

His mouth broke out into a huge grin. "Now where's the fun in that?"

I rolled my eyes dramatically and declared, "I'm here. So let's do this."

We were ten feet or so apart, with a dead man lying to our left. In an instant we could be at one another's throats. I waited for the right moment.

Caleb's demeanor remained non-plussed. "As much as I would like to end this game now, I can't. You added in an extra player and I have been forced to change my plans. This, right here, is my effort in sportsmanship, to let you know of the new rules. You see, you have something of mine and in return I'm prepared to take something of yours."

He spoke as though this truly was a competition, the ramblings of a mad vampire. The bits of his thoughts I could read were cryptic and confusing. I had something that belonged to him?

"Why do you think I'm going to play your games? The others will have caught and killed your men by now and I will kill you. You obviously didn't research me enough if you think I'm stooping to your childish level," I told him, adjusting my knees so I was crouching slightly, preparing to attack.

Caleb shook his head at me slowly while taking a step forward. "I wouldn't be so sure, Grant. Like me, you have the spirit of a competitor. I doubt you like to lose, especially when the stakes are so high." He revealed another image, this time of Amelia sitting with her friend at a table.

A low growl rumbled through my chest as I absorbed the picture. It was his memory, crystal clear. I could make out every detail of her delicate features. I realized the image I saw was from earlier this week. Amelia wore the same clothing she had on at work.

He howled with laughter, bouncing on his toes with excitement. "I knew you would be interested. Oh God, this makes it so much better, don't you see? I'd planned to just take what was mine. But your inability to resist the frail humans you surround yourself with has made this a much better game."

"Keep her out of this," I growled.

He ignored me. "You'll want to know that, as we speak, Sasha is gathering some information for me about your favorite human."

I hissed loudly and lunged, landing on his chest, forcing the two of us to fly across the pavement and smack into a concrete wall. Bits of stone fell at our feet. I pushed my shoulder into his throat and reached for the sharp blade strapped to my thigh.

He laughed, the pitch bordering on hysteria. Once he regained composure he said, "I should have known you were too impatient for this type of challenge. You're too temperamental and entirely too predictable. This is why it was so easy for me to draw you out in the first place."

I shoved my shoulder into him once again, crushing him into the wall. "Stop. Talking," I growled. The tip of the blade pushed into his side. "Your reign of terror is over. And you're wrong. I do decide where and when you feed when you are anywhere near this city."

I spun him around and had his face smashed into the wall. My foot was planted firmly in his back and all it would take was one easy twist to tear his arm clean off his body. Through gritted teeth he spat out, "If you kill me now, Sasha will exact my revenge. She's already in position."

He opened his mind again and gave me a view of Sasha and another vampire standing outside Amelia's apartment. He must have taken them there earlier. Anger shuddered down my limbs and as an act of incredible strength I dropped the blade, clenching his arm with both hands and tore it from his body.

I flung it behind me and faced Caleb, who now screamed in pain. Grasping his shoulder, he leapt to higher ground, on top of a mountain of lumber. He shouted, "Each time you take something from me I will do the same! You'll regret your lifetime of fear-mongering and intrusion into the lives of others. I will take the thing that is most important to you and turn it into mine. And then, when you least expect it I will return and take over this city and hunt you down."

I jumped up the pile of wood, scrambling up the side, but when I reached the top he was gone, completely out of sight.

"Grant!"

I looked down to find Olivia below me and Elijah kicking Caleb's amputated arm across the floor.

I surveyed the damage from above. Elijah's shirt was torn, revealing deep scratches across his chest. He grimaced as Olivia poked and prodded, assessing his injuries. She, on the other hand, was spotless, not a hair out of place.

"They're burning beyond the parking lot. In a pit," Elijah informed me, rubbing the spot where red teeth marks broke the skin. "That fledgling was a bitch. All teeth and nails."

I looked at Olivia and she shrugged. "That vampire underestimated my size and my ability. He thought too much. Definitely not spontaneous enough for a challenging fight."

I jumped down. Elijah nudged the arm again with his foot, watching it as it continued to twitch. He asked, "What happened to the rest of him?"

"He's gone. But Sasha knows where Amelia lives. She's there or going there now. I don't know." I heard the tremble in my voice. "Eli, take care of Caleb's arm. Olivia, call Amelia and keep her out of her apartment. Call me when you find her." They both nodded, wishing me luck. "I'm going on foot, it will be faster."

In a flash I was out of the mill, traveling through the wet, dark woods, fear taking over my body. I'd been late too many times as far as Caleb was concerned. He had the upper hand on me time and time again. It was understandable now that I knew he had been tracking me and had access to my mind. Regardless of my failures, I couldn't let the same thing happen with Amelia.

Driven to protect her, I felt the branches push past me as I traveled through the forest, each mile beneath my feet taking me one step closer to her or Sasha. I would deal with whichever one I met first.

***

I waited in the shadows of Amelia's apartment, phone in hand. Olivia was on the other end assuring me that Amelia was safe. Not only had she been able to see her, she spoke to her on the phone for clarification.

Unfortunately, Olivia had not been able to get a position on Sasha which meant she could be in the apartment right now. I used the traditional method and climbed the stairs to get to her unit. At her door, I took out the key I made and pushed it into the lock. The minute I opened the door I was struck by a wave of Sasha's scent. I listened intently but couldn't hear any noise from inside the apartment. I shut the door quietly behind me and entered the small foyer. There was nothing noticeable missing or any signs that a vampire had been in the apartment. In fact, if not for my superior senses, Amelia would have no evidence at all that there had been any kind of break in.

I quickly swept the apartment, noting that Sasha had spent the majority of her time in Amelia's room. Again, nothing seemed disturbed.

My phone vibrated and I pulled it out of my pocket.

"She's gone. Do you know where she went?" I asked, thumbing along Amelia's bookshelf and stack of mail to see if anything was missing. Everything seemed to be in place.

Olivia spoke quickly, "No, I can't see her. Some flashes but nothing concrete. Amelia is on her way home, though. I don't think you want her to catch you in her apartment."

"Thanks. Talk to you soon." I ended the call.

From the window in the living room I saw Amelia turn into the parking lot. She seemed hesitant to get out of the car and I wished I could go down there and ease her fears. Amelia finally got out of the car. She looked around the parking lot and then almost sprinted to the stairway. Was she always this scared?

Once she was out of view I tracked her movements by the sound of her feet as they echoed off the steps. I placed my hand on the door, feeling the vibrations of her movements as she approached. Her keys jangled, shaking nervously, as she fumbled them in the lock, dropping them once to the ground with a soft clink.

Her breath came out in gasps from her run up the stairs. I wondered what it would be like to feel her breath across my face. I pressed my forehead to the door, willing her inside. Outside, her heart sounded like a thousand drummers, ricocheting through my bones.

thump thump thump thump thump thump....

The knob twisted and the door opened a fraction. I saw her foot poke around the sharp corner.

I took one last look at her fingers wrapped around the edge of the door and slipped out the window, into the night.

29

Amelia

I stepped in my apartment and closed the door quickly behind me, triple locking it as fast as my trembling hands could move. I was freaked. Panicked. I took a couple of deep breaths to calm myself down from Olivia's calls. The first one was no big deal and I passed it off as a friendly, although random, call. The second one set me on edge when she inquired about my location. She sounded relieved when I said I was on my way home. Apparently, she had a hunch so she wanted to check on me.

A hunch? What the hell did that mean?

In light of the weird stuff with Sasha I wasn't taking any chances. I glanced around the house and everything seemed in place. I fought the urge to open the closet doors and peek under the bed. I had no doubt that if Sasha wanted me she would just come out and do it.

I went to my bedroom to change out of my work clothes. I walked to the dresser and began digging though my drawers, annoyed that I hadn't taken the time to wash clothes recently. I found a pair of gray cotton shorts and reached in to my T-shirt drawer and pulled out the first one. I sighed deeply when I saw the faded worn colors.

Let It Bleed.

The Rolling Stones had that right. I pulled it up to my face and sniffed the scent of laundry detergent. I'd washed it when I got home that night, horrified at the streaks of dirt and bleach that wouldn't come out. The bleach was so concentrated it actually ate holes though the fabric in several places. I felt terrible ruining Mr. Palmer's shirt and guiltily shoved it under the clean clothes, trying to put it out of my mind. I eyed the traitorous pile of laundry overflowing the hamper and cursed the fact my buried sins had floated to the top.

Tossing it on the dresser, I dug though the drawer looking for something comfortable to wear. I was left with a never been worn or washed freebie shirt from my bank and my ex-boyfriend's baseball shirt from freshman year.

Neither had much appeal.

Out of options, I put on the tattered, soft Rolling Stones shirt and a hoodie, refusing to look at myself in the mirror. On my way to the kitchen a sharp knock echoed off the door. I froze, wondering if I should open it or pretend I wasn't home. I was going with ignoring it until whomever it was knocked again. Only a little louder. Murderers and kidnappers didn't knock did they? Of course not. Drew probably lost his key again. I walked to the door and pushed up on my toes, peeking through the spy hole. All I could see was pale flesh and arguably the most angular jaw I've ever seen.

I quickly unlatched the locks and opened the door to find Grant Palmer standing in front of me doing that thing where he is trying to look calm but his jaw was clenched so tight I wouldn't be surprised if it snapped in half.

I pushed a lock of hair behind my ear and frowned. "Hey, what are you doing here? Is everything okay? Did I forget something?"

He awkwardly shoved his hands in his pant pockets and then pulled them back out. He was fidgeting. Mr. Palmer didn't fidget. Something was up. "May I come in?"

Realizing I barely had the door open at all, I swung it wide enough to allow him inside. He brushed past me, lightly grazing my hand with his own. A spark of energy shot up my arm. He murmured an apology, looking a little horrified. Was it because I'm an employee, or a woman?

I suspected neither one sat well with him.

"Wow. Do you keep the air on full blast in your car? You're like an icicle," I joked, rubbing the side of my hand where we touched, attempting to break the tension of my boss being in my house. Again.

251

We faced one another in the middle section of the apartment, the tiny area between the door and the living room, overlooking the kitchen. The entire living area was smaller than his closet. That only exacerbated the fact he was close to me, too close, and he smelled like rain and leaves. His nostrils flared slightly and he looked anywhere but at my face. If he wasn't gay I'd assume he was asexual.

He gave me a tight smile. "Something like that."

The room filled with one of our uncomfortable silences. I gestured to the living room. "Please, sit down. Can I get you anything?"

He shook his head no and he sat in the arm chair so I took the couch. He looked ridiculous sitting in our undersized IKEA chair, like a supermodel sent to a J C Penney photo shoot instead of Abercrombie & Fitch. I settled back in the cushions and tucked my legs under my chin.

"Why are you here, Mr. Palmer?" I asked, trying to desperately figure out what he was doing at my apartment so late at night. I nervously ran my fingers up and down the pull cord of my hoodie. "Is there an emergency? Do you need something done for work tonight?"

He took a deep breath and looked me in the eye. "I'm not sure how to explain all of this, Amelia, but I've been watching your apartment since the unfortunate assault downtown. I hate to inform you, but there has been a breach of your security this evening."

His words were formal and business like. I wasn't exactly sure what he meant. "You've been watching my house."

He nodded slowly and explained, "Yes. Well, my security firm has, since the attack by Sasha."

I felt my brow crease and my breathing picked up a notch. "And your security firm thinks someone broke in?"

"Yes, I'm confident that they are correct." He must have sensed my panic because he added, "It's okay, she has left the premises now."

I looked at him sitting in my affordable Swedish chair, in his five hundred dollar shoes, his perfectly muscular arms peeking out from under his black t-shirt, calmly telling me a sociopath had broken into my home. Today. Tonight.

I hopped off the couch and paced a small circle around the apartment. I didn't know which information was the most alarming. Sasha in my apartment or Mr. Palmer having people watch me. Something about my very small, insulated world had taken a turn toward the surreal.

I rounded the couch and stood in front of him. His long legs bent in front of him, cramped in the small space. "When were you going to tell me you've been following me?" I asked.

His eyes locked with mine. "I was hoping not to have to." I stared back, incredulous. He continued, "I hoped she would go away. That she would leave you alone. But she has not."

In that very moment I felt a sudden but distinct shift in our relationship.

I sat back down on the couch and wrapped my arms around my legs. Closing my eyes, I felt the tears pooling behind my lids and I wished them away. I wished for strength but it didn't come. What was happening here?

"Why me?" I asked from behind my knees. So quiet I was sure he couldn't hear me. "There is absolutely no reason for this psycho to have a hard-on for me."

"I'm not sure," he responded. "Amelia, I don't know why she picked you specifically, but she is very dangerous. You have to take precautions against her and the others."

I gasped. "Others? The boyfriend?"

He nodded solemnly. I rested my chin on my knees, trying desperately not to freak out, but I was failing miserably. My breathing accelerated and my palms turned slick. Mr. Palmer continued to sit across from me, perched on the edge of the chair, looking extremely uncomfortable.

"Amelia?"

The panic attack hovered over me like a wave, threatening to take me under. "Oh my God."

He blinked, uncomfortably. "What do I do? How can I help?"

"Talk. Say something. Do a dance."

This time he blanched. "Dance?"

The wheezing started and bile rose in the back of my throat.

"Uh, well, okay," he floundered. "Let's see...my other assistant, Genevieve, the one that interviewed you. She's a member of my family. I had another PA, before her, a graduate like you, but she got engaged and moved with little notice. I needed someone consistent for a while and she agreed."

The panic crested, not better, but at the same time it wasn't getting worse. I wasn't expecting this type of information but I was fascinated by his revelation. He raised an eyebrow and continued, "So you've actually met most of my family. That's pretty rare since I try to avoid them most of the time."

I gulped for air. "Why do they bother you so much?"

He shrugged. "It's complicated. They're intrusive and think they should have opinions in everything I do. They don't always approve of my lifestyle."

"Sounds like pretty typical family behavior."

"Maybe."

"If that's half your family, who haven't I met?"

We sat together, my steadying breaths the only sound between us. Occasionally I could see Mr. Palmer's Adam's apple lob up and down when he swallowed. "Ryan and Sebastian are twins. They're sixteen and completely out of control. Well, Sebastian's okay but he's gone through a lot in his life. Ryan is an absolute knucklehead.

"Again, pretty typical about sixteen year-olds."

"I guess, but that's the thing about my family, Amelia, everyone carries a lot of baggage. We sort of came together out of necessity—not genetics."

"Wait, you're not related?"

"Not by blood. The house in Black Mountain, it's more like a group home than anything else. We were all brought together by Miles, the real founder of the Palmer Foundation, and he's helped everyone assimilate from their old lives."

I couldn't imagine what sort of life Mr. Palmer had before this, but I got the feeling there were a lot of things I didn't understand or know about him.

Letting out a deep, uneven breath I relaxed, just a little. "What am I going to do? Should I call the police about the break-in?"

"The police are limited in what they can do in a situation like this." Moving fast enough to make me blink, he was crouched in front of me, balancing on the balls of his feet. His dark hair was close enough for me to touch and pushed back haphazardly. I felt his cool breath caress my face as he declared, "My security team will use all of its available resources on your case, Amelia. I promise to keep you safe."

As much as I wanted to believe him how could he make this type of promise? How could he guarantee my safety? He was only a man. Sure he was rich and had re-sources, but beyond that? It wasn't as though he was Bruce Wayne.

"Thank you, Mr. Palmer. I'm not sure how much you can do but I won't turn you away."

I leaned back into the couch, resting my head in a thick, soft pillow, exhaustion taking over. No one else was offering to protect me so I had no choice but to put my faith in him.

He was still there, crouching next to the couch. I could see the lean bands of muscle that stretched up and down his forearms as his hands clenched into balls. He gave me the most wonderful lopsided grin and said, "You're tired. I should go."

Alarmed at the thought of him leaving, I sat up and clutched the edge of the couch. "Will you stay? At least until I fall asleep?"

He hesitated, running his palm over his jaw. Caught in some kind of internal struggle, he shut his eyes. I'd asked for too much. He was just a man—not a superhero, I reminded myself, again. He was busy and owed me nothing. I should be thankful for the security watch.

"Of course," he said, returning to the seat across from mine.

"Thank you, Mr. Palmer."

I laid my head back into the pillow, shifting my jacket to get more comfortable.

"Amelia, before you go to sleep, two things...

I glanced over at my dark guardian angel cloaked in the shadows. "Sure."

He cleared his throat and said, "First, can you please call me Grant? Mr. Palmer seems a little formal under the circumstances."

I laughed. "Okay, Grant."

I heard the smile in his voice as he laughed with me and waited for him to continue. He paused long enough that I stole another glance in his direction. He was looking at me intently, eyes narrowed, crease in his forehead. Confused, I felt my hair and wiped my face, feeling self-conscious. "What?"

He stood up and walked over to me, lifting his hand. I scooted back under his scrutiny and felt his fingers as they wrapped around the zipper of my hoodie. In a quick motion, he tugged the zipper down. "Are you wearing my shirt?"

30

Amelia

Where did she go? *A cool breeze swept across my face. I shivered, wrapping my arms around my body. It was dark and the rough, damp ground scraped against my bare feet. I searched for the girl, but like everyone else, I couldn't find her.*

There! She streaked past me, running in the wrong direction.

"Come back!" I called, picking up my pace.

A cry echoed in the dark, followed by the sound of scattered dirt. I kept running and felt my feet slip from under me and I fell, arms searching for anything to catch hold of. My fingers desperately grabbed for the jagged edge scraping down my body.

I found her, Jenna, clung to the side of the cliff. We both hung precariously from the edge, a bright, flickering fire glowing beneath us.

"Help me!" she cried, the fire lapping at her heels. She kicked her feet, attempting to escape the flames. Tears streamed down my cheeks.

My fingers slipped, sweaty and cold.

"I'm coming," I yelled. My voice echoed back. The flames moved closer and closer to the girl. I didn't felt heat from below, only cold.

I searched around me for an escape, a way off of the cliff. Just above me, a withered, aged root sticking out of the dirt. I dug my toes into the clay, pushing myself upwards, struggling to reach the gnarled limb. I scratched and clawed, mud caking under my nails. I made contact with the root, wrapping my fingers around the cold, rough surface. The root came alive, reaching out, its long tendrils enveloping my arm, pulling me to solid ground.

The root morphed and changed to a strong, deadly hand. I looked to find the source of the hand and found a man with erratic hair and purple eyes on the other end.

"Grant," I choked, sobs filling my throat. I sat in a softer place, feeling the warm tears flow down my cheeks. In the darkness I felt him. I felt his cool breath washing over me. I felt the tips of his hair touching my forehead. The warm tears stopped, replaced by the icy trails of his fingertips as he wiped them away. I sighed as his thumb brushed across my bottom lip.

I blinked awake, trying to unscramble the dark. A sliver of light came from under the window shade and my eyes acclimated.

I was alone.

I sighed and lay back on my pillow and pulled my sticky shirt from my body. It was the third day in a row that I'd had the dream--or nightmare, I guess I would call it--and each time I awoke confused, covered in sweat and tears. The first one came the morning after Grant stayed the night, after Sasha broke in. I woke up on the couch, wrapped in a blanket. There was a note on the coffee table telling me he had to leave but that his security firm would be monitoring my apartment.

Every day I woke up the same way, feeling the pressure of his thumb on my lip, his name on my tongue. Each time I blinked, positive he would be there. The dream was so vivid. Jenna, the girl from the missing poster, fell off the cliff, then the gnarled root transformed into Grant's powerful arm. When I looked into his eyes I could almost taste his cool breath on my mouth. I would run my tongue over my bottom lip seeking a trace of him, but only found the salt of my tears.

I thought about Grant as I shook off the lingering feelings from my nightmare. My arms shot out, stretching to the edges of the mattress, and I kicked the covers off my legs. It was Monday and I finally had to leave my apartment and face the real world. I had to go to work. Things had changed between me and Grant over the weekend. He called once, informing me that his security team was in place. His tone was less formal, and I could hear the concern in his voice. I assured him I wouldn't leave without Drew and that all my doors and windows were locked. I searched for the security people, but no matter where I looked, I couldn't find them. I guess they were that good.

I pulled open my shade and looked out into the dreary rainy morning. Watching countless hours of bad TV and re-reading my favorite books gave me time to think over Grant's strange behavior. I was convinced that things were not exactly as they appeared. There was one thing I was sure of: Grant Palmer was a mystery, and I was dying to figure him out.

An hour later I had my keys in one hand, tea mug in the other. I struggled to throw my bag over my shoulder and open the door. Using my elbow for leverage, I managed to twist the knob enough to crack the door open. I pushed it the rest of the way with my foot and it flung back, crashing into the wall. There went the last of my security deposit. At this rate I'd never make it into work.

"Fuck," I muttered, knowing I probably made a dent in the wall. I peered behind the door and saw a dark scuff mark but no real damage. When I came back around I came face to face with him. Grant stood in my hallway with a tense grin on his perfect face.

"Good morning," he said, in his ridiculously charming voice. His voice never matched his face. Add that to the list of things about Grant Palmer that didn't add up.

I stared at him for a moment trying to figure out what he was doing outside my apartment and how long he had been there. I must have stood there for too long because he spoke again.

"I..." he hesitated for a moment, his eyes apprehensive, "I wondered if you would like me to drive you to work?"

Huh.

That was how the rest of my week unfolded. I would wake up, sticky with sweat, sobbing and reaching out to Grant in the dark. He caught me every time, pulling me off the cliff into his tight grip.

I'd prepare for work, open my door, and he would be on the other side waiting for me, hand out for my bag, which he would then carry to the car. We would sit, side by side, speaking only of the weather, current events or work. We avoided the subject of Sasha and why he was actually escorting me to work each day and how really, really weird that was.

On the upside, I did learn several things about him.

He had an innate sense of direction. No matter which way we traveled he seemed to get there just before the train passed or the light turned green. He managed to avoid back-ups entirely, driving a different way to work each day, always in perfect accordance to the traffic. At first I thought it was a coincidence but as he veered off the highway before a major jam, or hit six green lights in a row, it seemed like more than that.

I also found that he changed his cars with his mood or habits. He had several, three in the garage at his townhouse but I suspected more stashed away. He loved his cars, his eyes growing energetic when I asked him about them. On the days he had to go into his office, dressed in a crisp suit and tie, he would drive his dark gray Tesla, shiny and clean, with lightly tinted windows. The interior was pristine, the leather soft and cool to the touch. Other days, when he was more casually dressed, prepared to work from home, he would arrive in an SUV. When I asked about it I was forced to listen to a twenty minute lecture about how it was the new Lexus hybrid, unavailable to the public until later this year. Apparently, between the car and the fluorescent lighting, Grant was very concerned about our earth's natural resources.

Then his third car, which I'd never seen him drive, was tucked away in the corner of the garage, beneath a light blue canvas cover. I wasn't sure what day and activities warranted the use of that mystery car.

It was Thursday, Tesla day, apparently, and I decided to ask him about it specifically. "Tell me about your other car. The one you've got hidden in the back of the garage."

"It's not hidden."

"Then why don't you drive it?"

His looked over at me gauging whether or not I really wanted to know. His eyes bored into mine and his body relaxed, comfortable for once. It was one of those moments that if he wasn't gay I would think he liked me. I raised my eyebrows in encouragement and he said, "It's a 1968 Plymouth Belvedere GTX."

I had no idea what that was and it must have been apparent because he laughed again, a sparkle glinting in his eyes. He went on to explain how it was known as the "Gentleman's Muscle Car" and how it has some kind of enormous engine called the Commando or something. Oh, and it was a convertible.

As he spoke I realized how much I loved hearing him talk about the things that interested him. He knew so much about art and music. He could fix my computer or printer when it conveniently decided to not to work. And this, the talk about cars. A spark glinted behind his eye, like a little boy in a candy shop.

"How come you never pick me up in it?" I asked, envisioning his wild hair whipping in the wind, his muscular arm resting on the edge of the door.

He shrugged and said, "I don't know. I don't really drive it anymore."

His tone changed slightly, sounding sad so I attempted to veer this back in the right direction. "How did you get it? It looks like it is good condition. Do you maintain it yourself?" I asked, curious as to how he acquired his many collectables.

He his brow furrowed slightly at the question. I couldn't imagine why since it should be easy to answer. "I've had it for some time. Taking care of cars in our family is not really an issue. It's sort of a group hobby."

I laughed a little, looking down at my fingers laced together on my lap. "You couldn't have had it for that long. Contrary to the way you act sometimes, you're not really all that old, you know," I said, making a face at him.

"It was Miles'. He gave it to me when I was old enough to drive." He looked away at that last part, not meeting my eyes.

Miles. Grant mentioned him when he described his family the other night but very little about Miles specifically. I reached over and placed my hand on his arm, feeling the soft fabric of his suit. "It's really nice that he did that for you. He sounds like a great man."

He mumbled, "He is," and continued to keep his eyes forward. "I owe him everything."

I moved my hand and placed it back in my lap, wondering how he had gone from happily talking about his passion to closing off so quickly.

We spent the rest of the ride in quiet, the only sound from the speakers of Grant's musical choice of the day. I thought about how no matter how many steps forward I took with him, I always managed to push it too far.

31

Grant

After five days you would think I would be used to it. The trembling, the sobs, the sound of my name as it quivered over her lips. Each time, against my better judgment, I reached out and wiped the tears from her face and brushed my thumb across her thick bottom lip.

The first morning had been by invitation. She had asked me to stay, to keep her company after having her home violated by Sasha. I agreed, of course, it was my duty to stay and protect her. After all it was my fault she was in this situation in the first place.

That night she didn't try to hide her fear and it pained me to watch her cry, to worry and spill tears over Sasha and by default, Caleb. I had promised her I would keep her safe and there was no decision I had ever made that I felt more strongly about. She was so tired and sleepy, her eyes barely staying open and when she shifted on the sofa to get more comfortable, I saw my shirt under her jacket.

My eyes narrowed and fire licked the back of my throat.

Mine.

I returned the following night, after she and Drew were safe in bed, and repeated this dangerous trend over and over, taking liberties. Each one inappropriate and illegal, not to mention possibly bordering on perverse. I didn't really care. Because every morning, as dawn broke through her window, I heard her call for me, and it filled my empty heart with a sliver of hope.

Each time I tempted fate. Rubbing my thumb over her lip, wishing more desperately each day it was my mouth upon hers.

32

Amelia

Today was a Tesla day and I was alone in the townhouse completing the jobs left for me by Grant. He had left early to go into the office, his real office in Raleigh, to take care of some business for the Foundation. He was already so busy, add on his obsessive need to drive me to and from work, I had no idea how he had any down time. He assured me he was fine, so I let it go. Honestly, I was selfishly happy to have someone around.

The doorbell rang and I disengaged the alarm system to open the door for the postman, who had a thick package I needed to sign for. The envelope was addressed to The Palmer Foundation, with CONFIDENTIAL stamped across the front in bold red letters. Grant usually didn't get paperwork addressed to the Foundation at his home office, so I took a moment to call his office to find out what I should do.

"The Palmer Foundation, Mr. Palmer's office," the steady, official-sounding voice on the other end of the line said.

"Hi, this is Amelia Chase, Mr. Palmer's assistant. I think I have some paperwork at the house that may need to be at the office." I described the envelope to her.

"You're probably right. I can send a courier over to pick it up this afternoon," she told me.

I thought about it for a minute and looked at my watch assessing the time. It was still early morning and my work load for the day was pretty light. I said, "You know, I'd really like to see the main office. Maybe I'll drive down and deliver it in person. It would take just as long."

I hung up the phone, excited to observe Grant in his work environment. I'd never seen him with anyone other than his family and I was intrigued to witness how he behaved with other people.

A couple hours later, I turned Grant's SUV into the underground parking garage and pulled in one of the spots reserved for guests of the Palmer Foundation. Grant had given me permission to drive his cars while he was out since his daily transportation meant I didn't have mine at work. The Tesla was parked in the space closest to the elevator. The shadowy darkness of the garage was making me uncomfortable, but before the panic could fully take over the doors slid open and I stepped inside.

A last minute panic attack rolled over me as I glanced at my reflection in the mirrored elevator doors as I rode to the top floor to the PNT offices. I had on charcoal gray capris, a cream colored V-neck, capped sleeved shirt. My sandals had a heel and my hair was pulled back into a loose ponytail at the nape of my neck. No doubt I was underdressed for a visit to his corporate offices.

The elevator chimed and on the other side of the doors was an open reception area. The hardwood floors were a deep reddish brown, and the walls were adorned with beautiful artwork. One wall was solid glass, obviously tinted to keep the glare out. The view of the city was magnificent. The space had a very open floor plan with offices divided by large glass walls, so each employee was visible to the reception area. Large vases of yellow and white flowers brightened the area and filled the room with a fragrant light, soapy smelling scent.

I walked in clutching the package and stopped at the curved front desk occupied by an attractive woman in her early sixties or so. She had on tortoise shell half-glasses and her hair was grayish blonde, elegantly styled. Busy on the phone, she gestured for me to sit and wait until she was done. I found a chair by the windows and I scanned the room, my eyes eventually falling on an office furthest from the reception area. Grant's name was etched on the door. Through the glass, I could see him at his desk.

He was wearing the suit I'd seen him in that morning, his tie still perfect, his shirt crisp. His face was smooth and he had his typical professional air about him but as he bent over, writing with nimble fingers, I realized he looked so young. Like a boy sitting at his father's desk.

A young, attractive man in a suit and tie approached his office. I watched as he knocked gently on Grant's door. Without looking up Grant waved him in and the man tentatively approached, stopping several feet away from the desk. Their interaction was fascinating and I was completely enthralled to see him interact with another employee. Grant never looked up but continued to scribble on the paper in front of him, even at one point lifting his hand and retrieving a folder from his employee.

Grant always seemed one step ahead of those around him, including myself. He often seemed to appear from nowhere, startling me. I always thought it was just me being unobservant but watching him around others made me realize this was not the case. The two men in the office were polar opposites, Grant calm and nonchalant, the other shifting on his feet. His employee clasped and unclasped his hands nervously. After a second, Grant waved him off and he left the office, quickly and looking a little distressed.

"Can I help you?" I pulled my attention away from Grant and looked at the receptionist.

I stood up and walked over to her desk. "Yes, I'm Amelia Chase. I called earlier about the package for Grant." She looked at me quizzically glanced at me over her glasses. "Grant?"

I held the package out to her. I looked in his direction and found him staring back at me, the corner of his mouth barely turned upward. Before I could smile in return his eyes shifted and his face fell neutral. I followed his gaze and realized he was looking at the receptionist, who was watching both of us intently.

"Umm...Mr. Palmer? I'm his personal assistant."

"Of course, I was uh, taken back by the familiarity," she said, eyeing me carefully.

I peeked at Grant from the corner of my eye and he hadn't moved an inch. He simply watched me talk to his receptionist with a concentrated look on his face. I rolled my eyes at him and lifted my hand to wave. That broke his focus and he awkwardly waved back.

His eyes darted around once more and I realized that a small group of office workers had paused to watch our interaction. He pressed a button on his desk and at that moment the reception phone rang. She picked it up.

"Mr. Palmer would like for me to show you to his office."

33

Grant

I lifted the phone handle and called the front desk. "Joyce, please send Ms. Chase into my office." *Now*, I wanted to add, because she was here and there was nothing more that I wanted than to be with her.

I opened the door and watched her walk down the hallway. My eyes roamed over her neck and wrists, landing instead on her slim waist and curvy hips. I blinked as she came closer and ushered her in. "Are you okay? Nothing happened, did it?"

"No, everything is fine. Something was delivered to the house by mistake so I brought it in. I didn't mean to worry you."

I looked at her sitting across from me, ignoring the curious looks from the employees who suddenly became very interested in the area near my office, and frowned. "We have couriers, you know, you didn't have to come down here. That's not a short drive."

"I didn't mind. I wanted to see where you worked. It is an amazing office, beautiful, but I guess I wouldn't expect less."

The room was filled with her glorious aroma. I had the entire office filled with the scent of lemon, to replicate hers. I told myself I was doing it to desensitize myself but it was really so I could surround myself with something that reminded me of her. But now, with her actually in my office, I realized nothing compared to the real thing.

"Genevieve organized and designed the offices," I explained. "She had this whole concept for an 'open floor plan,' to make me seem more approachable."

"She's very talented."

Again, I fell for a loss of words. Talking to her in my home or in the car was one thing but having her here in my office, in front of other people proved overwhelming. I was very aware of how close I had let her get to me compared to anyone else.

"I had to drive your car to get here. I hope that's okay?" she asked.

My eyes were drawn to her mouth but I forced myself to respond. "No, I told you that I would rather you be safe driving back and forth to work with me. I'm not entirely convinced your car could make the trip anyway."

"My car is perfectly safe," she said, defiantly. It was an argument we'd had before.

I fought back a smile. I had found I rather liked it when she was upset. Her face flushed and her heart beat quicker, she became infinitely irresistible. I caught myself provoking her on more than one occasion to see what reaction I would get. So far, she had yet to let me down.

I watched as recognition registered in her eyes, aware now that I was picking on her. She puffed her cheeks and lips out in a pout. I smirked back, leaning my elbows on my desk.

"Wow. Look at that, Nancy, I told you he wasn't gay....what I would give to have him look at me that way...."

The curse of enhanced senses meant the voices slipped through my consciousness from an employee in the outer office who had a full view of our interaction.

"I don't care what anyone says that girl is more than a personal assistant for sure..."

She was right. Somewhere along the line, Amelia and I had passed the position of employee to employer and had moved somewhere else. Exactly where, I hadn't determined yet, but it wasn't nearly as scandalous as my employee suggested.

"Would you like a tour?" I asked, deciding that was an appropriate offer. "Genevieve made the break room terribly extravagant. I understand it's quite the hit with the staff."

She smiled, confirming my instincts. "I'd love to see everything."

I stood, intentionally ignoring the outside voices. Amelia never failed to show an interest in my work. She never failed to show an interest in my life, my family. Ushering her out of the office, I plastered on a brave face. Rogue vampires and fledglings I could handle. This woman and an office full of prying eyes? Terrifying.

34

Amelia

The streets whipped by as I rode in the passenger seat of the SUV. Casual day, of course. Grant sat next to me in jeans and one of his beloved T-shirts, Ben Folds, and a lightweight jacket. The funny thing about Grant was that although he was so private, so quiet, his behaviors were predictable. I often felt a false sense of familiarity.

We were quiet in the car, occasionally discussing some work to add to my schedule. During one of the quiet spells, his phone vibrated across the shelf by the stereo. He glanced at it quickly and pressed the mute button, ignoring the call.

He looked over at me and shrugged. I returned his vague gesture with a smile and said, "What are you working on today?"

Shifting his eyes to the road he answered, "I have some research to do. I'm a little behind on all the news-papers you've been bringing home for me and I need to go through some things. So I'll probably be locked in my study all day."

I studied the side of his face, completely fascinated by the fact his jaw and cheekbones had perfect symmetry. His cheeks were smooth and I noted he never looked like he needed to shave, regardless of the time of day. Knowing Grant, he probably shaved and showered twenty times to keep germs at bay. I really had no clue what he did up in his hidey-hole.

"What do you do with all of those anyway? All that data I enter?"

His hesitation was brief but I caught it. "I like to keep statistics on the surrounding communities to see what the true needs are for residents. Crime, poverty, housing numbers...it helps me keep focused. Many groups come to the Palmer Foundation looking for grants and funding, but often they are not reflective of the neediest."

"That's really wonderful," I said, and it explained a lot about the strange statistics I'd been entering for over a month now.

His phone vibrated and he clicked it off again, not even bothering to look at the number. Although I didn't expect an answer, I quirked an eyebrow at him in question. It was obvious he was avoiding someone.

Seeing my expression he sighed and admitted, "It's my family."

"And you don't want to talk to them?"

He hesitated, clenching and unclenching his grip on the steering wheel. "No, not particularly."

I kept my mouth shut, not pushing further because I was still testing my limits. I found that Grant was more likely to share information about himself if I listened, rather than if I pushed.

His mouth opened and shut once or twice and as he began to speak, his phone vibrated once more. We both looked down at the phone and he grunted unhappily. Through gritted teeth he said, "Yes?"

Suddenly the car became very small and I attempted to make myself busy for a moment by reaching into my bag and pretending to look for something. This lasted about twenty seconds before I realized I had eight pens from my desk stashed in my purse and little else.

He listened for a moment to the swiftly moving voice on the other end and said, "No."

He managed, quite amazingly, to keep one hand on the wheel and the other on the phone yet still have that hand clutching his hair while he listened to the voice on the other end. I marveled at his impressive motor skills.

"No. You know that is not acceptable," he said, glancing at me. "Fine. I'll be there in a couple of hours." He disconnected and placed the phone back in the cubby.

We sat in tense silence after the call. Grant turned up the music and I stared out the window, wondering if I had forced that issue. I felt like he answered the phone because of my intrusion and now he had to do something he didn't want to.

He cleared his throat and said, "So, I won't be home today after all."

I nodded, understanding this from his side of the phone call. I gave him a weak smile and said, "I'm sorry. You knew better than to answer the call and you only answered because of me."

His knuckles flexed white on the wheel and he said, "No. Not really. I was avoiding the inevitable. It was only a matter of time."

We approached his neighborhood and he drove down the back alley to his garage, his hand swiftly reaching up to press the garage door opener. He pulled in but didn't close it behind him as I expected. He walked me into the kitchen. I put away my lunch while he hovered near the back door.

"I left the list on your desk," he said. "But just so you're aware, Olivia will be here in forty-five minutes. You're welcome to ignore her."

I studied his face. He looked defeated, a look that didn't suit him. I took a step forward and asked, "Is it really that bad? Going home?"

He closed the distance, marginally, but it was there. We stood across from one another and I searched for his eyes, having to bend over a little, since they were cast down. I waited and when he finally met my own they looked darker, stressed. When he spoke, it came out un-wavering. "Going home isn't bad. Going home, for me, is simply hard."

With that he nodded and turned on his heel, leaving me in the wake of his distinct scent. As with most conversations with Grant Palmer, I had more questions than answers.

***

Olivia showed up thirty minutes later with a hot cup of coffee from my favorite café. She let herself in the back door, having her own key.

"That was fast," I said, taking the cup from her and feeling the welcome warmth against my fingers. "Grant said forty five minutes *and* you stopped to get this."

She smiled. "I may have left a little earlier than he thought."

Leaning back on the counter I eyed her suspiciously. "So you knew he would go home before he did?"

Olivia shrugged. "Grant is a bit predictable." I nodded at this, having had the same thought earlier. "I knew Miles was calling him today so I decided to go ahead and come down. Grant can say no to me or the others but not to Miles." She grinned. "I wanted to come see you anyway."

I smiled at this idea. Olivia wanted to be my friend and I wanted to be her friend, too. I told her I had some work to do at my desk and to my dismay, she said she needed to tackle Grant's closet. This idea made me uncomfortable at best.

"Really? I don't know, Olivia. He is going to be really upset with me if he comes home and you've messed with his stuff." I imagined his angry, tense face after I already made him cave to the phone call this morning.

"Amelia, I'm in charge of his wardrobe. Has he not told you this?"

"No, but that explains a lot." I stared her down, arms crossed and everything, in an attempt to stop this before it got too far. "It's just...ugh, fine. But you're taking the blame for it when he gets mad. Understand?"

"Perfectly."

An hour later, she'd convinced me to help and we were both knee-deep in all the clothing Olivia had deemed unacceptable. She had some sort of system that involved sorting items into 'classics', which we would put in storage, and 'never again', which would get donated to the luckiest Goodwill store in North Carolina.

"The Palmer foundation should set up some kind of used clothing store," I said, eyeing the enormous pile of brand-new clothes she was giving away.

"Amelia!" Olivia gasped. "That is an amazing idea."

"I was sort of kidding."

"Kidding or not, it's fabulous. Genevieve will love it."

She went back to her current task, meticulously removing and sorting the photos in the wardrobe books. She was very much like Grant, graceful hands, quick movements. I never would have guessed they were not blood-related. "Grant told me about you all sort of finding one another in the group home Miles started."

"He told you that?" she asked, eyebrow quirked slightly.

"A little. He told me about Sebastian and Ryan. He also revealed that Genevieve wasn't just his PA but also part of the family."

"Wow, he really opened up to you."

"Is that surprising?"

She snorted. "Big time. Grant is the most private person I know. Like he never tells anyone anything. Not even us. I'm impressed."

"At what?"

"You," she said. "You've accomplished a major feat."

"I doubt it's that big of a deal. I think I drive him a little crazy with all the questions and nagging." I shrug. "I'm not trying to be nosy. He's just an interesting person and it gets lonely working by myself all the time."

She paused, seeming to consider her next comment carefully. I looked down at the shirt I was folding, taking care to keep the edges clean even though it was going in the charity box. "Miles took us all in knowing we each had a difficult past. Abandoned, abused or orphaned. Miles showed us a new way of life and we were really lucky to have one another to bond with. Even so, Grant has always had a difficult time sharing himself with others, so if he trusts you, then it's a really big deal."

"Can I ask a question about him?"

"Yes. You can ask, although I can't promise to answer," she replied carefully.

I picked up another shirt and smoothed it on the floor, pushing out the creases. Olivia waited patiently as I formed my question. "If you're all so close then why does he spend so much time avoiding you? I know you're aware he dodges your calls and is hesitant to have you visit. Other than Genevieve, I've only met you and Elijah. No one else has come to the house."

"Oh, we know he avoids us. Grant had to make some difficult choices in his life. We're happy right now in our little spot on the mountain. Living the life we've built. Grant wanted more than that. He's always been a little bit of an outsider. He likes his private time if you haven't noticed." She laughed. "He loves us. But he can't live with us."

"What about, you know, other relationships? Does he have any of those?"

"That's one of the questions I can't answer. You should ask him."

"No thanks." I noticed her eyebrow lift, intrigued. I quickly added, "I want him to be happy. Once you get past the angry CEO thing, he can be pretty charming. Some guy is really going to be lucky to have him one day."

I stood up and took some empty hangers back to the racks to use later. My back was to Olivia and I knew my face was bright red. I hated to admit it, but I found my-self more and more attracted to Grant every day, which was wrong on so many levels. The greatest was the fact he was my boss. Then there was the problem of him be-ing gay. The whole thing made me feel pathetic and hu-miliated.

I heard Olivia shift behind me. The tension in the cluttered closet escalated from my discomfort. "Amelia, I'm going to tell you something because my cousin is possibly the most stubborn, control-freakish person you will ever meet. He takes everything to the extreme and nothing will ever make him change his mind once he sets it."

I took a deep breath, listening to the clank of metal against metal as I placed the hangers on the rack. I couldn't help but wonder what on earth she could want to tell me and why she felt the need to continue this con-versation. Did she know I was attracted to him? This whole situation was beyond embarrassing.

I had no choice but to deny any attraction or feelings for Grant. I would let her say whatever it was she had on her mind and we would laugh at his need for a date with some ridiculously hot guy and we would move on. Brac-ing myself, I turned and found her right behind me look-ing up into my eyes.

"Amelia. There is something about my cousin you need to know." Her tone was very serious. So serious a flare of butterflies burst in my stomach. "Grant is not gay."

"Um...what?"

"He's not gay."

Oh.

I tossed these words around a couple of times as Olivia stood in front of me with a mixture of concern and anticipation on her face. It was possible she thought I was having a seizure because I had no idea what to say about the information she had just shared.

Grant is not gay. Grant is not gay. Of course he was.

"Olivia, Grant told me he was gay," I corrected.

Her perfectly arched eyebrows knitted together. "No. From what I understand you determined that he was gay and he didn't deny it."

I gaped at her and said, "But, what man doesn't deny he's gay if he isn't gay?"

"Welcome to the world of Grant Palmer. Tickets to the freak show are on your left."

I felt my face grow hotter than before and I found myself cross-legged on the ground. When I spoke next, it was a tad strangled and embarrassed. "Okay, if he isn't gay. Then what is he? Because there is definitely something different about your cousin."

"You're right. He's not normal. He is sweet and loyal, and absolutely a gentleman. He cares so much about his family to the point it pains him. He works non-stop, carrying the burdens of others on his shoulders." She paused and looked me straight in the eye and continued, "And he is alone, and lonely, and because of that he puts up barriers so he won't get hurt."

I nodded, pretending to understand, but not quite sure I followed. She must have sensed my confusion. "Amelia, you are the first person in many years who has broken down his shell and even seen there is something behind the exterior."

I swallowed hard and nervously pushed my hair behind my ear. "What does that mean, Olivia? He's my boss. And yes, I do like him, I really do, but what do you want me to do?"

Leaning close enough to me that I could smell her sweet perfume, she pleaded, "I need you to be his friend. No matter what happens, or what he tells you, or things you may see or hear, please be his friend."

She was so serious and so entirely desperate that I could do nothing but nod my head and agree. To what, I had no idea, but I had apparently just bound myself to Grant Palmer and he didn't even know it.

35

Grant

The grass and rocks crunched under the wheels of my car as I drove up the winding mountainside toward my family home. Parking in the shade, I attempted to collect my thoughts before I saw the others.

I'd moved away from the coven almost a decade ago. I had been desperate, depressed and angry. Definitely lost. It had been coming for some time and although I was able to hide it from most of the group, eventually a series of events forced me from the home and into the real world on my own. At first I traveled, visiting the places I had been many years earlier: California, New York, Louisiana, various places in Europe and Asia. It was in these anonymous locations that I began my quiet vigilante work. But this only made me detach from people even further. I realized that after living with a coven for so long, I was actually used to companionship more than I would have thought.

So I approached Miles. I asked for his advice and blessing. To live near, but not with the family. He agreed wholeheartedly. He would support my decision and work things out with the Council, as long as it made me happy.

His kindness only made it harder, but I was determined.

The last move the family made was back to the house on Black Mountain and I moved to Asheville to create a new life. I laid the ground rules quickly. No unannounced visits, no peeking into my future. They could call and I could visit or ask them to come to me if I wanted, but for a long time I didn't. I just needed time alone.

Ten years, countless false documents, and several career changes later, I had evolved into a noted CEO during the daytime with a side job helping those in need and keeping the monsters at bay at night. I never would have predicted that path. Olivia probably would have if I had let her, but for the first time in decades, I enjoyed the spontaneity of actually living life.

Exiting the car, I realized it was unrealistic to think things could continue with such ease. Until recently everything was smooth, in place and under control. That was, until Amelia Chase entered our lives and Caleb brought a reign of terror down upon on our coven. Things were getting complicated. Fast.

***

"What's the status on Caleb and his companions?" Miles asked from the chair adjacent to mine. We sat in his office in front of a burning fire, the bald spot on the top of his head reflecting the yellow and orange light.

"Right now? Nothing different. I have Amelia's apartment on twenty-four-hour surveillance. Ryan and Sebastian, mostly. The abductions have stopped and there have been no additional murders since the security guard at the paper mill."

"Do you think he left the area?"

"No," I said. "He's still out there."

"I've been thinking about your altercation with him. You said he mentioned that you have something he wants. Do you think that 'thing' is Amelia? The female, Sasha, has made two attempts to abduct her, correct?"

"No. Amelia, unfortunately, is icing on the cake." I waited for the next wave of questions, not prepared in any way to answer them. "The clue he gave me, of the beds and the dark room. It seemed old—like something from years ago. I can't put my finger on it."

"I've approached Judson in Lost Cove. I wanted him to be aware of Caleb and his actions. If he makes a move too close to their community there may be some additional blow back."

"That sounds like a good idea." Miles nodded. I could tell he wanted to ask something else so I prodded, "Something's bothering you, care to share?"

Angel Lawson

"I'm sure you realize Olivia has told us about Amelia's take on your personal life."

I rolled my eyes. "I'm sure she did. I'm also sure it has caused a bit of amusement around here."

He gave me a guilty grin. "Maybe a little, but that has not been the main topic concerning your new employee."

I raised my eyebrows at him waiting for him to explain further.

"We're aware that you have become attached to the girl."

"I'm fond of her," I said carefully.

"That attachment could cause a problem."

I swallowed back the desire to lash-out, defending my feelings for Amelia. I couldn't. My actions were inexplicable.

"I need to know how you plan to proceed here, Grant. Exactly what are your intentions?"

Miles disliked intruding in my private life, but it was necessary. I would have demanded it as well, but it didn't keep the rage from boiling inside. I knew they would want to take her from me. To keep her from me. There was no way I would allow that to happen.

"She knows nothing. Not yet, but with the Caleb situation it has been difficult. I hate lying to her," I said, truthfully.

"If she finds out, there are only two options."

"I know."

Termination or transformation. I didn't require clarification.

"Are you prepared to make that decision? It's a heavy burden for the most emotionally stable of us. I have no problem admitting that I'm concerned about the aftermath for you if it comes to that."

"I'm prepared for the consequences." I hadn't been, but this conversation strengthened my resolve. I would not walk away from Amelia—under any circumstances.

This time he raised his brow and asked again, "Your intentions, Grant. What are they?"

I paused and looked around the room. I saw the collections of books, the paintings on the wall, some hundreds of years old. I was able to see myself in here, the way I collected similar objects, trying to remember my place in this world. Something that proved I was here. Miles had the Council, which had provided a lifetime of work, several lifetimes, in fact. I had only just begun to make my mark.

I braced myself, knowing I could lie to the others and lie to myself, but never Miles. I looked at him, eye to undead eye, companions for nearly a hundred years, and said the only thing I could.

"I'm not sure how, but I intend to make her mine."

***

I walked down the wide stairway from the second floor down to the main level of the house in Black Mountain. The house was quiet although Miles was still upstairs. Ryan and Elijah were engaged in a video game in the living room. I took some time to wander the house, stopping eventually in the art studio. Genevieve's easel faced a wall of windows that overlooked the valley below. A blood red, velvet chaise sat against the far wall.

The stainless steel counter in the corner held brushes and tools. Paints lined organized shelves. I ran a finger over the soft horsehair bristles and pushed back a familiar urge. No, this wasn't me anymore. I shoved my hands in my pants pockets and glanced around the room, at the large windows and open rooms feeling exposed.

"You know she keeps a stash of canvases in the corner for you. All of your old work is still on the wall..." Ryan said, coming into the room behind me.

I didn't respond. I couldn't. I couldn't be what they wanted me to be.

A fantasy of Amelia flashed before my eyes. I could envision her on the couch, neck exposed, back arched. I'd paint her hair a mixture of silver and gold.

If I couldn't be what they wanted me to be, how could I be what she needed me to be?

"How are you doing it, dude? How do you resist?"

"We all hold back every day. We make choices not to consume people all the time."

"Sometimes we make that choice. Other times, at best, we're simply delaying gratification, don't you think?"

Delayed gratification. Was that what I was doing with Amelia? Leave it to Ryan, the thickest one in the group, to hit the nail squarely on the head.

"Whatever you're doing, you're playing with fire, man. She's human. There's no way this will end well."

I looked at Ryan now, hulking in size, simple in thought, living in a world of black and white. "You don't know that. Even Olivia has said she's not sure. The only reason she is alive now is because of me. And I promised her I would keep her safe. Which trust me, is close to a full-time job."

His eyes narrowed and a mischievous grin formed on his face. "So, Eli says she's pretty. That helps, huh, with the not killing?" I glared at him. Unfortunately that didn't shut him up and he said, thoughtfully, "I guess this explains a lot, though."

I quirked an eyebrow in question, leery of where this was going. "Explains what?"

"I mean, if you were waiting all these years for a human to fall for then the whole Genevieve situation finally makes much more sense."

My hands fisted at my side. Ryan was venturing into a deadly area as far as I was concerned.

And he knew it.

With a final smirk he said, with vampire speed, "Because if you were looking for a Damsel in Distress, like your new little girlfriend, no wonder that whole thing blew up. Genevieve is certainly no damsel, well I wouldn't know of course, but...wait? Is Amelia a virgin?"

"Ryan," I said, patience wearing thin.

"I think to qualify as a Damsel in Distress you definitely have to be a virgin," he continued, until he saw the look on my face. I lunged but in a flash, he was gone, the back door slamming before I reached it.

"What the hell?" Sebastian said, racing to the porch.

"Your brother is an asshole."

"Tell me something I don't know."

"He's also a dead man," I said, catapulting over the railing. Ryan was already miles deep in the woods behind the house. That didn't stop me. I crashed through the tree line, hot on his trail.

"Can I watch?" Sebastian asked, appearing next to me, arms pumping.

"If you can keep up."

I flew through the woods, gaining on Ryan. It was only a matter of time before I caught him and he knew it. Ryan may be strong, but I was smarter. A lot smarter.

***

Hours later, I tried to ignore Elijah as he fiddled with the knobs and buttons on my car stereo. He hitched a ride back to the city with me so he could meet up with Olivia. I wished I was alone so I could process the afternoon but I wasn't so lucky; my passenger had questions and he really needed to stop molesting my dashboard.

Tired of waiting, I asked, "What do you want to know, Eli?"

"What did Miles say?"

"He reiterated that we'd have to be very careful with this Caleb situation."

"You haven't heard anything else from Caleb though, right?" he asked.

I shook my head. "No, things have been really quiet. I haven't heard of any murders or abductions. The police are still completely confused and are clearly trying to keep the information out of the press, because there has been little or nothing reported lately."

"But they haven't gone to Amelia's again?" he asked, and again I shook my head.

Elijah nodded in approval and asked me how patrolling was going. "It's hard to be in two places at once. In the city and protecting Amelia."

"So you've been staying with her?"

"She's been having nightmares and I felt the need to remain close." The look on his face told me he wasn't buying my excuse.

"How are you going to handle this? I mean, Grant, she thinks you're gay. And even if she doesn't, you're a vampire. A vampire. Undead. Lives forever. Drinks blood.

Okay, we drink animal blood, but didn't you say she's a vegetarian?"

I snorted at the irony.

"She's pretty cool, but no one is *that* cool. Plus her finding out you're a vamp is pretty much breaking every vampire rule we have."

I snapped my head toward him. "What do you mean even if she doesn't think I'm gay?"

"Look, you're the one who let Olivia spend the day with her. Who knows what she said. But if you did decide to do something, which I'm not saying you should, you may want to get on it sooner than later. It's not like you have forever to mess around with this anyway."

I narrowed my eyes at the windshield, considering what Elijah said. He was right. Our time in North Carolina was coming to a close. It had nothing to do with Amelia, it was the reality of our lifestyle. I had one shot with this amazing woman and I think I had decided to take it. Unfortunately, I was used to living a year like it was one day, and I no longer had that freedom. If I was going to do this, I had to do it now. Which meant that little games like my sexual orientation had to stop. As much as I wanted Amelia to know the truth, that story was nothing more than a distraction from the larger issue at hand.

I meant what I had said to Miles. The words came out of my mouth before I even knew they had formed. I did intend to make her mine. The decision had been made with or without my consent. I no longer really had control over it. It didn't hurt that lately I'd wondered if she was having similar feelings to mine. I noticed that her questions and gestures had taken a more familiar tone. My experience in such matters was minuscule. I couldn't be sure if she was comfortable with me because I was 'safe' or if she was just comfortable with me.

What I did know was that as long as she believed I was out of her reach, she stayed out of mine. Lately, her being out of my reach because of a lie wasn't enough anymore. It was getting harder and harder to stay away from her. And I hated lying. About everything, all the time.

"What am I supposed to do Elijah, come out and say, "By the way, I'm not gay?" I continued my false conversation. "And, Amelia, you know all that weird shit I do? It's because I'm a vampire. Apparently the traits are easily confused...when really she was just trying come to a reasonable solution—a realistic one."

Elijah broke into laughter and I groaned, rubbing my fingers through my hair.

"If it were you, what would you do?" I asked him, completely serious.

Elijah propped his elbow on the window of the car and leaned into his hand. "What would I do? Huh. I'm pretty sure I would've eaten her weeks ago."

A growl rumbled protectively in my chest at the thought, but he only spoke the truth.

"But," he continued, "honestly Grant, you are the only one of us who would ever get in a situation like this in the first place. You're going to have to figure this one out on your own."

His sincerity was more than I expected. Elijah had a long history of violence and destruction. It would have been easy for him to disapprove. The simple idea of considering a relationship with a human was dangerous. I placed the whole family at risk.

None of that detracted from the fact I wanted her. I wanted Amelia, the human.

I was so fucked.

36

Amelia

Olivia dropped me off after work and I stood, staring blankly into my refrigerator, trying to find some dinner. Drew was out with Jess. They were getting serious and he had been over quite a bit lately since Drew was worried about me being home by myself. It was Friday night though, and I insisted they go out. I was actually looking forward to relaxing and watching some TV alone. I had been trying to process all the information Olivia shared with me today, and I was still a little stunned that Grant wasn't gay. I believed her because she seemed so sincere, but really I wondered what I had gotten myself into with this family.

Olivia's comment about being Grant's friend no matter what I learned about him was totally cryptic. I wanted to be there for him and help him through whatever it was that haunted him. But at some point, he was going to have to open up and let me in. He had already proven he could be a good friend to me, and I really wanted to do the same for him.

Pushing these thoughts aside, I eyed the pathetic choices in my refrigerator and determined that the left-over vegetarian chili was not going to work. I dug though the kitchen drawer for the takeout menus.

Five minutes later, I was scrolling though the numbers on my phone looking for my local Thai restaurant when I heard a sharp knock on the door. I checked the spy hole. My favorite jaw line, attached to my favorite boss, waited on the other side. Even though I was annoyed with the fact he was a lying-liar, I was pretty happy to see him. I missed riding home with him. Happiness didn't fully explain the cheek-splitting grin on my face at the moment. It didn't justify the butterflies in my stomach, either.

I unlatched all the locks, knowing Grant would be listening to make sure I had the door secure. *That* was a conversation I did not want to have a second time. When I finally had the door open, he was waiting on the other side with a terribly sheepish look on his face and two bags of Thai food from the very restaurant I was about to call.

"This is a surprise," I said, flashing him a quick, controlled smile.

He gave me a killer one back that ignited the spark in my stomach. "I thought you may want some company and I brought dinner. You like Thai, right?" he asked and held the two bags up as evidence.

Incredulous, I nodded my head at him as he walked past me into the apartment and I relocked the door. He put the bags down on the table and began gracefully removing containers and placing them on the table.

I watched as he pulled out spring rolls, sticky rice, coconut soup and my favorite tofu and vegetable curry dish. I placed my hands on my hips and narrowed my eyes at the scene unfolding in front of me.

He glanced up and noticed my demeanor and with wide violet eyes said, "What? Is something wrong?"

I pursed my lips trying to figure out exactly how to approach this. "Grant, what made you decide to bring Thai for dinner?"

He was busy opening lids but his hands stopped for a brief moment before continuing. "I thought you would like it. I know you don't eat meat so I thought this would be a good choice."

I considered this for a second but wasn't deterred. "Did you know this is my favorite restaurant?"

He looked up, his ever-smooth face completely innocent. "Is it?"

I rolled my eyes, pulling my hands from my hips and wrapping them around my chest defensively. "Yes, it is. And this happens to be all my favorite food."

He turned now to face me and gave me another fabulous smile. "Really? Lucky guess."

I glared at him. "You guessed and happened to bring exactly what I was getting ready to order from my favorite restaurant? You're good Grant, but not that good."

He leaned back on the counter between my kitchen and dining area and crossed his arms back, revving up those butterflies again. Calmly, he said, "You're wrong. I am that good."

"Really?" I challenged.

"Really." He accepted.

I waited for him to explain, because he was going to.

He pulled a chair out from the table and gestured for me to sit in it. I did and he pulled out his own and sat down across from me. The spices and heat from the food tickled my nose and were making my mouth water. He must have noticed because he said, "Go ahead and eat. I'll explain."

I pulled a plastic fork and spoon out of the wrapper and took a tentative sip of the steaming hot soup. It was delicious. I raised an eyebrow at him to proceed.

"First, Amelia, you are more transparent than you think. You've brought leftovers from this restaurant more than once to work."

I grimaced. Stupid, observant boss. It made me wonder for a moment what else he had noticed.

"That doesn't explain you bringing it here tonight, just as I was going to call," I retorted.

He rolled his eyes at me this time. "Olivia called and said she had dropped you off so I knew you were home and hadn't eaten..."

He hesitated at the end a bit and so I prompted, "And..."

His eyes flicked to the table, the smirk gone a bit and the sheepish one returned. "And I checked your refrigerator this morning while you were getting your sweater. I knew you had nothing to cook."

I recalled opening the door this morning and greeting Grant. He'd suggested I get a wrap since it was fairly cool this morning. I went back to my room to get it, leaving him in the doorway, and came back moments later with him in the same spot. Grant was either really fast or really lying. I wasn't sure which one yet.

I pondered these things for a minute while dipping my spring roll in sauce and taking a bite. The sauce was thick and tangy, and a glob of it dripped down my hand as I picked it up. I noticed Grant watching me eat, his eyes shifting to the mess on my hand. Knowing he was such a clean freak, I decided to push his buttons a bit since we were in my house and on my time.

I put my elbow on the table and twisted my arm so I could see the sauce slowly dripping down my arm. I looked at Grant carefully and said, "Okay. But stop checking my refrigerator. It's creepy and it's not like you eat anything anyway." Before he could respond, never taking my eyes off his, I stuck my tongue out and took a long swipe at the sauce.

I expected him to be repulsed. Perhaps he would scrunch up his face in revulsion. I thought it was possible he would gag, run to the bathroom and return with soap, antiseptic or bleach.

He did none of those things.

Instead I watched him swallow hard and lick his lips. His eyes pulsed with dilation.

Busted.

Olivia was right. He wasn't gay.

Slowly, I pushed my chair back and walked into the kitchen, and turned on the faucet. I pumped some soap into my palm and washed the remaining sauce off my arm, all while keeping my back to him. It was time to confront him. I was just going to come out and ask him if he was or wasn't gay. No big. I mean, it couldn't be worse than how we got here in the first place.

I opened the refrigerator and pulled out a bottle of wine. There was no way I was doing this without liquid courage. Pouring myself a generous glass, I walked back to my seat where Grant was sitting exactly as I left him.

He eyed the glass and the change in my demeanor. "I won't go in your refrigerator anymore. Not unless you ask." He then made an attempt to change the conversation. "How was your day? Olivia said she kept you busy. What did you do?"

I took another bite of my dinner, chewing slowing and plotting my words carefully. "It was a good day. Olivia and I had fun. By the way, she is completely responsible for your closet. I was an innocent bystander."

"I can imagine," he muttered under his breath. "I'm well aware that you can't stop Olivia from doing whatever she has her mind set on."

I nodded and smiled, working up the courage to ask my question. I speared a chunk of tofu on my fork and looked up at him, innocently. "You know, Grant. Olivia was telling me about your family today and some things about you. She made me realize you and I may have confused some information awhile back."

Interest flickered though his eyes and he cocked his head slightly. "What do you mean?"

"Well, and I apologize for talking to her about your personal life, but I wondered why someone as successful and attractive and caring as you are, wasn't in a relationship." I paused and took a long sip from my glass, letting the moment grow. "I also asked her if perhaps you would be open to me setting you up with one of my friends. He's fantastic."

Grant was completely still across from me. Everything about him, from his hair to his hands to his feet, appeared frozen. I sat back in my chair, holding my glass, rocking my wrist back and forth to let the liquid swirl around in a circle. I was completely freaking out inside. I had no idea why I felt the need to push this man to his limits, but I did and I was.

There was a battle raging behind his eyes. I watched it unfold like a bad TV movie. He was working out his lie in front of me and for that I was going to take him down.

"That is really nice of you, but I don't think I have the time for a relationship right now," he said, convincingly. If I didn't know better, I would've believed it. I needed to file this fact away for the future. Grant Palmer was possibly a con man and had no problem lying right to my face.

"Grant, I know you're not gay. Olivia told me."

He gaped. Only for a second, but I saw it.

Fueled by anger and the fact I had caught him, I shouted, "What the fuck, Grant? You're not gay? Who says they're gay when it's not true?"

Not waiting for an answer, I downed the rest of my wine and slammed the glass on the table, surprised it didn't break. I stood up and walked into the living room and settled into the couch. I pulled the blanket off the back and draped it across my legs. Closing my eyes, I hoped that when I opened them he would be gone.

I waited for some time, listening to the quiet of the apartment, thinking about what he had done. I was stunned and I tried to remember what Olivia told me about Grant and his need for barriers. I had promised her I would remain his friend and I would, but it would take some time for me to trust him.

Minutes passed and I opened my eyes. "Holy mother of—" I shouted as my regained use of my lungs. Grant was sitting next to the couch, on the floor, staring at me.

I ran my hand over my face and sat up on the couch. "What are you doing here?"

He shrugged and said, "I never left."

I leaned my head back and closed my eyes again thinking that maybe this time he would leave. I opened one eye and looked out.

Nope. Still there.

"I'm sorry I lied to you," he said in the quietest voice.

"I'm sorry you lied to me, too." I spat back.

"I promise I won't do it again. No matter what, from now on I will always be truthful." He did that trick, the one with his eyes, where I forgot my name.

"Why did you do it, Grant?"

I thought he would hedge again but instead he moved, kneeling so close I could feel his cool breath across my cheek. The feeling was amazingly familiar and I reached up to rub the spot.

"I did it because in my entire life, I've never known anyone like you. And I was afraid that if you got to know the real me you wouldn't want to work for me anymore and you wouldn't want to be my friend." He looked down at his hands, giving me a view of the top of his thick, glorious hair.

I reached out to lift his chin so I could see him better. He flinched away from my touch, a look of pain crossing his face. My hand hung in the air for a second, feeling an ebb of electricity, before I returned it to my lap.

"Grant, I promise that I will always be your friend and there is nothing more that I want than to get to know the real you. But it's a two-way street. You have to give as much as you want to get," I said and I meant it. I suspected that other than his family, Grant didn't have much experience with this. I was willing to be patient. About some things at least. "No more lying. I'm serious, Grant. It's a deal-breaker."

He nodded and his lips pulled into the smile I suspected he knew I couldn't resist. I patted the sofa next to me and smiled back, giving him some space as he climbed in the seat. "I'm sure you don't watch a lot of TV," I said, rolling my eyes at him, "but I didn't get a chance to watch Sherlock this week. If there is one thing you need to know about me it it's that there's nothing I like better than a good mystery."

37

Amelia

L ingering over our lunch break, Drew and I sat on the patio of the coffee shop under the shade of a wide umbrella. It was the first chance we'd had in a while to catch up on each other's lives.

"So, you're coming with us on Saturday night to the music festival?" Drew asked.

I took a sip of my iced coffee before answering. "Yes, I'm going but Thomas knows this is not a date, correct?"

Drew nodded. "I told him and he knows. He's just happy not to be the third wheel again."

"I'm pretty excited to get outside and do something fun. I feel like I've been trapped indoors this summer either at work or at home." I said, pulling my hair over one shoulder, fanning the back of my neck a little.

"So how has work been since you un-outed your boss?"

I snorted and covered my mouth with my hand. "It's been good. We've both been busy so I haven't seen him much."

"But things haven't been uncomfortable?" he asked.

"Not really. It is a little weird that we are now 'friends' since he is my boss, but really I do like him. He's different. In a good way." I shrugged, trying to play off my actual interest. For some reason, I hadn't told Drew about my promise to Olivia and the intensity of my connection with Grant.

"Different? I'll say. As in he's gorgeous. And rich. And for some reason seems wants to be your friend when he shuts everyone else out."

I made a face and said, "Stop. Or I won't talk about him anymore with you."

He pushed his sunglasses on top of his head so I could see his eyes. He asked, "Isn't he still picking you up and dropping you off for work because he's worried about your safety? Or so he claims. I have a feeling it is more than that, Mel."

"Okay, I admit it. I'm pretty sure he may be attracted to me. You know, I just get that feeling, like there's energy or some sort of chemistry between us. But sometimes it feels like good, exciting energy and sometimes it feels dark and mysterious. There is definitely something going on with Grant Palmer that I can't put my finger on," I confessed.

"Ha!" He cackled. "Yeah, I know what you want to put your finger on..."

"Shut up, I'm serious." I felt the heat rush up my face anyway. "I'm done with this conversation, move on."

We talked a bit more about the upcoming music festival we had tickets to on Saturday afternoon and evening. It was primarily local bands, food, and drinks, but Drew and I had gone every year since we were freshmen in college.

"Gotta go," Drew said, glancing at his watch. He packed up his things to head back to work. I was going to sit for a bit longer and read my book and enjoy the warm weather. As he said goodbye a shadow passed over the table and a waitress appeared to clean up. I looked up and realized it was the pretty girl who normally worked the counter with the long black hair. I smiled and said, "Oh hi! How are you? I haven't seen you in a while."

She returned the smile. "I'm pretty good. I spent some time back home so I've been off for a couple of weeks. How about you?"

"I've been good. Where do you call home?"

"A little place called Lost Cove. It's deep in the mountains. My family has lived there for generations."

"Sounds cool."

"It's okay, but super small—and confining. Okay, it's sort of like hell on earth."

"That bad?"

"Asheville may not be the biggest city, but it's definitely bigger than where I come from."

"Any news on the missing girl?" I didn't mention my terrible dreams.

"No, her kidnapping seems to have hit a nerve though. Even back home they were talking about her."

"Really?"

She gestured to the chair asking permission to sit with me, I nodded and she quickly pulled it out and sat down. "Like I said, my family has lived in the same community for generations. They're old fashioned and have a fairly different view on life."

"How so?"

"No one really knows where the Melungeons, which is what we're called traditionally, descend from. Some say African, others Portuguese. Everyone has the same dark hair and light eyes. It's kind of our thing."

"Wow, I never knew about that."

"A fair amount of our ancestry can traced back to Native Americans—particularly The Cherokee." She shrugged. "But all those groups together just sort of created this weird community that was separated from the rest of the world for over a century. The Cherokee legends mixed with European and Southern religious beliefs. Not the normal shit either—the weird shit that gets you your own TV show on TLC."

"Holy crap, Laurel, you escaped a cult."

She laughs and nods. "Honestly? I did kind of escape a culty-environment. I mean, no one had to marry old guys or wear weird dresses from Little House on the Prairie, but they completely buy into the bizarre mixture of old-wives tales and religion and inter-mingle them into daily life. They don't marry you off but as a woman, there is no place for me there other than as a wife or a mother. I'm not interested in either of those things right now, so I left."

I made an exaggerated motion of shuddering at the thought and we both laughed at the idea of a commitment as serious and long-term as marriage or motherhood.

"What about the poster of the missing girl? What does she have to do with it?" I asked, still trying to figure out where she was going with this.

"I shouldn't really tell you. What happens during church council is supposed to be very sacred." She actually looked around the patio to see if anyone was listening. "But, I don't believe in any of it. It is all propaganda spread by the elders. Voodoo and supernatural crap."

"Please don't feel like you need to tell me if you're uncomfortable, I was just curious."

"No, I'm not kidding. I don't believe a word of their tales. When I went home they had a big church meeting and potluck, which was pretty normal, summer solstice and everything. The Deacons, which is what they call the old guys at the church, typically tell the same stories, half of them scare tactics. Fire and brimstone combined with weird voo-doo stuff. Seriously, it's insane. I'm embarrassed even talking about it."

"It can't be that bad," I said, laughing, but felt bad about making fun of her.

Angel Lawson

"Girl, you have no idea." Laurel rolled her eyes. "Well, this time was no different, except they mentioned Asheville and the murders going on here. My mother begged me to stay home and not come back, but I've spent my life resisting their twisted brain washing and this time was no different."

"Wow."

"They even pulled out the big guns. The head Deacon, Judson, launched into his favorite story about an enemy that they battled like, a hundred years ago. I'm relieved they didn't reenact it with a skit."

"Oh, sounds dramatic."

"Very dramatic. Did you know their so-called enemy was a bunch of wild demons that drank the blood of their victims for nourishment? Because it is. The demons have razor sharp teeth and play tricks with their minds. If they chose, they could turn you into one of their kind with a simple bite to the skin."

I frowned. "Wait...you're talking about vampires."

She rolled her eyes and said mockingly, "Yes, vampires. They don't call them that but the thought is the same. The elders have this ancient bible—handwritten if that tells you anything—and the stories inside warns us they are beautiful creatures that easily lure you in with their looks and enticing features. Our ancestors claim they visited these parts before and now they have returned, feeding once more on the innocent with a grand plan to build an army to take out all of humanity.

Frankly, I think this is their back-assed way of keep us from marrying white dudes from outside the community."

"And they think Jenna was taken by these demons?" I asked. I thought about the girl in my dream, calling for help, the flames licking her feet. Fire and brimstone, indeed.

"Yes. They suspect she is either dead or has been changed into one of the blood-suckers."

"What are they going to do about it?" I wondered, envisioning battles in my head. "Do they have vampire slayers or demon fighters? Because that would be awesome."

She laughed and said, "I know, right? Unfortunately, it's all just a story the old people like to share to scare kids from leaving the mountains. I mean, here's how they manipulate everyone. They claim there are two things that keep you safe. One is a different legend about our people being able to morph into their spirit animal."

"Any animal?"

"Supposedly. Anyone marked with the spirit can transform." She pointed to the birthmark on her cheek. "I'm one of the chosen. Oh wait, I'm not. I'm a girl." I laughed at her tone, not because it was funny. It all sounded insane. She shook her head and continued, "According to the myth, these mystical animals protect our people and land. There's one other thing that can protect us."

Angel Lawson

"What's that?"

"They say is our community has a covenant with some of these demons forbidding them to consume our people, in human or shape-shifting form. The only way to ensure safety though, is if you remain in Lost Cove." She sighed. "It's really very convenient way to keep people afraid and tied to the valley. It definitely works on the less-strong-minded of us."

"So you're telling me you come from a community that believes in shape-shifters and vampires and you don't want any part of it?" I joked. "You know, vampires in movies usually are pretty hot, you may want to look into that."

"I like how you think, Amelia," she said with a laugh.

"Oh," I said, leaning forward. "Speaking of super-hot, mysterious guys, guess what?"

"What?"

"You were wrong about Mr. Palmer being gay. I'm pretty sure you just aren't his type," I teased. "Definitely not gay."

"Huh. Interesting. If I'm not his type then I wonder what kind of girl meets his criteria?"

"He probably has a list," I mumbled, my face growing warm. Laurel announced she needed to get back to work before she got in trouble for socializing on the job. Checking my watch, I saw it was time for me to head back to work also. As I stood and collected my bag I asked her quickly, "Exactly where is Lost Cove? I'm not

320

originally from North Carolina so my geography of the area is limited."

"Lost Cove is in the middle of the Smokey Mountains, like way off the map. Trust me, you don't want to go there," she joked. "They may not ever let you leave."

***

I was working at my desk later that day when Grant appeared in the doorway.

"Do you need something?" I asked.

"Do you have any idea where my brown boots are?"

Grant had recently returned home from the Foundation office and had changed out of his suit. Now he stood in the doorway, shoeless, with thick brown and cream striped socks on his feet.

"I'm not positive, but I think Olivia may have given those away. They were not deemed 'classic' enough to keep. And I believe she may have commented that it is July and "who wears dark brown lace up boots in the middle of the summer."" I tried to look innocent.

"I wear boots all year. I always have."

"Well, maybe you should consider making a change," I said in an intentionally patronizing voice, knowing perfectly well this would never happen. This man was entrenched in his habits.

He considered this for a minute, or so it seemed, before he turned and went back upstairs.

I continued my work at my desk and started to type up the report for the day when he reappeared. He pointed down at his feet.

"See, I'm flexible. I found a different pair. And I'm okay with it," he said with a tense smile. "I am perfectly comfortable in these boots instead of the others."

I studied him for a minute trying not to roll my eyes at his absurdity. Everything about Grant was perfect as usual. His hair and fair, enviable skin, his T-shirt that pulled just so across his chest. The fabric clung to his biceps and showed a hint of what he probably had going on with his abs. His snug jeans hung exactly right on his hips. And then his boots. Which were also perfect, but basically, exactly, the same as the ones he had on before. By the look on his face I could tell he actually felt proud of himself and was consciously making an effort to push his boundaries. I couldn't help but smile, finding his stunted behavior charming.

Crap.

Only stupid girls with stupid crushes found stuff like shoes and obsessive behavior charming.

"Grant," I said. "I know you think you're trying, but this is not different."

He furrowed his brow in confusion. "But, it is different. I don't usually wear this pair."

This time I laughed out loud and said, "Come on, let's shake things up a bit."

He followed me to his dressing room. I got down on my knees and starting rummaging through his rows and rows of shoes. I finally found what I was looking for and pulled them out. I turned around and sat at his feet, sliding the shoes toward him. "Try those."

He eyed them skeptically but sat down on the floor across from me nevertheless. He held up the shoes, one in each hand, dangling them from his long fingertips.

"These? I don't know, Amelia."

"Yes, these. It's summer, and you are clearly going somewhere causal, and boots are for winter. Or hiking. Sneakers are for summer," I said. "If you want, I could find you a nice pair of flip flops."

Panic spread across his face. He unlaced his boots. I sat on the floor, mesmerized by his fluid movements. He paused before putting the new ones on. He seemed like he couldn't quite commit to actually wearing the sneakers.

I sighed and picked up the shoe in front of me and began loosening the laces for him. They were basic, navy, low top Converse. I had noticed them before while organizing the closet, and could tell they had never been worn. They still held the strong smell of new canvas and rubber.

"Let me see your foot," I directed, holding my hands out. He looked at me like I had asked him to take his pants off or something. I rolled my eyes. "Grant, just give me your foot."

He slowly moved his stripe-socked foot in my direction. His knees were up and his palms were back on the floor behind him. I picked up his foot and slid it into the shoe, meticulously pulling the long, white laces taut one row at a time. I kept my eyes on the shoe but I could feel Grant's eyes on my hands. In the quiet between us, I heard him take a deep swallow.

As I tied the top of the laces in a neat bow I found myself rambling to fill the silence. "When I was sixteen I got a job at the mall selling shoes. It was terrible. People would come in and want to try on shoe after shoe. They would tell me their shoes sizes and then I would have to go to the back of the store to find the style and size they asked for. There were these huge shelves of shoe boxes in the back. Rows and rows of boxes that all looked exactly the same and nothing was ever in the right place. Every time I had to go back there I would get completely confused and overwhelmed. They could've used Olivia to organize it for them." I took a peek at his face and smiled.

Then I picked up his other foot, adjusted the seam and smoothed out his sock before slipping the second shoe over his toes.

"What happened with that job?" he asked.

"After a couple of weeks I couldn't take the chaos anymore. I told my boss I had too much school work and my mother was making me quit. I wimped out, but that job wasn't right for me." I finished and felt Grant shift, wrapping his arms around his legs and placing his chin on top of his knees. My hands were still resting on the top of his shoes, occasionally adjusting the laces trying to get them to line up perfectly.

He looked thoughtful for a moment. "I wish I could have known you then."

"You weren't missing much."

"I doubt it was all that bad."

"It was worse than bad. I was awkward and gangly. Super nerd. I had braces and some sort of problem with my hair that I couldn't ever get under control. I would get so nervous around boys. I don't think I even spoke to a guy in my class until I was a senior and even then it was a hot mess."

He didn't look convinced. "I bet you were cute."

I felt the heat rush up my face and decided it was time to get out of this very close situation. I stood up, almost falling, and was caught on the shoulders by Grant's very fast hands.

"Thanks." I grimaced. "See? Awkward. By the way, those shoes look great. Change isn't so bad, huh?"

He looked in the full length mirror that hung on the wall, assessing himself. I also glanced over and saw us in the mirror together. Grant was tall and lean. He towered over me, and again I was struck how every part of him looked perfect, down to his shoes. I noticed though, that where he usually had been so distant and reserved with me, keeping such an intentional separation between us,

Angel Lawson

his current body language revealed something different. He leaned in my direction, almost but not quite, entering into my personal space. His eyes were fixed on mine. It was almost if I leaned backward we would meet somewhere in the middle.

He broke his gaze with me and looked down. "No Amelia, I'm beginning to realize change, although difficult for me, can be very good."

38

Grant

I followed Amelia up the stairs to her apartment, her black satchel slung over my shoulder. I allowed her to get a couple steps ahead of me for two reasons. One, with every step she took up the staircase I was enveloped in her scent. The second? I enjoyed the view.

Increasingly, I was faced with a difficult situation. My usual desires were being overshadowed by panic. I was truly entering into uncharted territory. I'd spent days formulating a plan for an opportunity to get to know Amelia a little better and break through some of the remaining tension. I'd almost done it today in the dressing room but the situation got away from me. One minute she was teasing me, the next we shifted into a more intimate moment. Amelia often calmed me, filling me with a sense of comfort with her words and movements. She made the most common moments so much more.

The boots were trivial, I knew that, but they were one of the things I clung to in my intentionally structured life. My inflexibility, and the stunted impact it had on my life, had become more and more apparent. I'd always thought this was something to feel accomplished about—my controlled, disciplined behavior—but Amelia was slowly showing me another path. One I'd never considered before. She constantly put me at ease, lulling me into a sense of peace.

The irony was that as a vampire, I was supposed to be able to do this to my prey. It was second-nature for me to convince them to come near me, intrigue and tempt them. I'd never prepared to be a fly in another spider's web.

We reached the top of the landing. I handed the satchel to her and she said, "Thanks, Grant. I'll see you tomorrow morning."

I didn't want to leave; every inch of my mind and body wanted to stay. It would be hours before I could sneak back. I needed to hunt and then resume my patrols for Caleb and his followers. I watched her fumble with her keys, restraining myself from helping her. I watched her long hair curl over her shoulders before allowing my eyes to roam down to the hem of her skirt, settling on the spot where it grazed the back of her thighs. I lifted my eyes upward as she finally inserted the key in the lock and twisted the knob open, giving me a final wave good-night.

I stopped myself before I turned the corner, gathering the courage to actually do what I had planned on all along. "Um, Amelia, I was wondering something..."

She turned away from the door and I could see her face in the fading daylight. She placed her hand on the edge of the door and leaned a little. "Yes?"

I was about to do something I hadn't done in my entire hundred years of existence as a human or a vampire. Thank God I don't sweat, I thought, as I fought to compose myself. I smoothed my face and made eye contact, hoping for once to use my abilities in my advantage. "I wanted to know if you would go with me to an exhibit tomorrow night?"

She paused, her face completely unreadable, but her heart pounded a bit faster. "An exhibit? What kind?"

I moved a little closer to her, near her fluttering heart. "An art exhibit. You had shown an interest in my collection at home, so I thought you may want to see some other work."

Her eyes lit up. "That would be great. In fact, I found a book at the library on impressionist artwork from the time period of your Jackson Pollock painting. I've been reading it at night."

The book was in her room, lying on the bedside table. That, along with her questions, prompted me to contact the local gallery and offer pieces from the Palmer private collection, along with a donation to the museum itself, if they would allow a small showing. When I told Miles I intended for her to be mine, I never said I would play fair. I planned on using every advantage I had to win over Amelia Chase.

Angel Lawson

I couldn't contain the smile creeping across my lips.

"So yes?" I asked, needing to hear the word.

"Yes, I would love to go, Grant. Thank you."

"Wonderful," I said, attempting to conceal my excitement.

"So, tomorrow...after work?"

"Yes, after work." I nodded like a fool.

She smiled again and pushed the door open, moving inside. I waited a moment, inhaling the last wisps of her scent in the night air, mentally congratulating myself on successfully asking a woman out. A task that only took a century to complete. Forcing myself to leave, I ran, faster than appropriate, down the stairs to my car, heading to the forest in a celebratory hunt.

Sometime later I stood over the remains of a large elk. I recalled my gorging from weeks before and my first visit to Amelia's apartment. The shades of my inner animal were less now and I could almost feel the humanity emerging from the depths of my soul. My hunger was tempered by other desires. Something I'd never known to be possible.

Consuming the flesh came in more than one shade of red. The lure of her body was nearly as appealing as blood.

The satisfaction from feeding from Amelia would be fleeting and if things went wrong, my despair would be eternal. The act was one sided—requiring that I take

330

and not give. Sharing our physical selves, if that was even possible? That was a shared action.

The thought of her proximity terrified me.

It was much more in my nature to want to keep a treasure like Amelia with me than to use them and cast them aside. I had rooms of knick-knacks, baubles, books and clothing to prove this point. Amelia was more than these mementos, a piece collected during my years. She was a living, breathing reminder of the fragility of humanity.

I buried the animal carcass and traveled back through the thick, dark forest. The air was cool as I traveled through the brush, using my senses to take me back to my car. I had hunted for several hours, making sure I was well fed, anticipating the strength I needed not only to resist Amelia, but to fight Caleb if necessary.

I scaled a large rock and scanned the area. A broken branch. Scuff marks on the ground. I moved faster, following the marks. I caught a hint of something foul on the breeze and inhaled.

"Get your fill?"

The voice echoed in my head and I spun trying to find the source. Nothing definitive jumped out. "What do you want?" I asked out loud. I refused to play the mind games.

"Just to check in with you. How have things been with your little pet?" Caleb asked.

"She's not my pet."

Angel Lawson

"No?" He shot me a memory of me climbing through the window at Amelia's apartment. Then another of us in the car together. A flurry of images rushed across my mind, like the pages of a flip book. He'd been tracking me the entire time. Dread mixed with rage pooled in my stomach. *"Maybe I'm wrong. Maybe you're her pet?"*

"You're out of your league, Caleb. Leave while you can. I won't follow you out of my territory."

"How generous. I'm afraid you don't understand what's at stake here, Grant. You've taken something that's mine and I will not leave until you return it."

I wondered for an instant if something in my collection was his. Had I poached a kill? Clearly he thought we had crossed paths before? "What did I steal from you? Tell me and we can negotiate. I'm sure I can pay you well above what the object is worth."

"Sorry, not interested. Some things are worth more than money. I think you're starting to realize that, no?"

"Don't touch her."

"Good night, Grant. We'll meet again soon."

From under the canopy of trees, I listened to the soft sounds of the night. Caleb was gone, if he'd ever been nearby at all.

***

It was past midnight when I left my car and quickly climbed the stairs to Amelia's apartment.

"Grant."

I stopped in my tracks and peered into the darkness. "Olivia?" I said, lower than a whisper.

Olivia appeared around the corner, near Amelia's door. By her side she held a package in her tiny hand.

"What are you doing here?" I asked.

"I had a vision, someone was here and it seemed faster for me and Elijah to check it out than to call you. Ryan's on his way down."

"Amelia?" My eyes darted to the door. Olivia's hand wove into mine, effectively keeping me from leaving her side.

"She's fine, listen..."

I focused and heard Amelia's faint heartbeat...*thump, thump, thump*...steady in its nighttime rhythm.

"Elijah is in the woods trying to pick up their scent."

"It's not Caleb, he was in the woods with me. Dammit! I'm sick of this mind-fucking bastard." I pulled her back into the shadows, but where we could still see the stairway and Amelia's door. After a couple of deep breaths I asked, "What did you see?"

Olivia closed her eyes and searched her memory. "I saw flashes of Amelia's door, not open, closed like it is now. I saw pale fingers attaching an envelope to the door. Then they were gone. They didn't try to get in the apartment."

"You saw them here, at the door, but not before they got here?" I asked putting the pieces together.

Angel Lawson

"Yes. No notice, they had already come and gone by the time I saw it." Olivia responded, her eyes flashing with irritation. "Somehow they manage the flow of information. I only see something when they want me to. I was worried it could be a trap for you."

"Caleb had me busy in the woods. They know I've been here at night. He wanted an opportunity so he distracted me." I picked up a rock and crushed it with my hand. I needed to let off some steam—or rip someone's throat out. "Will Eli catch them? Does he need our help?"

She shook her head. "No, it was a long-shot. He was hoping they would make a mistake."

I trusted Elijah to take care of it, but had little hope he'd be successful. Nodding at the envelope, I asked, "What's in it?"

She handed it over and I quickly opened it, inside I saw a delicate gold cross hanging from a chain. Another object was nestled at the bottom. I poured the jewelry into my hand, and Olivia quickly picked up the second piece. It was a golden brooch, designed like a flower. Its stem swooped into an elegant "A."

Olivia asked, "Is it Amelia's?"

I shrugged. "I'm not sure. I've never seen it before. It looks antique though, Victorian perhaps. This one," I held up the delicate cross between my fingers, "looks like the one the media has shown being worn by the missing teenager, Jenna."

334

"The brooch doesn't look like something a modern teenager would wear," Olivia said, her eyes narrowed as she took in the intricate detail. "Does this mean Caleb took Jenna?"

"Seems like that's at least what he wants us to think. That he's definitely responsible for the abductions, Olivia," I said. "He knows how I feel about her."

"He won't get her," she promised, a dark spark flared in her eye.

"Maybe I should give her up now. Leave her. It's too dangerous." The words came out like lead. One look from Olivia and she knew I'd never do it. It was too late.

"Elijah's coming back, let's go meet him," she said. I hesitated, not wanting to leave Amelia and Drew alone in the house. Olivia touched my hand. "Ryan will be here soon, let him keep an eye on Amelia. We need to go back to the house and work on these clues. Let's see if we can figure out what they mean. I have a feeling time is running out."

I listened once more to the sound of Amelia's heart, thumping peacefully while she slept. She would be safe with Ryan outside keeping guard. As much as it pained me to leave her, Olivia was right, she wouldn't be safe until Caleb and the others were destroyed.

39

Amelia

Where did she go? I wondered, and waited for the cool breeze to rush past my body. "Come back!" I called, picking up my pace. Why would she run away?

I heard her cry out and tumble, like always. I kept running and felt my feet slip from under me and I too was falling, my arms searching for anything to hold. My fingers desperately searched for the jagged edge I knew protruded from the side of the cliff.

I tentatively looked down and found her. Jenna clung for her life, the bright fire beneath us. "Help me!" she cried, her teeth gleaming from the brightness of the fire below. I watched, helpless, and felt the tears begin to stream down my face.

"I'm coming," I yelled, knowing though that it was of no use. I could never get to her in time. The flames moved closer and closer to the girl. This time though I felt the heat, the cold air that normally surrounded me was gone. Panicking a little at the change, I looked for my escape.

My eyes fixed on the root above me, and I felt a sense of relief as I scratched my way up the side of the cliff toward salvation. My fingers brushed the cold, rough surface and I waited for it to transform from a root to a strong, safe arm. It never happened. For once there was no transformation, instead the root crumbled under my touch shattering into brittle pieces.

My hand grasped at the dirt and debris and I shouted, "Grant!" desperate to find him, desperate for him to save me. But there was nothing to hold on to and he wasn't there. I fell, tumbling past Jenna and the fires below.

I woke with a start, the edge of a scream on my tongue, drenched in sweat. I'd had the same dream for weeks, every night, exactly the same. Something had changed and a feeling of dread settled cold in my chest. As weird and abstract as my dreams had been they had always been consistent. Like Grant. Weird, but present. I pulled back the cover, left with the lingering feeling of desperation. I had to wonder about my dream: where had he gone and why did he leave me?

***

After showering and getting ready for the day, my nerves finally settled down. Okay, the dream nerves dissipated. The ones about my plans with Grant for that night intensified. I heard Drew in the kitchen and decided to face the day and the many questions he was bound to have once he saw the extra stuff I planned on carrying to work today.

"Drew, do we have any more bagels?" I asked, entering into the kitchen with my satchel and a couple of hangers holding my clothes for the art exhibit.

He pointed to the counter and raised an eyebrow in the direction of my clothes as he finished chewing. I picked up a knife and slathered cream cheese on the top.

"Going somewhere after work?"

Placing the knife in the sink, I walked over to the stool on the other side of the kitchen counter. I shrugged nonchalantly. "Maybe."

He waited for me to continue, but I didn't. Instead I took a large bite of my bagel, trying to contain the smug grin that threatened to escape. Drew knew me too well.

"Amelia, are you going out with Grant Palmer?"

"Define going out."

Happy to play along, he said, "If he is taking you to dinner, or any other specific location, just the two of you, alone, wearing special clothes, and he asked you beforehand. That is going out. A date, in fact."

I pretended to think it over for a second. "Ummmm...then yes. Grant and I are going out. But, I don't think I would call it a date."

Drew literally began buzzing around the kitchen. "Oh my God, Amelia. Oh. My. God. Grant Palmer asked you out."

I couldn't help the smile that tugged at the corner of my lips, partially because my roommate looked like he may jump over the counter and sit in my lap out of sheer giddiness. But really, I couldn't hide my own excitement about my plans with Grant tonight. It wasn't a date, I knew that, but at the same time it was something other than two friends going to an art exhibit. I told Drew this and explained the Jackson Pollock painting and how he offered to take me to a special exhibit of this type of work.

My phone rang, and as I picked it up, Drew said, "Amelia, I don't care what you say, that is a date."

I picked up my phone, glancing at my watch, and realized it was time for Grant to pick me up. "Hello."

"Good morning, Amelia." My heart beat faster at the sound of his voice.

"Hey, are you here? Do you want me to come down?"

"Actually, I can't come get you today, I'm sending my cousin. There was an emergency at work and I can't leave right now. He should be there any minute." Before I could respond a sharp knock sounded on the door.

"Elijah?" I asked and swung the door open. "Err...not Elijah." The largest boy I had ever seen stood in my doorway with a frightening grin on his face. I eyed him, trying not to gawk at his massive size. Once I moved past the fact he was a giant it dawned on me that he was gorgeous and way, way, wayyyyyy to young.

Increasingly, I was suspicious that Grant grew-up in some strange foster care system of genetically superior people.

"No, my other cousin, Ryan. I'm so sorry," he apologized, and broke me out of my ogling.

"Its fine, Grant. I'll see you in a little bit."

I slung my bag over my shoulder and took in the hulking man in front of me. "So you're Ryan." I tried to focus my eyes on his face and not the ridiculous size of his hands.

"I am. And you must be Amelia." His voice was softer than I would have expected. He held out one of his giant paws for my bag. "Grant said I'm supposed to carry that."

I rolled my eyes. "I know Grant thinks I'm helpless but I'm not. I'm actually capable of carrying my things on my own."

He nodded, flashing me another brilliant smile. I walked past him, holding my head high. Too high, it seemed, since I tripped on the threshold, causing my bag and clothes to tumble to the ground. Fortunately, I never actually fell since I was being held several inches off the ground by the two enormous hands I had previously been studying. He gently placed me back on my feet and I sighed in embarrassment before stealing a look at Ryan, who was shaking with laughter. I took a moment to straighten my shirt and hair, my face turning ridiculously red. I picked up my bag and forcefully shoved it at him. He took it without a word and followed me down the hall. At the top of the stairs I turned to him, making as much eye contact as possible with our height difference, and said in my most authoritative voice, "Do not tell Grant this happened."

A huge grin broke out across his face and he gave me the most adorable boyish grin. God. What a heart-breaker this kid was going to be. He winked and said, "Are you kidding? If I deliver you to his house with even a scratch, I'll never hear the end of it. This is strictly between you and me."

I grimaced at the accuracy of his statement. I suspected he was right. Grant, for whatever reason, had definitely accepted the role of my protector whether I'd asked him to or not.

"Good. Now, let's go before he drives over here to find out why we're late." I said, and we both laughed as we walked down the stairs to the parking lot.

40

Grant

Bracing myself for his arrival, Ryan bounding up the stairs immediately upon depositing Amelia at her desk.

"I like her."

"Excuse me?"

"She's feisty. Absolutely stubborn and has a classic combative personality. She's perfect for you."

The gleam in his eye was a bit too intrigued. "Ryan, don't make me regret letting you drive her to work."

He stood across from me, hulking in size, and rolled his eyes. "I won't. And you're welcome. I knew you weren't eating her because she was pretty. Don't even try to deny it."

"I'm not denying anything. Or admitting anything. Not to you," I said, childishly. Ryan had this tendency to bring out my inner sixteen-year-old even after all this time. Like all of us, some extreme traits had seemed to freeze at the moment of our transition.

We were in my bedroom. Elijah and Olivia were next door in the office on the computer. I had a stack of papers lying across the bed and skimmed through them for some notes I had taken earlier. Ryan, rarely invited to my house, looked at the shelf on the wall that held some personal objects. I watched as he picked up my signed Shoeless Joe Jackson ball and practiced his windup.

"Do you think you would have gone to see him in the World Series if you hadn't changed?"

Ryan loved to talk about baseball. He loved it as a kid, listening outside of bars or wherever he could catch it on a radio. When he discovered this part of my collection, he badgered me with questions for a month.

"Probably," I answered even though he already knew this. We'd had this discussion a million times.

"Would you have gone with your dad?" he asked, again knowing the answer, but obviously wanting to pretend he hadn't. When you live together for over fifty years, subjects tend to come up more than once.

"Yes, he loved baseball. He worshipped the Yankees. He was the one who told me to keep an eye on Babe Ruth even though he was still in Boston." I said, trying to remember as much as I could. It no longer hurt to remember but it had become difficult to place the memories from before I turned.

"I would have loved to have seen Babe Ruth. Just my luck I became immortal the year he decided to retire," he said wistfully. I laughed at the irony of the fact we can have anything we want unless it is bound by time or humanity.

Mid-pitch he said, "So how long has it been."

I flipped through the papers, barely listening to him. "What?"

"I'm curious. How exactly is this going to work, you being a vampire and Amelia being a human? You know, sex and stuff."

"You're kidding me." I glanced up. "Really? That is where this is going?"

He nodded and I was shocked to see his face was completely free of humor or mocking. I shouldn't be surprised. Ryan and Sebastian grew up in a world of loose morals. Sex was a daily part of their lives from a young age. A job even. That was how their mother put food on the table.

"Don't tell me you haven't thought about it. I mean, we've all thought about it at one time or the other. Not you and Amelia—just humans."

"Look, I'm not going to deny I've thought about it." I shifted my gaze away from Ryan down to my hands. "I thought about it, a lot, but I don't know the precedence on this. If there even is one."

"Vampire-human sex isn't new, Grant."

I thought about his history—how he was created. "No, it's not. I apologize if I'm being insensitive."

"You're not and whatever this is with you and Amelia, it's not the same thing that happened to my mother. You're giving her the choice."

"I don't know if I even want this to be a choice—if it should be."

"Sebastian will have a hard time with this. He's not as open-minded as I am."

"Undoubtedly."

"He'll come around."

"Look, you're way ahead of the game here. I've kept my distance—barely even allowing myself to touch Amelia right now, not until she knows the truth about what I am. It's not fair to trick her into something she doesn't understand. Beyond the ethics of the situation, I don't exactly trust myself with her."

"That bad, huh?"

"If you mean amazingly good, then yeah, that bad." I swung my chair around and gazed out the window. The sun was already out full force. It would be a warm day. "I'm going to have to tell her at some point. Sooner than later."

I already regretted those words. I wasn't sure if I ever could tell her the truth. I wanted to, and I had promised not to lie to her anymore, but I was terrified of her reaction.

***

I assessed myself in the mirror as I buttoned the cuffs on my shirt. The fabric was pale green, one of Olivia's selections. She picked it out, along with an entire outfit, laying it on the dressing table for me to see when I walked in. Now I found myself analyzing the mop of hair on top of my head. It was its usual catastrophe, sticking up and in total disarray. There was little I could do at this point, yet I continued to poke and prod it into some kind of submission. Nature made my hair this way, while immortality froze it in place. Nearly a century later I continued to fuss over it like a school boy.

Amelia was downstairs changing for our evening together. With every passing minute, I was convinced this was the longest day I'd ever lived. The afternoon was spent discussing the tokens left by Caleb and what they could mean. Elijah hacked into the police system. We quickly determined that the necklace and cross were definitely Jenna's. There was an inscription on the back that said, 'Love, Mom and Dad' which matched the information in her file.

The brooch was harder to determine, as Amelia had not made a police report or told me of any missing items from the break in. We suspected it must be hers, but had no concrete evidence. I was hesitant to bring it up—an ugly reminder of the violation of her home. Elijah searched the files of the other missing people and murder victims that matched our profiles and wasn't able to connect any of them to the brooch, which only convinced us further it was most likely Amelia's. At this point it didn't really matter if we confirmed the jewelry or not. Caleb had targeted Amelia. It made the most sense.

I hid upstairs all day, away from Amelia, terrified to face her before tonight. What if she changed her mind? Or came to her senses? What if she realized after all this time that I was truly a monster—a demon—who should be feared? Part of me almost hoped she had a revelation before the evening came and I could put this entire fantasy to rest.

I took one last look over my shoulder into the mirror, compulsively trying to make the hair on my head do something other than what it was. It was mostly nerves, I knew, I'd looked exactly the same for the last ninety years. Some things never change. *That's enough*, I told myself, forcing my body out the door and pacing myself at human speed, one step at a time. I stopped at the landing at the bottom of the stairs.

I smelled her before I saw her, lemons mixed with shampoo and adrenaline. It was her specific, delightful scent and I begged the vampire in me not to respond. I followed her trail to the library where she stood before the shelves, scanning my books. She touched each spine gently, using the soft pads of her fingers. I soaked her in. Her hair was knotted up on the back of her head, loose tendrils falling haphazardly down her neck. I could see my favorite spot, the one under her ear, and it was all I could do to keep my distance. Amelia turned around, letting the skirt of her black sundress flutter around her legs. The fabric was pitch-black, with white embroidered designs. The color accentuated her pale flesh and showed more skin than a vampire could ever resist. I smiled when I saw her and rejoiced when her entire face lit up in response. She was possibly the most beautiful creature I had ever seen and I opened my mouth to tell her these very words.

Except I couldn't. Warring desires choked me, lodging the compliments in my throat. When she turned in my direction, I floundered helplessly. She smiled, lifting her eyebrow in anticipation. Oh god, I'd failed already.

"Grant," she said, cutting through the palpable tension, by pulling a thick, black binder off the shelf. "Is this what I think it is?"

Huh? I tried to focus on the book in her hands and not the gentle curve of her neckline. "Umm...what do you think it is?"

She opened the book and held it up. "Comic books. Lots of them. Individually wrapped and numbered and tagged." She was now flipping through the plastic folders, running her fingers over the covers with an excited look on her face.

"Oh, yes. Those are mine." Her excitement amused me. Only Amelia would find this to be the most interesting thing in a room full of first editions and rare books. The comics were a loaded subject if she asked me where

Angel Lawson

and when I acquired them. The weight of my promise to be honest with her weighed heavily on my mind.

I cleared my throat to get her attention and she closed the book slowly before looking up. She took in my appearance for a moment, starting with my hair, (my godforsaken hair) and ending at my feet.

She took a step forward, her lips curved evilly. "Have you already forgotten our conversation about trying new things?"

I pulled up the hem of my pants and said, "No, look. Not boots. Shoes. Brown yes, but not boots." I couldn't help but succumb to her infectious laugh. "I'm change-able, and with the right motivation, I find I can do almost anything."

I dropped the hand holding my trousers. My words hung in the air. It had been so long since I was around someone I cared for, if I ever really had, and now I'd said it out loud.

We stood in the library, me in the doorway, Amelia still near the shelves, neither knowing exactly what to do next. Her hands smoothed the fabric of her dress, and mine were precariously close to running compulsively through my hair. It was clear she was waiting for me to do something. Anything. For a brief second, I considered running. She could never catch me. I caught sight of myself in the mirror across the room. I was shocked at the actual panicked expression on my face. I focused on my freakish purple eyes and wondered if I could pull

350

this off. Like Ryan implied, there was no way this could possibly work. I was a monster and she was an angel.

Oh god. What the hell was I doing?

"Grant, do you know who my favorite superhero is?" Amelia asked, snapping me out of my spiraling break-down.

"No." I answered.

"The boys were arguing about this at the bar a couple weeks ago. The night you showed up to save me from Sasha." She took a step closer. "Since Drew is dating Jess and they're around all the time, I've managed to now see every current and not-so-current superhero movie available. But that night they fought about Su-perman vs—"

"Captain America," I said.

"How..."

I shrugged.

"After you showed up in that dark alley and saved me, I knew who my favorite superhero was."

"Who?" Me?

"Batman."

"I don't think that was one of the choices," I said, ut-terly lost.

"He has such a sense of conviction and drive. He was overcome by the tragedies of his past but decided to help people instead of hurting them. I know he doesn't have real super powers but he uses discipline, strength and intelligence to fight for those in need. But he has such conflict in his life and it shows in how he chooses to live. Batman chose his path, which kind of makes him more awesome than someone like Superman. He lives with darkness, not just the light and righteous, like Captain America. Living a solitary life but also surrounding himself with people he trusts." She closed the remaining distance between us and handed me the book she still held in her hands. With a cocky grin she said, "Not to mention he drives the Bat-mobile, which is pretty much the coolest car ever."

"Batman," I repeat.

"Oh and don't forget, he has a jawline the ladies swoon over."

Placing the book on the table by the door, I returned her smug grin with one of my own. "The Bat-mobile, huh? What if I told you I could possibly challenge your idea on the coolest car ever?"

She rolled her eyes. "Doubtful. But if you want to try, I'm game."

"Follow me," I directed, leading her to the garage. Amelia's shoes clicked on the floor behind me and I flipped the light switch. Walking across the garage to the far side, I stopped at the sea of blue covering the car. I hesitated for a moment, thinking about what I was about to do. I glanced at Amelia. She waited eagerly to see what was under the cover. So eager to experience what I had to show her. I rubbed my jaw and grabbed a fistful of the tarp in my other hand, yanking it off in one quick swoop.

I'd forgotten how beautiful she was.

I turned and looked at Amelia, whose eyes were wide and had the most gorgeous smile on her face. I placed my hand on the slick, canvas roof and said, "Amelia, this is the coolest car ever."

41

Grant

I stood over by the car, tarp in hand, and looked at Amelia with what I'm sure was the widest grin I may have had on my face in years. Instead of a smile back, her head was cocked and her expression a bit skeptical. She finally said, "This is the coolest car ever? Better than the Batmobile?"

I nodded and ran my hand down the side of the car before placing my fingers on the door handle.

"Your convertible? I mean, it's beautiful and hot, but superhero-worthy? I'm not so sure." She scoffed in the direction of my baby.

"Amelia, I can assure you this car is more than just superhero-worthy. Let me show you," I informed her and walked around the car, opening the passenger side door for her. "The Batmobile is a fine machine, but it's a bit flashy for my taste. I think something a bit more understated is appropriate."

She had a gleam in her eye that was absolutely wicked, and she followed me around the car, quickly ducking in, saying, "Thank you."

To my dismay she adjusted her dress, covering her alluring legs, when she sat down on the shiny, soft leather.

Her scent whirled around me, making me heady and warm. I shut her door and walked around the car in exaggerated human speed. I needed to compose myself. I had been on the precipice of ruining the evening when Amelia had managed to soothe me by pulling out those comic books of all things, making everything right. She made *everything* right.

Stopping behind the car, I contemplated the new emotion spreading through my body. I couldn't be sure, because I had no experience with this, but I was almost positive what the feeling was. I'd seen it in movies, read about it in books and heard others think of it for years. I had even forced myself to pretend I had these emotions on my own, trying to make it work, to fit in with the rest of my family. But it always felt false. And now, I knew for a fact that it had been.

Just because I knew what it was didn't mean I was ready to admit it out loud. What if she didn't feel the same way? What would I do then?

I watched Amelia sit in the car and marveled at how this woman had changed the course of my life by simply being herself. I opened the driver's side door and slid inside next to her.

"You want the top up or down?" I asked, pretending like this wasn't the most important night of my life.

"Whatever you want, Batman," she said with an arched eyebrow, still not looking completely convinced.

I suppressed a smirk at the irony of her calling me Batman, if she only knew, and pressed the lever that folded the top into itself before easing down into the back of the car.

"I thought you didn't drive this anymore," she said.

I gave her a sideways look, my fingers on the key inside the ignition. "I didn't, but I told you, Amelia, I can change with proper motivation."

The admission surprised me more than anyone. There was no reason I should stop doing the things I loved to punish myself. There was no changing who I was, there was only acceptance. Amelia helped me accept who I really was, even if she didn't have the whole picture yet.

I cranked the engine and it roared with life. An enormous hum vibrated off the walls of the garage. I backed out into the clear evening.

Amelia's hair fluttered around her face with the movement of the car. With the top down and the engine purring, her scent and heartbeat where lost under the power of the machine.

"Sebastian worked on the car last. He's never satisfied unless he's upgrading something." I drove the car down the street. Amelia had no idea of my power behind the wheel of a high-performing car. Other than running, there was no place I was more comfortable.

"He removed all the original electronics here and installed a state of the art GPS navigation system. It also has a built-in phone and tracking system. If someone even thinks of touching this car the information goes right back to the computer in my office so I can find it." I explained while pointing out the features. "Plus, this car has an enormous engine. It was original to the car, but it's been upgraded to modern standards."

We had been traveling through the city at a normal speed but I maneuvered us onto the highway. Once I was sure there were no police or traffic problems ahead, I asked, "Is your seat belt secure?"

She hooked a finger through the belt and tugged. "Yep."

I shifted into gear, and as my tires squealed against the asphalt I said, "Hold on tight."

We shot off into the night to see exactly what a superhero's car could do.

***

Exiting the highway, I stole a glance at Amelia sitting next to me. I could tell she loved the speed as much as I did. The whole time we were moving she laughed and squealed and even though I saw her fingers clenched around the leather upholstery I could tell it was out of excitement, not fear. She acted scared but the wide smile on her face told me faster was better, and I was happy to oblige.

"Okay, you win. I admit it," she confessed breathlessly. "This car is amazing. Who taught you to drive like that?"

"I taught myself. It's instinctive." I found myself gazing at her hair, loosened from the tie at her neck. It was wild from the high speed and open roof. I couldn't help but grin.

"What?" she asked, and she realized where my eyes were and she instinctively touched the top of her head. "Oh crap." She groaned and pulled the visor down to see the damage.

While she wrestled with her hair (I couldn't even look at mine after my near hair freak out earlier) I attempted to walk, not run, to the passenger door to wait for her. Apparently satisfied, she snapped the visor up. I was surprised to see a conflicted look on Amelia's face.

"What's wrong?" I asked.

"Nothing. I look like a rat built a nest on top of my head," she said and narrowed her eyes. "You should have warned me."

I laughed. "You said it was my choice, and anyway, I think your hair looks beautiful," I said, this time without gagging on my words.

Amelia's face rushed with blood and my desire grew. I silently prayed for it to pass and focused on the long strands of hair flowing around Amelia's face. My fingers twitched, and before I could stop myself I reached out and pushed a strand smoothly behind her ear, grazing her skin.

"The wild, untamed look suits you." If I could have blushed I would have, but I couldn't, and it only encouraged me.

"Thank you," she mumbled and her heartbeat quickened as her own blush deepened.

As we casually walked down the street Amelia pointed out a series of posters plastered to the side of a building. "Oh, Drew and I are going with some friends to the music festival downtown tomorrow night. You should come with us?"

I forced myself to pause as though I was considering her offer. I wanted so badly to say yes but large crowds were difficult for me. The smells and sounds were so invasive.

Normally I would have lied, but in an effort to fulfill my promise I answered truthfully. "I don't really do well in crowds. But thank you for the invitation."

"Okay," she said. The hint of rejection was undeniable. I suppressed a frustrated sigh. What a way to start a date.

In an attempt to make her more comfortable, I began talking about the exhibit and some of the different artists we would see. As always, she seemed so interested in the things I had to say, which caused my ego to soar. We came to the front of the museum and Amelia stopped short. "We're going to the Asheville Museum of Art?"

"Yes."

"But, Grant, the museum isn't open at night. We're way past closing time," she said.

We climbed the steps to the front door and a man in a suit waited for us with the front door open. As we approached, he said, "Mr. Palmer, I'm Michael Barnes, director of the museum."

"Good evening, Mr. Barnes. I appreciate you opening the museum for us." I glanced at Amelia, who had a look of confusion on her face.

I gestured for Amelia to go ahead and she walked through the door into the main lobby.

The director stopped and said, "I think you know your way around, right?" I nodded. "Good, I will be in my office if you need any additional assistance."

He said 'good night' and walked off. Amelia gave me a hard look.

"What?" I asked, feeling the grin on my lips.

"Grant, did you pay them off or something?" she asked in a hushed whisper, suspicion filling her eyes.

"Shall we?" I asked, ignoring her question, and started for the staircase to the second floor. If Amelia was ever going to fit in my life, she would have to realize at some point the Palmers don't live like other people. We have money, resources and connections. We used them all when the time was right.

As we walked through the exhibits I allowed her to set the pace, pointing out the pieces that inspired or drew her attention. Amelia was drawn to color; bright hues and abstract work seemed to be her favorite style of artwork. She spent a tremendous amount of time looking at a series of Kandinsky paintings, commenting on the subtle differences in each piece.

She walked toward one in particular and looked up at me with amazement in her eyes. "I love this one. It's so different with the black background."

Her bright, innocent eyes were shining under the spotlights and I could almost hear the wheels turning in her mind. If only I knew thoughts instead of guessing. I was forced, as usual, to prod her for further information. "The irony of this painting is that Kandinsky was noted for his dislike of the color black. This painting is actually his final one. Composition X is its title."

She turned away from the picture, a sly smile lifting the corners of her lips, and said in a falsely impressed voice, "Mr. Palmer is there anything you don't know?"

Plenty. Like, how did this woman have such a powerful hold over me?

We continued through the museum like this, Amelia pointing out a painting or sculpture, and me answering her questions effortlessly due to the years of sleepless nights and a near photographic memory. We walked slowly, taking in each piece, and I listened as Amelia spoke in a hushed, reverent tone. It was quiet here, not a voice to be heard, a whisper to block out. Just me and Amelia, alone.

It was close to perfection.

She wandered a bit ahead of me and I wistfully looked at her hands gently swinging by her sides. I wished I could simply clasp one in my own. I shook my head slightly at the foolishness of my desires. Until I'd met Amelia, I'd never understood the need to touch another person like this. But now it was an ache. An overwhelming need to thread my fingers through hers. To rub my thumb over the creases in her palm or to simply cup the sides of her petite face in my hands.

"Are you coming?" she called, her voice echoing off the high ceilings from the next room, pulling me from my fantasies.

I walked in and found her engrossed by a collection of regional artwork. As I opened my mouth to give her history of the painting before us but Amelia turned and asked, "Isn't your family from Black Mountain?"

"Yes. They've owned property there for generations."

"Have you ever been to Lost Cove?"

Lost Cove? I looked over her shoulder at a photograph of members of the Melungeon community from the early nineteenth century. Even in the black and white photo their specific brand of beauty was mesmerizing. Had Amelia read about them? My confusion quickly turned to unease.

Angel Lawson

Knowing my promise to be truthful would be tested, I braced myself, admitting, "Once."

"Oh," she said and wandered over to the next one, a painting. The Melungeons had the body of a person but faces like an animal. "This is called Spirit Animal."

I followed her for a bit, responding to her comments and thoughts until curiosity got the best of me. I turned to her and spoke her name to get her attention and then asked, "Why were you asking me about Lost Cove?"

She looked around and found a bench across the room. Amelia motioned toward it and together we walked over and sat down.

She paused for a moment before speaking, her upper teeth biting down on her lower lip, drawing my attention to their perfection. "I haven't really told you this, but ever since my house was broken into I've been having nightmares."

"You told me you were having problems sleeping. Nightmares? What about?" I asked, feeling myself hovering over the line of honesty. I had wanted to know the truth about her dreams for weeks. I'd caught bits and pieces when she mumbled in her sleep, but the clearest part was my name at the end.

"It's the same one. It's horrible. I'm chasing after that missing girl, Jenna, the one from all the posters?" She paused, crashing her face in her hands. Amelia knew about Jenna. What else did she know?

364

"I chase her and she falls, then I fall and well, the only way for me to get away is to climb up a cliff, but I can't do it alone. Then in the end, you come and save me." Her face flushed a bit, but she didn't seem truly embarrassed. She looked almost thankful.

"I'm sorry you've been having bad dreams," I told her. "I don't understand though, what does this have to do with Lost Cove?"

She sighed. "No, I'm sure you don't. There is this girl at the coffee shop. Her name is Laurel. You know, the dark haired one, she's a Melungeon."

Of course. The girl was a Melungeon. I hadn't made the connection during her attempts to secure me as a potential mate. I held back a snort. What a pair we would have made.

Amelia took a deep breath and continued, "She told me this crazy legend about how her family believes in vampires and how they used to hunt in the Smokey Mountains. The church leaders in Lost Cove think they're back. Her community is convinced Jenna is a victim of a vampire attack." She rolled her eyes at the end, making me think she didn't fully believe the story.

Who would?

I wasn't exactly sure how to respond and finally spit out with a nervous chuckle, "That's an interesting story. Did she say anything else?"

Amelia hopped up from the bench and walked over to another painting. "She went on to tell me about shape-shifters and all this totally weird religious stuff." She looked over her shoulder at me and smiled. "She wasn't much of a believer. It's so strange, me having these horrible dreams and then she told me these crazy legends. I felt like they were connected. Your family is from that area and you're in my dreams. It all seemed like maybe it was more than an odd coincidence."

I pushed off the bench and stood behind her, watching her as she studied the painting in front of us. I wanted to tell her everything but she was so unnerved, and disturbed by the information, I was worried I would only make it worse. Instead, I leaned in and said, "I am sorry about your nightmares. I don't want you to worry. I promised you I would make sure that you are always safe."

She turned and we were now facing one another, so close I could see my reflection in her eyes. I absorbed her face, soaking up every detail. The smattering of pale freckles across her nose, her long feminine lashes, the crease under her left eye...I felt a jolt of energy spreading from my left hand up my arm.

She'd placed her hand in mine. Her skin was warm and soft and filled me with such a strong current of electricity I thought my heart may actually start beating. Amelia's eyes widened and I heard a small, but sharp, intake of breath come from her mouth but she didn't let go.

Please never let go.

She dipped her head for a moment, forcing me to lose eye contact, and I heard her softly say, "Thank you for keeping me safe." The back of her neck burned scarlet and she whispered, "In real life and in my dreams."

Intentionally this time, I found the strength to lift my free hand and placed my fingers under her chin, tipping her face upwards. The softness of her body amazed me and it took all the control I had not to run my fingers down her neck and push my nose into her hair. With one hand clasped in mine and the other cupping her face, I met her eyes. "You're welcome."

42

Amelia

"**A**melia, you have to wipe that smile off your face or Thomas is going to get the wrong idea," Drew scolded.

I tried. I did. I even used my fingers to push the corners of my lips downward but couldn't. They were permanently stuck upwards. Like the Joker.

The Joker. This made my smile widen even further as I laughed to myself thinking about comic books, Batman, and the best date I'd had in my life. Drew rolled his eyes while I giggled at one-sided jokes, and eventually directed his attention to the large stage in the middle of the park and the roadies setting up the next band's instruments. Jess and Thomas were attempting to get beer in the staggering lines across the field, and we saved our spot laying on blankets that we'd spread across the grass.

I was beaming. I knew it. I could feel the girly, pathetic, "I'm falling for him" giddiness emanating off of my body. My non-date with Grant took a sharp and sudden turn when I slid my hand into his very smooth, cool one. It was forward of me, I knew from experience that he wasn't fond of touching, but as he towered over me and promised to keep me safe, I knew I had to see what would happen if I did. I wasn't disappointed. Separate, we were two people muddling through life. Together we were electric. I knew this the instant we finally, physically connected.

"Amelia, you're almost vibrating." Drew looked me up and down slowly with narrowed, suspicious eyes. "Hell, did you have sex with him? You have this post-coital glow going on."

"What?" I shouted, a little too excitedly. "No! God. No. Nothing like that." The thought horrified and excited me at the same time. Grant was barely receptive of me touching him. At this point I could hardly imagine anything further.

That was a lie. I had imagined it. For weeks now, if I was honest with myself about it. The thought of his perfect lips on mine and those freakishly long fingers roaming around my body. Fantasies that had distracted me more than once when I should have been focused on other things. I considered it the whole time we drove home from the museum.

He walked me up the stairs as usual. The only difference was, he walked a little closer and once or twice I felt his tentative hand graze my back, which was enough to cause shivers to run down my spine. I thought for sure he would kiss me at the door, and I waited eagerly as he stared at my mouth instead of my eyes. I noted how his gaze kept shifting down to my exposed neck, hunger and desire present behind every blink. But behind the desire, I could see the smallest hint of fear and doubt filling his violet eyes. Something held him back, and I wasn't going to blow it by shoving my tongue down his throat.

"No. He didn't even kiss me," I confessed unhappily.

"So you're acting like this and you didn't even get a kiss? Wow. Remind me not to be there when you finally do take this further."

I blushed, but it was more about my own silliness than his innuendos. Drew and I had discussed sex more often than was probably normal. We didn't keep secrets, but something about my relationship with Grant kept me teetering on the edge. I wasn't even sure it was a relationship. I was close to squeeing just from simply holding his hand. That was very fourth grade and not impressive, but with Grant something told me it meant much, much more.

"I have no idea where this is going so don't get your hopes up. Grant is...well the more I get to know him, the more questions I have."

"That doesn't make any sense," Drew said.

"Well, Grant is..." I stumbled, looking for the right way to say it. "Grant is, you know, wealthy, intelligent, young, amazing looking, talented, but..."

"But? He sounds perfect to me."

I grimaced a little and stretched my legs out on the red and blue blanket we had brought with us. "But he's not perfect. At all. He is completely compulsive to the point he can hardly function. He is alarmingly socially awkward. And half the time he acts like a 45 year-old, repressed man hell bent on maintaining a perfect lifestyle at the expense of actually living his life."

Drew leaned back on her palms, his legs crossed. "And the other half of the time?"

I smiled at the thought of the other Grant. "The rest of the time he is like a twenty year-old who loves gadgets, fast cars and hiding from his family."

My fingers found a tuft of grass on the edge of the blanket. I tugged at it softly. "But then, there is something else. I don't know what it is. It runs deeper. Sometimes it scares me and other times it just pulls me to him like whatever he's hiding is the most amazing thing I could ever desire. Like *he's* the most amazing thing I could ever desire." He caught my eye and I confessed, "He also has this whole 'tortured soul' quality. Somehow, he's damaged, and I want to help fix him."

I continued my grass molestation while Drew was oddly quiet. The field around us was filling up with happy festival-goers. Drew said, "Amelia. That sounds really intense. But, you can't save people, you know that."

372

"I know. I don't know why, but I am so drawn to him. Well, part of it may be the fact I think he may be Batman. You should see his car." And I rambled on about the convertible for a while and our date trying to lighten the mood. I did not tell him about Lost Cove, Jenna or the spark that flared when Grant and I touched. Those were my thoughts to ponder and I wasn't prepared to share.

Luckily, Jess and Thomas came back carrying plastic cups of beer and the music started. From there, the night flew by. Thomas was great, he seemed perfectly clear we were nothing more than friends, which made it more bearable to listen to his conversations about B movies and horror film costumes. By dark, we were having a great time dancing and spilling drinks all over ourselves. I inhaled the cool summer night air, realizing how nice it was to get out and enjoy life a little. I had definitely spent too much time cooped up indoors all summer.

Before the final act began, I decided to make a bathroom run while the crowds were low. "Hey guys, I'm going to go run to the restrooms over there, the one by the beer truck," I said, pointing to the well-lit pavilion.

"Do you want company?" Thomas asked.

I laughed. "No, you know it will take you half the time in the men's room as it takes me in the women's. Plus you'll miss too much of the show. I'll be right back." I darted off though the crowd. The line snaked out the door and around the side, still crowded, even at this point in the show. I waited patiently until something caught my eye.

Leaning against the wall was a small girl with long dark hair. Her back was to me but when she turned I saw the side of her face I immediately recognized her. Jenna.

I hopped out of line and called out, "Hey!"

She didn't respond and turned away.

"Jenna!" I yelled over the music and crowds, picking up my pace. I searched for her in the mass of people. I should have gone for the police, or gotten help but I had this intense connection to the girl. I couldn't let her out of my sight. Maybe, I thought, as I pushed past a couple making out, this was what my dreams were about. Maybe I was supposed to be the one to find her.

She was several people ahead, swiftly ducking between people. The girl moved easily, just beyond my reach. I struggled against the crush of the crowd, stepping on one woman's foot and had a full beer cup spilled on my shoes as I searched the crowd.

"Jenna!" I called again, panic swelling in my chest. I lost her.

I spun in a circle. I spotted the shiny black of her hair as it broke through the swell of people. I followed, scooting past the First Aid tent and into a darker area of the field. Pushing my way through, I eventually freed myself from the throngs of people.

"Jenna! Wait!" I shouted, louder this time. She had quite the distance on me. To my relief, she slowed her pace and looked around for who was calling her name.

I started running a little. If it was her, I had to catch up. I had to help her. I'd been dreaming about her for weeks and I knew her parents must be worried sick. I couldn't believe she was here. Right in front of me.

What I couldn't figure out was why she was back here all alone. If she wasn't being held against her wishes, why was she wandering around the festival? I stopped running as it dawned on me that maybe things weren't as they seemed with this girl. Maybe she was a runaway? What if she didn't want to be found? It was too late for me to stop though. I had to know if she was okay. She'd haunted me, and there was no way I was letting her loose until I found out she was okay.

We were close to the edge of the field but the lights from the concert were still illuminating the area, casting a shadowy glow over the grass. I was breathing heavily from running and was glad to see her finally stop and turn around.

"Jenna? Is that you?" It was hard for me to see her face the way she was standing.

"Who are you?" she said, in a small weird voice.

I took a tentative step forward. "I'm Amelia. I saw your photo on a poster at my coffee shop. Your parents are looking for you. Are you okay?"

Her upper lip curled slightly and I watched as she in-haled deeply. The gesture was oddly familiar and Grant's face flashed in my mind. She turned to face me and said, "I've been looking for you."

"For me?"

"I was sent here to find you. Thank you for making it so easy." She took another breath through her nose. "You smell nice."

Sent to find me? I peered at her in the darkness while my internal alarms began to sound. I found her eyes in the darkness.

Black. Soulless.

Jenna's face was pale, her cheekbones hollow. Her eyes sunk into her skull and she had a maniacal expres-sion on her face. This was not the little girl whose pic-ture I obsessed over and dreamt about night after night. This girl was a monster, like...

Oh no, oh no, oh no.....

I heard a branch snap beside me and I looked over quickly. In the odd lighting I could see the spikes of short dark hair. No. This couldn't be happening.

Not again.

"Aw... you're not happy to see me?" Sasha purred. "I've really missed you. So much that I've come to visit you more than once. We even left you a gift. But I was a little disappointed that you didn't send a thank you card. You know, one of those pieces is an antique and very spe-cial to Caleb."

What? I never understood this woman's crazy mind-fuckery. I did know from the dark glint in her eye she wanted to hurt me and this time I wouldn't be so lucky. "I don't understand. What are you talking about?"

Under Sasha's booming laughter, Jenna hissed. Glad they thought this was so hilarious. "Your boyfriend did-n't tell you about your gift? How selfish of him."

The police always said to keep an attacker talking and never let them take you to a second location. Great Amelia, that seemed really helpful against a psycho-pathic stalker, who bragged about breaking into my house. I tried anyway. "My boyfriend?"

Unnaturally fast, Sasha appeared in front of me and reached out. Her ragged fingernail scraped across the contours of my cheek and she brushed my chin with her disturbingly smooth and cool hand.

Smooth and cool.

I shook her off, but for the second time, the image of Grant appeared in my mind and this time it made me stop. "You think Grant's my boyfriend," I stated more than asked, finally making the connection. I hastily took a step backwards, trying to get some space between us.

She gave me an odd smirk and said, "Of course he is. More than that even. He's your mate. Or he wants you to be." She laughed and stole a glance at Jenna who looked like she was coming down from a high. Sasha made a cooing sound in her direction. "I know you're hungry, young one, but you know the rules. Only Caleb tastes the blood of this treasure."

Her words slid around me like pieces of a puzzle, sometimes they didn't fit but others were interlocking and everything looked clearer. Before I could stop myself I whispered, "You're a vampire."

Sasha cackled and clapped her hands. "Welcome to the game, Amelia! Everyone has been playing, now you can join in, too. Although it is too bad you don't get to pick which team you want to play for."

I saw the evil glint in her eye. My feet moved instinctively, fight or flight kicking in. I raced toward the crowds but it was futile. Before I moved five feet Jenna was behind me, hands clasped around my upper arms. I could feel her cool breath on my neck as she panted like an animal. She smelled fresh, like flowers, but when I looked down her hands were filthy, covered in a thick coat of grime.

I felt pathetic, but there was no way I could fight her off. She and Sasha were vampires and had been stalking me for weeks.

Vampires.

My whole body shook with the realization she would take me to Caleb and I didn't have any way to stop her.

Sasha settled her hard eyes on Jenna. "Young one, you can touch, but do not taste." She laid a hand on top of Jenna's head and said in a vicious tone, "Do not damage her or we will all pay."

She spoke so freely of my death, as though it was inevitable. Desperate, I tried the last thing I could think of, hoping someone would stumble upon us and save me from this impossible nightmare.

"What do you mean Grant wants me for his mate?" I asked shakily.

Jenna never loosened her grip but Sasha did pause for a moment before giving me an amused eye. "You really don't know?"

I shook my head nervously confused by this whole line of conversation but enthralled at the same time. "I don't understand any of this."

Sasha's amusement turned to hysterical laughter. She tossed her head back, flinging her black hair out of her eyes. From behind me, I heard small giggles coming from the demonic girl holding me prisoner.

"Well that makes everything so much more interesting. See, Caleb is my mate. My partner, my other half. We've been companions for decades."

I knew my face betrayed my disbelief as I processed this information. Decades? Sasha couldn't be older than me. She moved closer, so close, I could see the thick rows of freckles across her nose and cheeks. Her movements were unnaturally fast and disconcerting, and my eyes couldn't keep up with the level of speed. She smirked. "It's how our kind declares commitment to another immortal. Grant is completely, eternally, committed to you."

Images began to unfolded, almost like a series of photographs. The first picture was of Grant. I thought of his habits, the secrets, the lies. Why he was so young yet appeared so old. His cool touch and cryptic words. I considered the lack of food or drink in his home, his strength and beauty.

The look of hunger in his eyes. My heart lurched into my throat.

No.

"I'm not immortal."

"Not yet," Sasha declared. "Your boyfriend is exactly like me. And like Jenna. Well, not exactly like us. He has chosen an 'alternative' lifestyle." She rolled her eyes. "It doesn't matter that you belong to him. Caleb wants you more, and whatever Caleb wants, I will give him. Because that is what a mate does for the other."

"Does Caleb want me as his mate, too?"

Sasha's hand flew through the air faster than I could comprehend. I heard the hollow slap at the same time I felt the sting from where her palm met my cheek. Tears welled in my eyes. "Caleb is my mate, bitch. That's not what he wants you for."

"What then?"

"Revenge. He'll train you to tear the Palmers apart. One by one, until there's nothing left other than what he came for in the first place."

She turned and walked into the woods with no other words. Jenna's fingers dug into my arms harder as she pushed me along taking me with them, back to this man named Caleb. Also a vampire.

Grant was a vampire. Sasha and Jenna were vampires. The entire Palmer family? Holy shit.

Jenna released my arms when she realized I was no longer resisting, and pushed me ahead, into the forest. I stumbled and fell more than once, and her small hands yanked me up from the ground. I flinched, knowing the bruises would be worse than last time. I blinked. The harsh reality that bruises, cuts, and heartache no longer mattered. These two creatures were marching me to my death.

43

Grant

melia.

Where did she go?

I closed my eyes in the middle of the crowd and tried to get my bearings. One minute she was standing in the line for the restroom and the next she was gone. Her scent mixed in with the thousands of other concert go-ers. Raking my hands into my hair, I dropped to my knee in frustration in the middle of the park. I knew I was overreacting, but ever since she told me she was coming here I had a sense of dread. There were too many people. It was too easy for them to get to her and for me to lose her.

I rocked back on my heels and listened.

"This band is great....hey, ass face....if he touches me one more time...I wonder how long the beer truck stays open after the band finishes..."

My gift of exquisite hearing was a blessing and a curse. In a crowd of two thousand people it was a curse straight from the devil himself. I heard so many people—so many different voices that it was impossible to shut them all out. Finding Amelia among this crowd was literally like looking for a needle in a haystack. Even my vampire senses weren't that good.

I pulled out my phone, stabbing my finger at the button going to the only person who could maybe find her. "Where is she?" I spat.

"Amelia?" Olivia asked, knowing there was only one person I would be concerned about. "What's wrong?"

"You can't see her?" I asked, the unfounded panic rising again.

"Um...." Olivia went silent and I began pacing around the park, looking for any sign of Amelia. I couldn't catch her scent over the overpowering odors of food, drinks and sweat. Between that and the noise I was truly blind.

"Olivia?" I asked, tentatively this time.

"Grant, all I see is her in the woods at some point. She won't be alone and she isn't going willingly. Other than that it's shifting and moving too quickly. The only thing I know for sure is you need to find her in the forest."

I disconnected and wove through the thick crowd. I had no choice but to ignore the blaring thoughts and obnoxious odors. I passed a couple engaged in a deep kiss and had a brief sense of relief smelling Amelia on the back of the man's shirt. She must have come this way and brushed against him.

I saw the First-Aid Tent ahead and peeked inside. She wasn't there but I found indentions in the grass beyond the tent. There were two sets of footprints, one possibly running behind the other, both leading to the shadowy darkness of the forest.

What would make Amelia come into the darkness like this? I wondered and was instantly hit by a flowery scent wafting in the breeze. I'd smelled it before, at Amelia's home and on the necklace left on the door.

Jenna.

Dammit. Only the little girl could lure Amelia away from safety and I berated myself for not telling her to stay away if she encountered her. But what could I do? Comments like that would only force her to ask more questions and force me to tell more lies.

I picked up my pace and opened my thoughts, trying to track their direction. I pushed aside the faint murmurs from the distancing crowd and the fading music from behind me. I smelled Amelia, her scent becoming stronger as I approached the edge. Suddenly, I was struck by a different aroma, Sasha's. Amelia's odor was replaced by adrenaline and fear. Panic took hold.

I raced through the woods until a wave of images flooded my head. *Blonde hair, blue eyes, angry scratch marks on pale skin.* Caleb. Was he near here? I took a deep breath-searching for his scent. Nothing, yet he had to be close to hijack my mind. I was slammed with an image of Jenna's tiny hands clutched tight around Amelia's arms. Everything about her was unfocused, immature, and unpredictable. Her eyes lingered on Amelia's neck. *My neck.*

The vision sent me into a rage and I pushed Caleb out of my head. I pummeled through the trees, trampling brush and foliage with a viciousness I'd never felt before. Up ahead I saw them. Three figures. Small and wild, dark and dangerous, and lastly, timid and scared. My eyes zeroed in on Amelia being manhandled by Jenna as I crashed through the brush. I cringed at the sight of her, filthy. At the way fingers were bruising her very human flesh. The thought of her pain caused my fury to rise even higher. Her body was mine and mine alone to worship. Their disrespect would cost them heavily.

Ahead, Sasha heard me coming. Her eyes flicked left and right, processing escape plans. Beyond that, I could see the conflict on her face. What would be the cost with Caleb if she failed to bring his treasure back? Death? She wavered for a moment, glancing between me and Amelia. She made her decision quickly, flight being her best weapon of defense. Before I fully reached them, she fled into the darkness of the forest.

Jenna lurched at the sudden disappearance of Sasha and jerked Amelia to a stop. Amelia yelped and whimpered from the pain. I winced with her, quickly determining how to proceed. The fledgling was very powerful. Hungry. And absolutely zero self-control.

Without Sasha to guide her I only had seconds to save Amelia.

I made my decision without hesitation.

"Jenna," I said, in a tone lower than Amelia could hear. "Release her."

The fledgling turned to me, placing Amelia between me and her. Amelia's eyes widened with...hope? Fear? I wasn't sure. I was never sure. I tilted my head to the side, longing to reach out for her.

The sound of a hiss snapped my eyes back to Jenna.

"Take your hands off her and I'll make your death quick and painless."

Her fingers fumbled but her teeth glinted sharp. One look at Amelia proved she was close to slipping into shock. Her eyes were unfocused and she had yet to utter a word of recognition.

Jenna spoke, her voice young and high pitched, "You can't save her. No one saved me, and look at you. You're no different. Your heart is as cold and dead as my own. Your soul? You can feel the hole from where it's missing. The only actual difference is you're pretending to be better than the rest of us. You're a fake. The real enemy. The failure of our kind."

"Jenna. Take your hands off of her. Or I will take them off for you. Like Caleb. You saw what happened to him. Next time I'll kill him," I said. Her dirty fingers moved to release Amelia, but instead of dropping to the side, they latched onto Amelia's head and twisted, exposing her neck.

I heard, rather than saw Jenna's teeth scrape against Amelia's flesh. I cried and lunged forward, thrusting my body between them, shoving Amelia aside as gently as possible. She stumbled to the ground, but Jenna was my priority. She growled and hissed like a wild animal. Barely two months old, hunger and the desire to fight were the primal urges that coursed through her infected veins, and now that Sasha abandoned her she had no reason not to follow her instincts.

I dove at the fledgling and tore into her with my teeth and nails. She fought back, slashing at my arms. I drew a blade from my pocket and she stilled, pressing her back to the trees.

"Your time is up," I said, slicing the blade across her throat in one final arc. Jenna howled like an animal in pain as thick blood spilled from her wound. "It never should have been this way. You're too young—too innocent." With both hands I ripped off her head and dropped it to the ground.

She may have been stronger, but I was smarter and more disciplined. I was a killer. The dead body and dripping blood from my hands proved that. Amelia moved behind me and I spun, finding her on her hands and knees. She crawled away from me and retched in the dark, dank forest. A feeling of absolute dread settled in my bones.

I knew all along she wasn't mine to have. At the very best I was placed here to protect her. The worst? To kill her. My need for her was irreversible but now that she knew, really understood, that I was the very real monster that haunted her dreams, there was no way she would want me in return.

"Amelia?" I called, now on my hands and knees.

She was sat on the ground, shorts smeared with dirt from kneeling on the forest floor to vomit. Her pale arms were covered in purple bruises and she rubbed her hands absently over the painful welts. She looked at me with confusion and apprehension in her eyes.

"I'm so sorry. I promised you and I failed."

My knees pressed into the soft dirt and we sat in the quiet of the forest together. The energy between us had shifted, no longer filled with hope and possibility. Instead we were enveloped in the stench of death and fear.

"I won't hurt you. Let me take you back," I said in an even tone, unsure of what she was thinking. "I'll carry you."

"No."

The word came out loud and forceful. She was in there, thank God.

I attempted to help her to her feet, but she flinched violently at my touch, so I distanced myself from her once she was stable. Her eyes clouded and she fell mute. The only sound came from our feet on the dirt and her erratically beating heart.

She stumbled through the forest, arms wrapped around her body. She couldn't see clearly, as it had grown too dark. I was forced to speak, point out a tree or branch. Once I caught her when she stumbled on a root. She recoiled on contact.

It was so far removed from our gentle touches last night. The excitement and flare were gone. I repulsed her.

I'd lost her.

I had her and I lost her.

We made it to the edge of the forest and we could see the lights on the field. The music had stopped and people were gathering their things to leave. I had to address the situation. I had no choice. It was for her safety and my own.

"Amelia," I said softly. "Speak to me."

Her head tilted upwards and her eyes slid over mine but never fully focused.

I forced myself to be honest. I owed her that much. "I know what you saw back there was disturbing. But I really need you to keep what you saw to yourself. Caleb and Sasha are both still out there. I'm going to catch them. Then I'll destroy them."

She swallowed deeply and finally spoke, her voice was shaky and low. "Who would I tell Grant? What would I say? That I'm being hunted by a pack of deranged monsters? That deep in these woods you left the ravaged remains of a missing little girl? Mutilated by..." she swallowed. "Do I tell them I finally thought I found the man of my dreams and he's..." She gasped for air as the words and tears rolled down her face. "Not human?"

Her words hit me like a ton of bricks. The man of her dreams? Me?

Amelia steeled herself for a moment. She wiped her eyes with the back of a dirty hand and I watched as her chin jutted out in determination. "I'm not telling anyone anything, Grant. Your secret is safe with me, but promise me one thing."

"Anything."

"Don't come looking for me again. I quit. I'm done. You'll have to find someone else."

She pushed forward, limping and holding her neck. From my spot in the dark I watched her go, barely holding on by a thread. Like the feral nature controlling Jenna something deep down and instinctive told me she belongs with me—*to me*. I held back, fulfilling my promise to keep her safe. She stepped into the crowd, the overhead lights reflecting off her hair like a halo. Without even the smallest glance back she disappeared and I knew, no matter how painful, this was right. She was right about everything—but one.

I'd never find someone else.

Epilogue

She knew I would come.

Cowards have their own particular aroma, making it easier to track her down. The further she traveled the more distinct the trail she left through the forest became. In a valiant effort to throw me off track she circled and wove erratically through the woods. Unfortunately for Sasha the pain and loss I suffered seemed to heighten my senses. In a grove of hardwoods, I climbed and waited.

Dusk lowered and Sasha broke through the trees. As predicted she runs beneath me, oblivious, and I pounce—claws out. Teeth bared.

Any mercy I'd shown in the past was gone.

"I told you to make this stop," I said. She lay beneath me, arms and legs pinned down. My sharp blade pressed against her neck.

"There's no stopping him," she said. "None. Not until you're all dead."

She kicked and fought but I had the upper hand. She knew either I would kill her or he would—mate or not. She's lost another fledgling and she failed to bring him Amelia. Killing her would be a kindness.

I plunged the blade into her gut and a small smile flickered on her lips, her chest heaved. She enjoyed this. Like her mate it was all part of a twisted game. "Do it! This way I die a martyr for the cause—and his vengeance will be twice as powerful. Beware, Grant Palmer, that little pet will be his before this is over, and the things he'll do to her..." she laughed, choking on her death. "You'll regret the day you crossed him."

Gripping her throat, Sasha's eyes bulged and I whispered close to her ear, "No one touches what is mine. Not my city, my family or my girl."

Flinging the blade into the trees I tore at her flesh with my bare hands, until her body scattered across the forest like discarded waste. When there was nothing left I stood over the remains and brushed the death off my hands.

There are some things even a vampire can't come back from.

Amelia and Grant's story continues with *Creature of Habit (Book 2),* available at Amazon.com.

Acknowledgements

In 2008 I'd just started writing and showing my work to others. I had an idea and mulled it over for a while, sharing it with close friends. "It's about a vampire who's kind of like Batman—or maybe more like Angel. He's a vigilante, working quietly to help the people in his city, yet isolated and lonely. He has OCD and I have this great idea for a scene where the love interest confuses his vampirism for being gay."

They all pretty much told me this was a terrible idea. Like, "Huh, Angel, that sounds great, except no one will want to read it."

They were right. No one did want to read it. Not at first, but I had a vision and a stubborn streak and I did it anyway. Apply those same characteristics to the last 6 years and you pretty much can sum up my entire writing career.

Creature of Habit is one of those stories that required a lot of help on. Back then and now. The book above is greatly altered from the original work (Book 2 is even more so). I bugged the crap out of anyone that would listen to me brainstorm and plot. I owe them much. All I've got is a thank you and some eternal fan-girling. Author Beth Bolden is one of the ones that told me it sounded like a terrible idea. We laugh about it now. I love her for her honesty. I can always go to her for the truth. Author Bev Elle encourages me in all my projects, and trust me, encouragement is worth more than you can even imagine. Vanessa C. has been with me through all the stories, all the books and does the dirty work with grammar that I am unable to do. Alicia N. listens to me talk about all of this over cheese dip and Diet Cokes (and margaritas) which is invaluable. I drag her to book festivals and panels and all the other stuff no one else wants to do. Rochelle Allison, Author TM Franklin, Elizabeth Vincent & Annie J (street sleepers) have provided unwavering support, listening ears and friendship.

There are others I want to thank, people I don't communicate with much anymore but please know they are the reason this book ever happened. They are why I fell into fandom and embraced a new creative outlet. Barb H, LolaShoes (for bringing me to, and introducing me to the wonders of SDCC way back when), Wime09, Kirsten A, Tammy N, Kristen and Jess (Jandco's work always inspired me to be better), Halojones (omg halo.jones. *sigh*), Author Kira Gold, Jessica N, Elaine L (we were right), Cartnee, Claire G, Jan R (the always, always supportive Jan!), Valerie R, Amy F, Lorena, Audrey, Autumn (a shout out to April S. for some last minute edits!) and all the others I know I'm missing (because I suck, not because anyone is forgettable.)

Of course I say thank you to AG, because obviously.

For the record, Captain America beats them all. Also, you can find me on twitter @theangellawson or on facebook at Angel Lawson or Angel Lawson Author. Come say hi. I do have cookies but they're gluten free.

Angel Lawson

Printed in Great Britain
by Amazon

86130451R00231